+

DEATH'S ANGEL

A Detective Al Warner Novel

By

George A Bernstein

Award winning Amazon Top 100 Novelist

Other Al Warner Novels by George A Bernstein

Born to Die
The 2nd Detective Al Warner Suspense
Available in e-book, print, and audio

The Prom Dress Killer
The 3rd Detective Al Warner Suspense
Available in print, e-book, and soon in Audio

White Death
The 4th Detective Al Warner Suspense
Available in print and as an e-book

Sniper
The 5th Detective Al Warner Suspense
Available in print and as an e-book

Taken
The 6th Detective Al Warner Suspense
Available in print and as an e-book

Other Bernstein novels

Trapped
A parapsychologic romantic suspense
Available in e-book, print, and audio

A 3rd Time to Die
A paranormal Romantic Suspense
Available in e-book, print, and audio

GnD Publishing LLC
Palm Beach Gardens, Florida 33418

Publisher's Note: This is a work of fiction. Names, characters, and incidents are a product of the author's imagination. Locales and public names are sometimes used for atmospheric purposes and may have been altered to meet the demands of the story. Any resemblance to actual people, living or dead, or to businesses, companies, events, institutions, or locales is completely coincidental.

Book Layout ©2015 - BookDesignTemplates.com

Cover Design by Priority Designs Studios

Ordering Information: Quantity sales. Special discounts are available on quantity purchases by corporations, associations, Bookstores, and others. For details, contact the publisher.

DEATH'S ANGEL/George A Bernstein. -- 1st ed.
ISBN 978-0-9894681-4-5

DEDICATION

I'd like to first dedicate this book to all the Writers Conferences & seminars I've attended, where a plethora of experts helped shape my ability to tell an engaging story.

At a 3-day seminar by Donald Maass, one of the very top fiction agents, he hammered at us, "What's the worst thing that can happen to your protagonist?" Then he asked, "What can be even WORSE than that?" Then, "even worse than that?" I learned that good storytelling takes more than just raw talent, and hopefully, you'll agree I learned that trade, as you read this novel.

Good story-telling is an art not practiced often enough.

Also, my thanks to my editor, Dave King, for his valuable insights, continued patience and encouragement. His suggestions helped make *DEATH'S ANGEL* the best it could be.

And lastly, thanks to Google, where with a little work, you can learn oodles about anything. I was able to download a complete symposium from the FBI's BAU conference on Serial Killers, an invaluable insight.

DEATH'S

ANGEL

PROLOGUE

Free!

Free at last!

Imprisoned so long behind that dark wall.

It took a stranger, a kindred spirit, to shatter my bonds.

Finally, my chance to deliver sinners for redemption. Fear will fill their immoral, lust-filled hearts before I bring them to God's ultimate glory.

Soon, I will begin my quest.

Soon, the world will know the virtue of my glorious mission.

Soon, they will learn I am among them, returning order and morality to their shallow lives.

Because I am finally free.

Free at last!

ONE

Jodi Gannon lifted her glass, leaving a circle of condensed moisture on the scuffed mahogany bar top, and studied the pale imprints her pink lips left on its rim. She took another sip of the cold vodka, rolling it on her tongue, its sweet, cloying odor filling her senses. She swiveled around, drink still in hand, her shoulder-length corn-silk hair rippling with subtle sensuality. Resting bare elbows on the stained bar top, she surveyed the dimly lit room. A smug smile teased the corners of her lips.

Life was good, and with the magazine already on the stands, things promised to get better.

A lot better.

A full page, in all her natural blond, erotic glory. None of the other girls could compete with that. Might *Playboy* even consider her for a centerfold? Either way, this was a big boost to her modeling career, and maybe even a chance at the movies.

Seeing her own nude photo prominently featured in *The Girls of the Southeast* pictorial in this month's issue was a real turn-on. Only seven days, and she'd already been approached by two new agencies vying to represent her. Then there was the deluge of male attention that might intimidate another girl, however gorgeous.

But Jodi Gannon always handled guys fantasizing about wrapping their arms around her slim waist, burying their faces between her glorious C-cups. Rebuffing randy college kids at the U. of Miami, where she was a junior, was no challenge.

Nothing wrong with a hot night with the right guy, but she'd had her fill of hormone-ridden, inexperienced boys, too much in a hurry to get off. Jodi Gannon craved a virile, mature lover who knew how to give a woman pleasure.

And *there* just might be the guy, at the same little corner table the last four times she'd visited the lounge.

She knew nothing about him except lately, when she was at the Hurricane Bar, he was there, alone in the dim lighting. Each time he'd send her a drink via the buxom little waitress. Cute, but not in Jodi's class. Jodi wondered at the absence of a note, but all she got was a barely perceptible nod. No follow-up, no invitation to sit with him, just those dark, magnetic eyes appraising her. It was kind of sweet, and not at all pushy.

He was getting to her. She found herself looking forward to this evening's possible encounter. He just might get lucky tonight because god knew, she was ready.

A covert glance revealed him staring openly at her again—a guy of maybe thirty-five, totally out of place in a joint full of college kids.

Why is he here? To see me, of course.

Goosebumps tap-danced down her spine, bringing a familiar wetness. Good thing she was wearing panties for a change. If he sent a drink today, she might even overrule that nagging little voice lurking in her head. Make a cautious move and test the waters. She suspected once she went for *that* swim, she might paddle clear across the lake.

She shrugged. Though innately hot-blooded, she wasn't promiscuous. But he'd been a gentleman, patiently wooing her from afar, and his hook was in her now. This evening might end with some (hopefully) hot sex. Maybe she wouldn't even *want* to get away after that. She hoped not!

Rotating her stool, Jodi took another sip of cold vodka. Glancing at the gilt-framed mirror, she saw him. Despite deep shadows, she sensed his eyes riveted on her. She flinched, startled by a light tap on her shoulder, nearly spilling off her perch. Fran, the waitress, was holding a tray with a fresh drink. This time a small piece of paper lay on its surface.

"From your ardent admirer again. Waxing poetic is he,

Jodi? Some gals got all the luck. A little T and A in *Playboy*, and the world's your oyster." A playful smile ticked up her lips.

"Thanks, Fran. Yeah, they're all hot for my bod, but that's nothing new. Guess it's a curse to be beautiful, but I'm not trading it in." She leaned closer to the waitress. "He seems like an okay guy, Fran? Not a psycho or anything?"

"Acts pretty normal to me," the barmaid answered. "Good tipper, too. Never got a real good look at him because of the ballcap, but he seems kinda rugged looking. Real well built. Wish it was me he was sending drinks and love letters to." Fran laughed as she moved off to serve two young men at another table.

Glancing at the man across the room, wrapped in a mantle of dark shadows, Jodi picked up the paper. Could that be a little smile there? Flipping open the note, she read the brief message, neatly printed in simple, block letters:

HAVEN'T WE PLAYED THIS GAME LONG ENOUGH?

She turned back to the room, her eyes measuring him, certain now a smile played across his lips.

Hell. Why not? He'd been a gentleman. Not a bit pushy. If he turned out to be a jerk or a pervert, she'd split. She had a brown belt in karate and could take care of herself.

Feeling reassured, she smiled, the glow illuminating the lounge. Three young men, hungrily watching the exquisite blonde, silently groaned and glared at this fortunate interloper, enfolded in the soft tapestry of darkness at his corner table.

Jodi picked up her drink and the small piece of paper and slipped off her stool. A bead-studded leather belt divided her short white skirt from a flowered silk sleeveless blouse, unbuttoned well into her cleavage. The outfit accented her slender waist, the sway of full hips, and the jiggle of her breasts. She flowed across the room, a sensual cat, prowling. Reaching his table, she smiled once more and held out her hand.

"Hi. Thanks for the drink—again. I'm Jodi Gannon."

"Hi to you." He pressed her crimson-nailed finger to his lips, his face still thickly shadowed by the peak of his ballcap.

"I'm Angie Dedios, and I *know* who you are. Just like any other red-blooded guy who reads *Playboy*."

His head tilted, and his fathomless obsidian eyes engulfed her, igniting hot sparks dancing across her skin. The flutter of hummingbird wings assailed her heart, flooding her with delicious anticipation of—what? She wasn't sure.

"You're the most beautiful women I've ever seen." He still held her hand, his thumb lightly caressing her palm.

"I can't believe I actually ran into you."

Goosebumps ridged her neck and back, spinning her into free-fall, swallowed by the dark abyss of those haunting eyes.

"Glad you joined me, despite that corny little note." He stood, pulling out a chair for her. "Frankly, I'm a little nervous. First time I've done something like this."

"That's so sweet." She sat, back in control, crossing her legs, her laugh the tinkle of silver chimes.

Jodi sipped her drink. Tearing herself away from those hypnotic orbs, she saw him clearly for the first time. She understood Fran's assessment. The face looked hewn from granite—definitely attractive in a rugged sort of way. About six feet tall, broad shouldered and hard muscled without being massive, he exuded a lithe grace. His skin was darkly tanned, the hands strong but nicely kept. An Armani sport shirt bespoke of affluence—maybe a lawyer or a businessman? His smile radiated warmth.

And those eyes. Those galactic black holes pulled at her, the roar of her own pulse filling her head. She barely heard him say *Playboy* should consider her for a centerfold. She'd be a lock for *Playmate of the Year*.

She blinked, looking away. Sipping her drink, she fought

to calm her thundering heart. Guys *never* got to her like this.

"Yeah, I'm getting a new agent, and I'll be discussing that with them. It's all very exciting." She smiled, back in control.

"It should be. You're sensational!" He had taken her hand again, gently stroking her fingers.

"Coming here isn't like me. But there was something about you in that photo—something more than just beauty. *Playboy* must have seen it too, giving you the only full page. I wanted to see you in the flesh—no pun intended." He chuckled.

"I guess I wasn't so unique." He nodded toward several tables, filled with mostly college men, openly staring at them.

Jodi shrugged, mesmerized by the gentle warmth of his voice and the haunting depths of those eyes.

"I never expected to meet you," he softly squeezed her hand, smiling a little sheepishly, "and I'm flattered you accepted my very corny invitation. Geez, I'm prattling on like a love sick kid." His smile broadened as he searched her aqua eyes. She grinned, back in charge, despite the heat infusing her.

"Oh, the note was kinda cute, and I like that you're *not* one of these college guys. Frankly, I'm tired of over-hormoned, self-styled studs that only want to get me in the hay." She flipped a fall of blond hair back over her shoulder and grinned. "They're in such a damned rush, a girl doesn't feel very special.

"You're a mature guy, and that's different. I'd like to get to know you better."

"Good. So, tell me about you... where you're from and how you decided on U of M?"

TWO

As they talked, she covertly appraised him. A little older than she first thought, and just a bit better than average looking. Nothing special to account for his magnetic sensuality. His obsidian eyes caressed her, firing tingly little bumps across her neck and arms. She preened, knowing she looked magnificent.

Jodi Gannon, a Nordic goddess who strolled through life with an easy, athletic grace, pursued modeling and hopefully, a movie career.

Few men passed without snatching a wistful second look. Since her early teens, she'd learned to capitalize on her beauty, and very little eluded Jodi's grasp if she wanted it badly enough—especially from men.

She smiled, porcelain-white teeth catching the dim lights.

"Are you into sports, Angie? You look like an athlete."

"I don't go in much for the team stuff. I love the outdoors: fishing, hunting, camping. Things like that.

"Joined the Marines when I was a kid and had a short stint in Afghanistan. Took a bullet in the shoulder. Just bad enough to keep me out of action. I was glad to get out of there alive." He grimaced and looked embarrassed.

She nodded and squeezed his hand.

"I'm busy with my work, and don't get out much. The dating scene's very intimidating, with all the AIDS, herpes and psychos out there. But when I saw your photo in *Playboy*, I had to find you. I had this sensation, as if I knew you from another lifetime." He chuckled. "Figured nothing would come of it, but I was compelled to try. I'm happy I was wrong."

His bottomless eyes pulled at her and triggered a delicious

shiver, her heart jumping into her throat. She moistened her lips with the tip of a pink tongue.

"Mind if I ask what you do for a living, Angie?" She wouldn't hook up with some loser, however attractive.

"Got my own company, doing a special type of security work. Only one client, but he's the biggest in the world. Top secret, though, so I can't talk about details. Maybe, when we get better acquainted. . .." His wink sent more eruptions cascading across her spine and neck.

Gotta be Uncle Sam. Who else is that big? His own company, too.

Yeah. Haven't lost my touch. His probable connections wouldn't hurt her career. She'd probably go to bed with him, regardless, but this was so much more exciting.

Hook him first, then see what he can do for me. Her eyes searched his, unaware they were harboring surprisingly different views of the future.

Three U of M students began setting up musical instruments on a small podium along one wall, near an open area used for dancing. They played three nights a week at this popular lounge. Soon, the strains of a new country song filled the air.

"You dance?" she asked, taking his hand and standing.

"Sure, if they stick with the slow stuff." He followed her to the quickly filling dance floor.

Finding an open spot, she snuggled into his arms, resting her head on his shoulder as they began to move to the slow, erotic beat. Her nipples, swollen and erect, teased his chest through his thin cotton shirt. She undulates against him as they swayed to the music. Not surprisingly, an obvious hardness grew there. Her fingers caressed his neck and the back of his head, as he buried his face in her hair, gently nibbling an ear.

Angie seemed unembarrassed by his obvious arousal, which

16

excited her. He was very hard and very large. She'd intended to play him along for a few days, but flaming ardor filled her now, jack-hammering her heart against her ribs. She needed that big thing in her, and soon.

Can't wait another night. Pampered all her short life, she freely indulged her lust for instant gratification. Jodi had no doubts about this man, trusting her judgment implicitly, never considering for a moment she may be wrong.

After two slow dances, they returned to his table where they continued their Q and A.

"I'm a drama major, and do some modeling," she said, sliding her chair close to his. "Well-built chicks are in demand these days, so I've been doing pretty well. They say the camera really likes me. And now the *Playboy* spread is bringing more dividends."

As she talked, his hand found one of hers, fingers lightly interlocked. Her other hand came to gentle rest on his thigh. They verbally preened, two peacocks in a mating dance. Then, without speaking, they knew the time to go had arrived.

Courting was finished. Mating was about to begin.

They departed the noisy lounge arm in arm, leaving the green beast of envy glittering in the eyes of the young men who remained inside.

The evening air had cooled, but their passions flowed like hot lava, each inflamed by their intense lust.

Angie pulled her into his arms, eyes locked, answering questions silently asked. The kiss was slow, lingering—tentative, yet demanding, searching for a truth not easily discovered amid such carnal heat.

Eventually they separated, gasping slightly for a fresh breath. She looked again into those bottomless orbs, her smile radiant, simultaneously heart-stopping and pulse-racing.

"Do you live nearby?" she whispered huskily, animal

excitement rasping her voice. "Can we go to your place?"

"I live way up in North Miami Beach. Can we wait that long? D'ya live off campus? A roommate?"

"Yeah, and the roomie's no problem." She pressed against him, arms around his neck, her fingers playing in his hair.

"She's spending the night at her boyfriend's."

"Swell. We can take my car, and pick up yours later. I can't tear myself away from you, even for just a few minutes. I've waited so long to be with you—this chance to fulfill my destiny."

Jodi stared at him, charged by a sudden flutter of anxiety. What a strange thing to say. It almost sounded as though. . ..

She thrust fleeting doubts aside, reveling in the obsessive behavior she ignited in men.

THREE

Angie drew her to a stop next to a shabby blue Ford, generously decorated with dings and scratches. Confidence wilted as uneasiness again assailed her. He shrugged, grinned, and ran a hand over the badly oxidized finish.

"Not a thing of beauty, is she? A surveillance car— something no one would notice. I came directly from work, not expecting to really meet you." He shrugged. "I should've gone home for the Mercedes. Can't judge a lady by her looks, though, 'cause this baby runs smooth as a top."

Jodi's budding concerns melted. Yet, she was again assailed by a ripple of indecision. Was she really considering a roll in the sack with a stranger, however alluring? He'd been a total gentleman, putting no real pressure on her. It was *her* ardor she struggled to corral—and was

losing the battle.

"You look apprehensive, Jodi. Look, I don't want you to feel like I'm pushing you into something . . .."

"No, it's okay." She thrust a gag in the little inner voice, whispering caution to her. What could go wrong? And he's so *hot!*

"My place is less than a mile."

"Good. I'm glad you didn't change your mind, because I'm really looking forward to having a glorious time together."

She shivered. He made it sound almost like a religious act. How exciting to be deified.

Angie held the door for her and held her hand as she slid in. Closing it, he leaned through the open window.

"You know, you'll be my first—love—since I've been set free. You can't imagine how eager I am to begin again." He stood back, then circled the car, as she wondered . . .

Recently divorced? And I'm his first. Wow.

He slipped into the driver side and reached over, strapping her in. They kissed, and his hand trailed across her breast, over her flat stomach, finally resting on her thigh with a gentle squeeze.

The parted and she gasped for air, her heart tripping over itself.

"Go south on Dixie," her voice a horse whisper. "I'll show you where to turn."

She planted a quick, hard kiss on his lips.

"I can hardly wait," he said and started the car. An almost wicked grin flickered across his lips, kindling another tickle of doubt.

What the hell was she doing? She barely knows this guy. Was she so horny she'd screw the first mature stud that looked good to her?

Well, he *acted* like a gentleman—a damned sexy one. At least he wasn't a weirdo. If things didn't work out, it'd just be a one-night-stand. He *did* seem special. Very special. And she was so *hot.*

Everything would be fine. Probably *better* than fine. She could handle herself pretty well, too, if things got out of hand.

Self-reassured, she directed him to a parking spot a half-block from her apartment. They walked the difference, hand in hand.

"We'll have to be careful. My landlady's not too happy about guys in our rooms, but she's hard of hearing, so it should be easy." She studied him again, a shiver of nervousness rekindled.

She was about to let a stranger jump her bones. She rarely acted so impetuously, but the cumulative excitement of the last weeks had her so charged, she couldn't control her own rampant lust.

Sure, Angie was different—a real man. Not some college punk. Anyway, she was too turned on to chicken out now. It was going to be okay—probably the fuck of her life.

So, she justified what, in her heart she knew may be a mistake, fueled by an ardor always difficult to keep in tight rein. Everything was happening too quickly.

She paused in front of the four-flat building, then turned and gazed at this rugged, sexy guy, and hesitated, still battling indecision.

Hell, they were just heading for a wonderful romp in bed. Not like he was forcing her. She wanted it just as much as he did. What could go wrong?

"I'll see what's going on with the old lady. I'd like to avoid any hassle, if I can."

"Hey, I don't want you getting into trouble, but I don't think either of us can wait. We'll go somewhere else, if you think . . . .."

"No. It's okay. If she hears us, just be quiet and try to make

20

yourself look smaller. She doesn't see that well, either."

"I'll be like a ghost. Good thing her hearing's not good, though, because my heart's pounding like a bass drum."

She smiled and planted a quick, wet kiss on his lips. Feeling better again, she skipped lightly up the porch steps. She opened the outer door and peeked inside, then beckoned him. He took the stairs two at a time, joining her on the stoop. Pulling her to him, he nuzzled her hair and neck, kissing her lightly on the ear.

This was perfect. Just perfect. He trembled, clearly seething with an impatient equal to hers.

FOUR

They sped through the doorway into a little foyer, heading for the stairs.

"Quiene va alla?" a shrill voice cackled from the room to their right, the door slightly ajar.

"It's Jodi, Mrs. Ramos, from 2B."

"Who wit you?"

"Gloria, my roomy. Just the two of us, coming in for the evening."

"Okay. *Buenos noches.*"

Grabbing Angie's hand, they raced up the stairs, turning left at the top. Five quick steps brought them to her doorway. She turned, giggling and looking radiant. He swept her up in his arms and their lips fused, tongues fencing, their bodies aflame, quivering deliciously.

"Wait. Let me . . .."

Hands shaking, she fumbled with the key, finally springing

the latch. Once inside, he kicked the door closed and again snatched her close in a steamy embrace. Four hands roamed freely, his busy fingers exploring the firm fullness of her body, and hers the lean hardness of his. Electricity stormed every nerve, sapping strength from her legs.

Finally breaking away, she dragged him across the room.

"C'mon. In here. I'm too horny to wait a minute longer." She was dazzling, glowing with the heat surging through her. His eyes consumed her, as if photographing the memory.

Spilling into the bedroom, he pawed at the buttons on her blouse.

"Wait. Wait." she panted and shoved away his fingers. "I'm gonna undress you and then treat you to a sexy strip. To set the mood."

"I don't need any encouragement, beautiful." He groaned softly, and his tongue darted between lips as she twisted, spinning from his grasp, arms raised and intertwined above her head.

"You'll love it, baby. I promise it'll be worth the wait."

A hungry smile split his lips. His dark eyes devoured her, and he nodded, as if answering an inner voice.

Jodi avoiding his grasp as she slowly unfastened the buttons of his shirt, moving around him like an ethereal forest nymph. Slender, red-tipped fingers lightly stroked his chest. Teasing kisses peppered his neck, chest and belly. She slipped behind him, stripped away his shirt, and snuggled tantalizingly against him while unfastening his belt.

He was as still as a bronze statue as she unzipped his fly, pulling down his pants. Crouching in back, her hands constantly fluttered over him with butterfly wings. Finally, onto her knees, she lowered his boxer shorts as her long nailed, perfect fingers trailed up and down the insides of his thighs, fleetingly caressing what had grown there.

She deftly fended off his clutch and gently shoved him into a sitting position on the bed. Jodi stood, feet spread, hand on her hips, her tongue darting across smiling lips.

She began swaying, hips undulating with an ancient provocation. The last of her blouse unbuttoned, she teased him with fleeting views of her luscious breasts. A slow pirouette, and when she faced him again the thin silk top rested in her hands, barely covering those lovely mounds. She swayed erotically in place as she slowly uncovered one, then the other. Her large nipples stood fully erect. His midnight-dark eyes glittered with a smoldering, almost maniacal passion.

Wonderful. I'm driving him absolutely crazy. This is going to be so-o-o perfect. I can hardly wait.

She eased down her short white skirt and twirled once more as her sheer bikini panties vanished. One last spin gave him full view of the woman he'd bargained for. Hands on hips, she arched her back, naked perfection—Aphrodite incarnate.

Caution long dismissed, she enveloped him, kissing, licking, stroking them both into a frenzy. His mouth, tongue and hands devoured that glorious body, as they whipped each other into a wild froth. She flipped around on the bed and took his hardness greedily into her mouth, while his tongue licked and sucked engorged lower lips, drinking in her freely flowing juices. They were on the verge of a wonderful madness.

"I can't wait any longer! I need that big beautiful thing in me—now. Condom?"

"No worries," he said. "You'll never get a disease from me."

"Oh, shit. I never . . . Promise you're not . . .."

"Yeah, yeah. No STD's from me, Babe. We gonna do this?"

"Oh, damn, can't stop now."

Flooded with passion, she crawled over him, straddling his body, taking his iron hard spear slowly into her. Then she started to move, rocking back and forth as she raised and lowered herself, trapped him in a wet, velvety grip.

"Oh, god, I'm coming already," she wailed. "Oh, damn. Not so soon. Please. Not so soon. Oh, god!"

"Yes. Me, too. Do it to me, whore. Fuck me, while you call to God. Too late . . . to redeem yourself. Oh, Lord, forgive me the pleasure. Arggghh."

He exploded, his fingers gliding across her hips, her thighs, her breasts, as his release ignited hers, filling her with mind-numbing ecstasy. In a corner of her brain, shrouded by the shuddering glory of her climax, a thought bloomed.

He's talking dirty, but . . . so strange. What's he trying to say? Lost in the throes of her orgasm, the full impact of his passion-slurred words didn't register.

His hands crept higher, caressing her shoulders and neck, sowing ridges of goose-bumps. She barely heard his murmured words, his tender tone belying a dangerous message.

"Wanton whore. Immoral harlot. Now it is God calling for *you*. Pray you find redemption at his side."

Still trapped inside her, he began hardening again as he drew her closer, kissing her breast, then her lips. His roaming hands gently circling her neck. Still trying to make sense of his words, raw ardor clouded her thoughts as his thumbs caressed the lines of her jaw, stealing tantalizingly down the front of her neck.

Smiling whimsically, his lips lightly brushed hers, followed by a gentle sigh. Suddenly those thumbs became rigid posts, boring into her windpipe, his grip tightening like a vise.

Jodi gurgled and pried at his wrists, clawing weakly—ineffectual efforts casually thrust aside. His black orbs glittered, his lips twisted into a cruel smile as her eyes bulged, filled with terror.

"Don't!" Her voice a hoarse whisper. "You're hurting . . .."

Shit. I shouldn't have . . . Her hands fluttered, the wings of a crippled bird, as her body went slack. Her karate brown belt meant nothing.

Dedios drew her close, the pressure from his thumbs never relenting, as he planted a gentle kiss on her forehead.

"Listen and you'll hear him. Your journey to glory awaits you."

Her last, fleeting memory in life was his final three words, ringing in her ears . . ..

"The Lord calls."

FIVE

The patrol cruiser careened down a dark alley, ricocheting off one wall, then off another. Its siren pulsed, an ear-piercing wail, echoing off a massive stone barrier looming ahead. The car was out of control, about to annihilate itself against that impenetrable pile of rock. He clutched the wheel and pumped the brakes with no effect. He tensed and burrowed back into the seat, braced against what was surely his impending death. The repetitive squeal of the klaxon echoed off the brick canyon, as if summoning him . . ..

Al Warner lurched awake, groggy and disoriented. He fumbled in the dark and cursed under his breath as he groped for the insistently trilling phone, surely the siren in his dream. It fell in a jangling crash as he knocked the noisy contraption onto the floor.

"What the fuck time is it?" he muttered, as he scrambled for the hand piece. Shaking away cobwebs, his eyes focused on the LED of his clock radio: 5:40 AM.

"Yeah?" he growled. "Whatizzit?"

"Al? Is that you?"

"What other asshole'd be answerin' this fuckin' phone at this hour?"

"Hey." The voice was indignant. "That how you talk to your boss? You still asleep?"

"Not anymore." He sighed. "Sorry, Cap'n." Warner perched on the edge of the bed, stifled a yawn, and knuckling sandy eyelids.

"I *was* asleep, and havin' one hell of a scary dream. What's up?"

"Good then, that I woke you. Anyhow, we got us a murder over near the U of M. Strangled coed, maybe raped. CSU's on the way. Get your ass down there before someone fucks up the crime scene. I get real nervous about a campus murder, ever since Gainesville."

Detective Alan Warner, now fully awake, turned on the night-stand light and scrambled for his note pad and pen. He copied an address and the few details Captain Santiago had. He hung up and stretched, trying to loosen the dream-cramped muscles in his back and get his still sleep-fogged mind into gear.

Damn. He needed coffee. Hadn't had a good night sleep in at least a week. Those goddammed, crazy dreams. The doc said he was fully recovered. Physically, maybe, but he never had nightmares like these before. Post-traumatic stress over crazy Leordano, Doc said.

He stripped off sweat-soaked pajamas and hurried to the bathroom. Tepid water from the "cold" faucet splashed across his face did little to dispel the remnants of sleep.

He grunted. One of the few things he missed from his childhood in northern Illinois was cold water from the tap.

Warner's fingers sought the still slightly throbbing right side of his head. Close-set, dark-brown eyes examined the area

26

above his right ear in the mirror, tracing the three-inch-long furrow, well-hidden now by his mop of curly chocolate hair. The dull ache, always amplified by the nightmares, was beginning to fade. His slightly hawkish face, usually ruggedly pleasing, was a crumpled road map, seamed by occasional scars earned over the years at his hazardous occupation.

He looked wrung out, but so many weeks without a real night's sleep can do that to a guy. So what. He didn't think he was anything special to look at, except maybe when he went running on South Beach. He was compact and well-muscled, the rewards of vigorous rehabilitation after the Leordano fiasco. At forty, he was in the best physical condition of his life.

He slipped on tan, cargo-pocketed slacks and a beige short sleeved cotton shirt. The air had cooled, as it did most falls, but never cold enough for Warner. In the kitchen, he mixed a large mug of strong, instant coffee and grabbed two chocolate doughnuts from a box on his counter, examining them for ants. Lucky the little bastards hadn't found these yet. As an afterthought, he stowed the box in the refrigerator.

He shrugged on his shoulder holster and light sports jacket and was out of his cookie-cutter town-house, pausing only long enough to toss Mrs. Gerber's *Miami Herald* up against the foot of her front door. Any steps he could save those eighty-seven-year-old arthritic hips was a moment well spent. She had no immediate family nearby, so he always made time to run errands for her, however busy his schedule. She frequently rewarded him with plates of scrumptious brownies or slices of apple pie.

He sped along the freeway, avoiding his siren, as traffic on I-95 was light at that early hour. He made good time and arrived in his green Dodge Charger at 6:25. Two patrol cars and a black, Chevy van crowded the street, along with an unmarked cop car he recognized.

Warner hated being the last at a murder scene. Too many ways for eager amateurs to screw up evidence. And the average street cop *was* an amateur when it came to homicide. In his haste to park, Warner's tires crawled onto the sidewalk.

Fuck it.

He jumped out of his coupe and flashed his badge at the officer guarding the door of the two-story yellow stucco building. Warner hurried across the brown-tiled foyer, finding another policeman slouched against a doorjamb of one of the downstairs apartments. A constant singsong lament poured from the open doorway.

"*Madre de Dios. La pobre nina. No en mi casa. Dios, no en mi casa. La pobre nina. Madre de Dios.*"

Warner looked at the cop, his eyebrows arched.

The young officer grimaced. "The landlady. She found the body. Sneaking around, checking on her tenants, I guess, and saw the open door. She's freaked." He gestured toward the stairs with a toss of his head.

Warner raced up, two at a time. In the door to his left a small, scruffy guy knelt, studying the carpet. Warner spotted two pairs of eyes peering through a barely ajar door of the other apartment on the floor.

Witnesses? That'd be a change. He crouched next to a diminutive man in the doorway.

"Hi, Moe," Warner said. "Findin' anything useful?"

"Nope. Just getting warmed up, Detective. Finished with the stiff, though. What a dish. One good look at her, and you might get a little stiff yourself." He stood, proffering his hand.

"Glad you're back on the job, Detective. Not enough good men in Homicide to let a guy like you sit on the sidelines."

Warner nodded to the short, pencil-thin man, round-shouldered from years hunched over lab tables and microscopes.

Maurice Gold was an unlikely looking cop, with thinning, light-brown hair and a scrawny little mustache. Thick, shaggy eyebrows hovered like wings over a huge Semitic beak, one of the things earning him the nickname, "The Hawk." And like that raptor, his piercing eyes rarely missed even the tiniest detail. Dressed in a crumpled, tan polyester suit, he seemed innocuous and bumbling, until you noticed those intense, cocoa eyes.

Moe Gold was only small in stature. His analytical brain seldom missed much. An ability to put together an accurate assessment of a series of events from limited pieces of evidence had won the Dade County D.A. a high rate of convictions.

"You ain't gonna like this one, though. Déjà vu," he said.

"What're you talkin' about?" Warner enjoyed the little man's often dry humor.

"The vic, Al. The vic. That's one beautiful dead sweetheart in there, buddy. She could have given even an old cocker like me a good hard-on. Take a look." He returned to his inspection of the entrance. "You can move her a little if you want. I've done my prelims. Oy, what a waste."

The detective chuckled as he headed for the other door. He saw her immediately, sprawled across the bed. Her head dangled over the side of the mattress, sightless, distended dark blue eyes, now clouded by the signs of asphyxiation, glared angrily at the ceiling. He walked around to the other side for a better look.

God, she *was* gorgeous. Used to be, anyhow. What a terrific body. Familiar looking, too. Damn, he'd seen her—or her photo—somewhere. But where, damn it? Well, it would probably come to him. He pivoted, taking his time, slowly scanning the room, searching for something that might strike him as wrong or out of place.

As Metro-Dade's chief homicide detective, Al Warner got the real murders, not the obvious drug-related shoot-em-ups.

Just off injury leave, his caseload already overflowed. It was wearing him down. That and the recurring nightmares plaguing his sleep since the Leordano affair.

The often-restless nights—and plenty of bad dreams like the one he had that morning—conspired to make him tired—very tired. What sleep he got didn't bring much real rest. But he couldn't take off any more time.

Just too many loonies out there, and it was his job to catch them.

SIX

The Hawk's comments made Warner leery of something scary, and he'd had enough of that with Leordano. His stomach churned at that memory, the acidic fumes of bile sliding up this throat as he looked at the dead young coed.

Her once exquisite face was bloated, eyes and tongue distended, the normal results from strangulation. He could see the dark discoloration at the front of her throat where the perp buried his thumbs. Lifting one of the girl's shoulders, he noted the raw bruises on the side and back of her neck.

Probably strangled by hand from the front, both thumbs crushing the larynx. Put her out of action almost instantly. No signs of a struggle—no defensive wounds he could see. Checking her hands, the ruby finger nails seemed clean. No obvious skin residue from fighting a rapist. She knew the guy, and they were fucking when he killed her. That's pretty damned callous.

He moved up the bed, crawling onto the side to peer between her legs, searching the sheets beneath.

"Pervert," Gold giggled, standing in the doorway, arms crossed.

"Yeah, they'd completed the act. Lots of sperm all over. Ain't these kids ever heard of AIDS? He sure didn't use a rubber."

"Looks like she must have known him. No forced entry. No signs of rape. Nope, this honey was a willful participant. She let the guy bang her, then kill her. Much to her surprise, I suspect. You got any idea on the time of death, Moe?"

"That's the M.E.'s job, Al."

"Don't feed me that shit, Gold. You got an opinion on everything. I'm not gonna carve it in stone. Just a ballpark to work with, 'til the M.E. finishes. Give me a head start, will ya?"

"Geez, what a pushy bastard. Well, based on her current temp and rigidity, I guess One, maybe Two AM. Don't go quoting me to Luis, now. Okay?"

"What're you worried about, Moe? They gonna send you to the principal's office?"

"Touchy, touchy this morning, aren't we, Detective? You know, you oughta get more sleep. You look like shit."

"Yeah? Well, it ain't for lack of tryin'. I've hit the sack early three or four times in the last week. I sleep, but don't seem to get much rest. Lots of nightmares since Leordano. I guess my little dance with that bastard ain't been so good for my dreams."

"Yeah, well that was nasty, all right. And you were pretty lucky at the end. I tell ya, Al, the world's full of crazies. A normal guy like me wouldn't do something like this. Our mommies taught us better. With a beauty like this, make love, not war.

"Anyway, back to work. Find this mamzer quick, Al. My kishkes tell me this guy might make Leordano look like a boy scout."

"Why? You think this ain't just a one-timer, Moe?" Icy fingers skipped down the detective's spine and prickled the

31

hairs on the back of his neck.

Another serial-killer, so soon after the last crazy bastard? He shuddered, his hand tentatively stroking the hidden scar.

"You ain't been in the bathroom yet, huh?" Gold asked.

"Can't seem to tear myself away from the stiff. Seems familiar, or maybe I've seen her photo somewhere. Just can't place it yet." Was he looking for a good reason not to move?

"So, schmuck, go in the bathroom."

"What's there?" Warner's reluctance was a useless stall. Unnatural panic rippled just below the surface of his control, a beast ready to rear up and engulf him. Was he really ready for this, so soon after coming back on The Job? His stomach knotted in expectation of something he knew he didn't want to see.

"Go. Then tell me what *your* gut says."

Warner sighed and accepted the fact he had to see what Moe was talking about. Damn. This was his job, and all the nightmare of Leordano, and all the bad dreams weren't going to keep him from doing it, and doing it well. Still, as he started toward the open door, another wave of apprehension washed over him. The last thing he need now was another lunatic.

Worse than Leordano?

Shit, he hoped not.

He paused for a moment at the threshold, his jaw in a vice-grip. Sighing, he stepped onto the white tile floor of the small room and glanced around.

It hit him like a blast of Arctic cold, snatching his breath, numbing his mind. He feared something like this from Gold's comments, yet was still unprepared for its shattering impact.

Shit. Oughta be used to it—water off a duck's back. But after Leordano, everything changed. *He* changed. He leaned back against to doorjamb for support.

Fuckin' red lipstick. Why do they use that damned red lipstick? Fucked up loonies, runnin' around killin' people. They love the dramatic, but this one's pretty damned trite.

He hunkered, motionless for several moments, barely breathing, trying to absorb every nuance of the message, scrawled across the vanity mirror in vivid, blood-red block letters. A stark, single word, foretelling more terror and death.

"Shit." he muttered aloud, his stomach doing its own version of Rock and Roll. The sour taste of last night's TV dinner in his throat, he turned and stumbled out of the room, shivering from an unnatural cold.

Better finish up and get the hell out of there. He'd return later once he settled down. An oppressive weight, a leaden drape, dragged at him, smothering the very breath from his lungs.

Not again.

Shit. Another maniac, with Leordano barely cold in the ground. Not again.

SEVEN

Al Warner slouched at his battered oak desk and stared vacantly into space. His usually nimble mind was in "Park" from lack of sleep. The scene that morning in Coral Gables was just bitter frosting on a cake of exhaustion. The thump of footsteps coming up behind him barely registered.

"So, what ya got, Al? This one gonna be straight forward, I hope?"

"Don't think so, Cap'n." He glanced up at his boss. "The vic's name is Jodi Gannon, a knockout U of M beauty who was doin' the horizontal rumba when her lover turned out her lights.

Strangled, his thumbs doing a number on the larynx." He massaged his eyes.

"Looks like she was humpin' him willingly. And no, I doubt this is gonna be easy. Moe's 'kishkes' tell him this guy could be worse than Leordano, and his tummy has an awfully good record on this sort of thing."

"Shit. What else?"

"He left us the red lipstick message on the bathroom mirror. Not very original, but it's likely this may be only the first of whatever crusade he's on. I got a bad feelin'. Very bad."

The detective shoved his camera phone in front of his boss. Captain Santiago stared at blood-red call to death, splashed across the mirror like a gruesome knife slash. The reflected sight of the photographer and the hot flare of his flash seemed to be hiding behind the one-word scrawl. It was surreal.

"This is *it*?" he asked, eyebrows arched, his handsome dark face screwed up into a grimace. "Shit. Another deadly fucking screwball. Why has Miami suddenly become serial killers' city of choice? Sure am glad to have you back on The Job, Al."

"Thanks, Captain." He grunted and scowled. "Just so happy to be smack in the middle again, my first week back."

"Feeling sorry for yourself, Detective? I can always . . .."

"Forget it, Cap. This is my kinda ballgame, like it or not. That blond kid was the most magnificent dame I've ever seen. If you're gonna feel sorry for someone, make it her—and her family. And all the other young girls he's probably gonna snuff if we don't catch him soon? Feel sorry for *them*, Captain."

Warner's anger wasn't aimed at his boss, who just stood in the line of fire.

"Yeah, you're right, amigo. This gotta be pretty tough, you just back and swamped so soon. You getting any sleep, Detective? You look terrible."

"Geez, thanks. Moe Gold said the same thing this mornin'.

Yeah, I'm gettin' plenty of sleep, just no real rest. Leordano's gone, but he's left me with heaps of dreams. Bad, scary ones. I wake up all rung out."

"I'm not surprised, especially after bouncing a bullet off your thick skull. The public thinks we're too tough for these guys to get to us. What do they know?"

Warner nodded and rubbed the back of his neck.

"You need a break from serial-killers, Al? I can assign this to . . .."

"Nah, don't do that. I'm in it already. We don't even know for sure this guy is serial, but if he is, we gotta get him quick, and I'm the most experienced detective on these nuts. I'll be okay."

"All right. But let's not get ahead of ourselves. So far, it's one girl. Maybe it was personal, and it stops here. Don't want to get the press all fired up again until we know more."

"Yeah, well like Moe, my gut says this ain't gonna be just one girl for long. Then what?"

"Well, it's our job to nail him. What d'ya got going?"

"Gold's still at the scene." Warner stretched and sighed. "I'm waitin' to see what kinda magic he works. The place was wiped clean, includin' her neck and throat, so there's no prints."

"Pretty clever. Most guys don't know you can leave prints on skin."

"Right. There *was* sperm, so they'll run his DNA for a match through our system and the FBI database. I doubt we'll get a hit, but at least we'll know who's who when we nail him.

"I got three uniforms prowlin' the apartment building and surroundin' area, lookin' for anyone who mighta seen or heard something. Sent a photo and a few details to the Herald. A beauty like this'll make the front page. Maybe someone saw her last night with the guy. It's a shot, anyway." Warner glanced at his notes.

35

"Harris and Olvida will hit the U of M after they check out the vic's apartment building. Interview classmates, friends—the usual. Her roommate's missin' for the moment." He lurched to his feet, flexing his shoulders and neck, trying to relax tension-knotted muscles.

"I'm goin' over the contents from the scene. The usual personal stuff. And I guess I gotta call her parents. Bloomington, Minnesota. How I love *that* job, but I don't want 'em hearin' it second hand. Might as well get *that* over with."

He slid into his chair, leaning back, looking up at his boss.

"Anything I mighta missed, Cap?"

"Nope. Looks like you got things under control. I don't envy you that phone call, man."

"Wanna make it for me, Boss?"

"No, sir. It's your case, so it's your call. I just supply the quarter."

"Thanks a heap. Well, I guess I'd better get at it."

Warner picked up a small, well-worn personal phone directory he'd found in the girl's desk. There were lots of names and numbers needing follow-up. He flipped it open to "G" and found, "Mom." He sighed, clenching his teeth, as he punched out the number. The phone was answered on the second ring.

"Hello?" The voice was soft and musical.

"Mrs. Gannon?"

"Yes. May I help you?"

His hands were sweating, his jaw clenched. He didn't give a damn about tears pooling in his eyes. He was about to destroy all the melody left in her life.

"My name is Alan Warner, ma'am. I'm a detective with the Miami-Dade Police. It's about your daughter, Jodi . . .."

"What's wrong? Is she all right?" Panic propelled her words across the fiber optics, and he could almost see her wilting. It was going to get worse, very soon. Warner bit his lip, wishing he could just hang up, but knew this unhappy job had to be done.

"I'm afraid that there's no easy way to say this, ma'am. I'm sorry to have to tell you, Jodi was murdered in her apartment, early this morning."

A soul-wrenching wail hurtled into his ear, followed by the clatter of a dropped phone and a loud thud.

Oh, shit. She's fainted.

Warner heard a frantic male voice and the soft moaning of the woman. The phone banged around some more and a strong, hoarse voice boomed loudly over the line.

"This is John Gannon. Who the hell is this? What did you say to my wife? She's fainted, damn you. Who *is* this?"

"I'm sorry, Mr. Gannon," Warner said softly. Their pain was squeezing the breath out of him. He reluctantly began his message of agony and despair again.

"I'm Detective Alan Warner, in Miami. It's about your daughter, Jodi . . .."

EIGHT

While Al Warner reluctantly shattered the lives of Jodi Gannon's parents, Detective Rafael Olvida was talking to the young couple living in the apartment directly adjacent to the murder scene—and not getting much. The guy kept looking pensively at his watch.

"Look, Mr. Sims, I know you're eager to get going, but Jodi Gannon was brutally strangled by someone she knew well enough to let in. We gotta know what you saw or heard last night, and if you've seen her with any particular guy recently.

Here or anywhere else, for that matter."

"Yeah. Sorry. Okay, Detective. We don't know much. We both work—which we're late for this morning, by the way . . .."

"Yeah, you keep telling me. I'll write you a note. The quicker you answer my questions, the quicker you can trot outta here. So . . .?"

The man sighed. "Well, like I said, there isn't much to tell. We didn't see her often. The walls are thick in this old building, so we didn't hear much, either. She wasn't the noisy type. We think we heard her come in last night around eleven-thirty or twelve."

His wife nodded in agreement.

"Yeah, it was around midnight. We heard a few sounds a little later—you know, passionate-like. It's hard to tell." He blushed. "We were kinda busy ourselves at the time. That's about it." His wife nodded again.

Todd Sims was going to miss Jodi Gannon. He'd watched her more than he would ever confess to Dot. Jodi was the major character in his fantasies when he was making love to his wife.

He didn't realize Dot would miss Jodi, too. She was fully aware of the part their lovely blonde neighbor had played in providing her such a happy sex life. Their sex was so much better, and much more frequent, since that beauty moved in last year.

Questions, answers and personal erotic fantasies were all noisily interrupted by angry sounds erupting in the hallway.

Olvida went to the door. A very tall, irate young woman was aggressively towering over his partner, Jack Harris, who was blocking the door to the crime scene.

"Who're you?" he was asking.

"Who the fuck are *you*?" she responded, arms akimbo. "And what the hell are you doing in my apartment?"

"Your apartment? You live here?"

38

"You bet your ass, buddy. And if you don't get out of my way, I'll call the cops."

"I *am* the cops," Harris shouted, flashing his badge. This job was tough on his blood pressure. Seeing Olvida in the other doorway, he yelled.

"Hey, Ralph, will ya see they get this damned door taped off." He turned back to the confused young woman, and began again in a more civil tone.

"I'm sorry miss, but you can't go in there. Not until we're finished."

"Finished? Finished with what? What the hell's going on here?"

"Oh, shit. No way you'd know what . . . You Gannon's roommate?"

"Yeah. Gloria Roberts. What's happened? Did she do something stupid?"

"Yeah, she did something stupid. Like bringing home the wrong guy for fun and games. I'm sorry, Miss Roberts, but Jodi was murdered last night."

"What!" the girl shrieked, throwing her hands to her mouth. "Ohmygod. She's—she's dead? Jodi's dead? Oh-my-god."

The girl swayed drunkenly and started to collapse. Harris sprang forward, supporting her, and steered her toward the Sims' apartment.

"Can she sit in here for a while?" Olvida stepped out, snatching her other arm, helping Harris hold her up.

"We can't let her back into her apartment until Crime Scene's done sweeping for evidence"

The young couple nodded dumbly.

"Good going." Olvida muttered to his partner. "You handled that like a real diplomat. Ya gotta polish your act, Jack. Learn to be a little more sensitive."

"Yeah, Yeah. I know. I wasn't thinking." The two detectives

helped the blubbering young woman into the Sims' apartment.

"Hey, get her a drink of water, will ya. Ralph, you take her statement when she can talk. I gotta get back next door and see how Moe's coming."

"Sure. Sure. Sit here, Miss Roberts, was it? Take a couple of breaths. I know this is a shocker."

"Huh?" she looked up at the swarthy face in front of her. Her eyes were beginning to focus again, and her breathing was returning to normal. She buried her face in her hands, crying softly.

"Oh, god. Jodi. Jodi." Her long, angular body heaved convulsively. "Oh, poor baby. You had so much going for you." Reality was sinking in. Racked by hoarse, choked sobs, she collapsed into a chair.

Shit, this is never easy. Some lunatic snuffs an innocent life for reasons only he understands and smashes a bunch of others along the way. What a miserable fucking job.

Olvida hoped he'd get a chance to put a couple of rounds in the bastard when they finally caught him. He'd save the State some money, and the family lots of grief.

He looked at the young woman, drowning in pain.

Gotta find something else to do—another department. Homicide is starting to get to me. The dust's just settling over Leordano, and we got another one.

Another murderous lunatic.

Son-of-a-bitch.

NINE

The two detectives left the apartment forty minutes later with little to begin an investigation. Gloria Roberts took a half-hour

40

to sufficiently pull herself together to answer questions. She supplied names of several of the victim's male friends but didn't think Jodi was seeing any of them very seriously and doubted she was sleeping with anybody recently.

"Jodi was a passionate girl," she said, "but she wasn't promiscuous. She was serious about modeling and acting, and wasn't into innocuous affairs with what she called 'college studs.'

"She said if she did get involved, it'd be a 'real man.'"

"Do you know what she meant by 'a real man?'" Olvida asked.

"Someone older, more mature, I guess. Maybe a guy who could help with her career."

Gloria was fading as she listlessly ticked off the names of her dead roommate's favorite haunts around campus: restaurants, bars, and workout clubs. She slowly descended into the dark caverns of shock-induced stupor. They laid her out on the sofa in the Sims' apartment. Todd got a spare blanket, and Dot decided to call in sick. She'd stay home and help her young neighbor through the day.

Who says people don't care about each other anymore? Detective Olvida shrugged, as they left.

Now the two homicide cops began the grueling task of checking out the few people and many places they learned of from the roommate. The job entailed plenty of footwork, little of it fancy, and a lot of talking, little of it productive. The key was finding one tiny gem amid all the muck they would rake through. One or two little, precious jewels that might, just maybe, lead them to the mother lode—the killer.

This painstaking job took time and patience. They couldn't be seduced into careless boredom by the tediousness of the mission, or that little gem might be missed—thrown out with the rest of the garbage. It was a miserable task, but it wasn't thankless if it lead to their prey. Anyway, it was all they had.

They headed back to headquarters in Olvida's battered Chevy. They'd split up to expedite coverage of all they had to canvass, looking for a lead. Harris needed his own vehicle to speed up the task.

The search for truth and guilt had begun, less than ten hours after Jodi Gannon gasped her last breath.

It would take a long and frustrating path.

TEN

Detective Warner scrawled mindless doodles as he mulled possible new avenues to expand the search for something—anything—giving him a lead to the author of this senseless killing. He waggled his jaw, trying to loosen cramped muscles and clenched teeth.

It was only the second day of the investigation, but a pressing urgency filled him to unearth something quickly. The ominous message, shouting angrily at him from Jodi Gannon's bathroom mirror, surely promised this guy would kill again. Where, when, and how he selects his victims—those were the questions. One death didn't create a pattern.

Al Warner was *the* serial killer expert on the South Florida Gold Coast. He had attended two FBI schools, including stints with the BAU, devoted entirely to the psychology and motivations of these seriously disturbed psychopaths. The book on these lunatics might provide an insight to help catch him.

Some serial killers were born that way—without a moral compass. Environment and parenting (or lack thereof), while still a factor, bore less of an impact in current thinking than

DNA. Many of these monsters are born without any link to a conscience. Most were medically—but not legally—insane. They knew the consequences of their actions, understanding the moral code against them, but didn't care. Often, they had suffered serious abuse as children, usually at the hands of their parents, exacerbating their innate predilection.

They progressed from petty crimes to more gruesome acts of violence, often with small animals before evolving into homicidal psychotics, obsessed by a particular target for a very specific reason, usually known only to themselves. Their victims were the deadly results of their imagined goals, selected often randomly from those who, in the mind of the killer, met his particular parameters.

But being crazy didn't preclude them from being very bright (often with genius IQ's) and very clever. They were among the most elusive of all criminals. Many were never caught, since these wily lunatics often appeared similar to everybody else: normal, healthy guys (seldom women), concerned with the usual routines of life. They might be pleasant, mild mannered, and charming, until suddenly transforming into monsters, dispatching innocent victims for their absurd purposes.

Now he may be faced by another such madman, that reality wedging open a vault buried deep inside Warner's mind. Entombed visions slithered into his consciousness—bitter memories of his first and only actual confrontation with Luis Leordano . . ..

He slowed his Dodge, searching the canal bank, lined by shin-high, brown grass. No way across the water here without some sort of flotation. He was already three miles past the Indian village. The anonymous caller said two-and-a-half miles.

Probably just another sick prank, but the guy sounded genuinely frightened. Pulling off the road, he got out of the car.

A grassy plain, broken by an occasional clump of melaleuca trees or live oaks, spread to the limits of his vision.

He should have waited for Jack Harris. Common sense (and department policy) dictated you don't go after a dangerous perp without your partner. Especially a madman like the Baby Butcher. But he had a date that night with Sharon and didn't want to be late. He left Jack a note, but this would probably just be a wasted three hours. Another look in a blind hole for that clever bastard.

Seventeen dead teenagers and still nothing to work on.

Back in the car, he headed slowly back toward Miami. There was a large hammock of live oaks along the canal. Might as well stop and take a better look. He pulled onto the narrow shoulder.

Moving through the shaded glade under the big trees, he was surprised to find a narrow, rutted path. Examining the moist ground, he noted recent tire tracks. Following the path south, he stumbled upon a small flood control dike across the Tamiami Canal, shielded from the road by the stately old trees. It looked like a vehicle had crossed it sometime earlier that day.

Just what the caller described. Peering across the canal, he saw a small wooded area. More live oaks. Could there be a hut of some kind back there? Damn.

He should have waited for his partner after all.

ELEVEN

Jarred back to the present by the sound of his name, Warner shuddered and shook his head, dispelling the remnants of those agonizing memories. Captain Santiago was clearly agitated.

"How's the Gannon investigation coming, Al? It's been two days. You got anything?"

"We're beatin' the bushes, Bob. The usual preliminary foot work. You gettin' pressure from upstairs already?"

"Yeah," Santiago responded, "they're pretty anxious, with this so soon after that last crazy son-of-a-bitch. Brief me."

"Okay, but there ain't much to tell. First of all, we're still canvassin' the area surroundin' the victim's apartment. Got street cops startin' at the site and are workin' out from there." He shuffled some papers on his desk, selecting a single sheet.

"Harris and Olvida are runnin' down a list of names and places they extracted, between cryin' jags, from the roommate. She came in at my request and told us what little she knew about Gannon's sex life. Took half the mornin', with all the bawlin'. She's really shaken by this thing." He shoved out of his seat and began pacing.

"Seems like Jodi Gannon was a busy, motivated gal in the midst of a fast-bloomin' modelin' career. In love with life and havin' a very good time." Warner sighed and shrugged his shoulders. "Until two nights ago.

"We're still waitin' for the Hawk. He's finished collectin' his tidbits from the apartment, includin' any clean prints. We'll process anything not belongin' to either girl, but I don't expect much. Moe said lots of things were wiped clean. Anything that might be remotely related to the killer was bagged and tagged for the lab. They've stripped the linens from the bed and are testin' 'em for semen and pubic hairs for a DNA profile."

"Hopefully we'll get a hit from that." Santiago halted Warner's prowling with a touch on the shoulder.

"I ain't so sure, Cap'n." He turned to his boss, hands on hips. "Something tells me he's new at this."

"Wonderful. Nothing's ever easy."

Warner shrugged and returned to his desk, consulting his notes on a yellow lined pad.

"Harry Klein's goin' through the girl's phone directory, callin' every South Florida number in the book. It's the kind of thing he does well, and he wants to be a part of catchin' this prick."

"Old" Harry was due to retire in just over eight months, so he seldom went into harm's way anymore. Not that he was afraid. Harry Klein had been a tough cop in the Miami Department, long before it became Metro-Dade. Over the past forty years, he'd been in his share of scrapes and was forced to kill three times in the line of duty.

It was the captain who kept Klein off the streets, a sort of deference to all his years of service, and the old detective didn't mind desk duty at this stage in his life. He had a gentle manner and a quick, bright mind, with its own built-in calculator. And he was the best in the whole department at doing what he was doing now. Few men Warner knew could wheedle as much information out of people, however scared, tight-lipped or belligerent.

"I've put a uniformed cop on the phones, monitorin' calls generated by the articles in the Herald and the Sun-Sentinel. Both had it on their front pages, which ain't surprisin', gorgeous as she was. The guy's supposed to separate the wheat from the chaff and only to give me the good stuff. He'll handle the rest himself. There's always plenty of crank calls after a crime like this."

"Getting anything worthwhile? Somebody musta seen something. We got a grand reward on the TIPS line."

"Nothin' yet. I've talked with three guys and one female, all students at U of M, but there wasn't much there. They knew Gannon, and all obviously had the hots for her, includin' the girl. All they really wanted was the details of what happened, stuff I'm not givin' out at the moment."

"Well, so far there's been no panic," Santiago said. "I've taken your suggestion to temporarily keep the information about the lipstick message from the press. It's being treated like an isolated event. The apartment's remaining sealed, with a uniform always on the door." The captain looked at Warner.

"There's gonna be a loud wail from both papers when they find out we've withheld that detail."

"Too bad," Warner said. "No need to foster wholesale panic over another serial nut-case—or spawn a copycat."

"Yeah. The specter of Leordano is still too fresh."

Nodding, Warner looked at his list again and sighed.

"There ain't much more to do, Bob, except wait for Gold or the people on the street to turn up something. Give us some direction for the investigation."

Santiago nodded, giving Warner an encouraging pat on the back, and headed for his office. Meanwhile, Warner could only wait and hope someone calls with something of real value.

A direct line number was listed in both papers. This hapless waiting was the toughest, because Warner knew this lunatic may already be stalking another victim. If not now, then very soon. Some of these guys waited months between kills. Others, rarely, just days.

TWELVE

The ring of his private line broke Warner's meditation. *Now what?* He lifted the receiver and grumbled a terse greeting.

"Yeah? What?"

"Oh, Al, you charmer, you." A rich, contralto chuckle caressed his ear, a sound filling this rough-edged man with a sense of—what? "Awe" was about right. And a surprising feeling of tenderness. Unfamiliar sensations, always followed by a gentle fluttering of his heart.

47

"Ah, Counselor. If I'd known it was you . . . well, things are always different around you. Thank god."

Sharon Clark was a special, unexpected treat in Warner's normally stark existence. This tall, shapely, hazel-eyed brunette with the all-American girl beauty was both intelligent and passionate. That she, an educated woman from an upper-class Northeastern background, found attractive a gruff, graceless, hard-core cop was a miracle he never fully comprehended. Nor did he try. He just hesitantly accepted her love for what it seemed, a true mystery of life, one in which he reveled.

"How's your case comin'?" he queried, enveloped by the warm glow her phone presence brought him.

"Slowly. I don't think we'll even get to our side until next week. Probably not until Wednesday or Thursday."

"Ya know, sometimes I wonder how you do it, Sherry."

"What is it exactly that you don't understand, Al?" she asked with a musical little chuckle.

"The bastard's clearly guilty. He raped and beat two little teenage girls, and thought he'd get away with it just because they were black. I know *you* know he's guilty. Don't it keep you awake nights, defendin' scum like that?"

"It's not always easy, but that's a Public Defender's job. The law promises everybody a proper defense. I have to give it my best shot, or I couldn't live with myself. You know that's me—dedicated to my tasks, whether defending a bad client, or loving a surly cop." She laughed.

"Anyway, luckily for the public, I doubt my best will be nearly good enough this time. The stupid redneck bastard was so cocky, he's buried himself at every turn. Your buddies have hammered out a pretty ironclad case, but Coggins is so steeped in prejudice he can't conceive he'll be convicted. He won't let me try to plead it out, so don't lose any sleep over him. I suspect he's going to sleep, permanently, even though it may take ten

48

years. Off the record, of course."

"Yeah, well sleep's a sore subject with me right now. I'm pooped. Hit the sack early, sleep through the night, and wake up exhausted, all wrung out. Lots of bad dreams. The aftermath of Leordano, I guess. Now we got this U of M gal."

"Yes, I saw her photo in the *Herald* this morning. A real beauty. Was it rape? There weren't many details in the article."

"That's how we want it for now. What I'm goin' to tell you is strictly off the record, Sherry. Not for discussion with anybody else. And I mean anybody."

"Sure, honey. No problem. You sound nervous. Is it that bad?" She was genuinely concerned, and Warner loved her for it. Hard to believe this fantastic gal truly cared for him.

"Worse. It looks like we've got ourselves another loony. Another Leordano, or somethin' similar."

"No. Seriously? How do you know, if this is the first one? There *is* only one so far, isn't there?"

"Yeah, as far as we know. But there was the classic note left at the scene. It's got all the markin's of another crazy on some sort of self-appointed mission. We kept the part about the note out of the papers for now. Don't want to start another panic, or encourage copycats." He paused, then went on.

"I tell you what worries me, Sherry. Looks like they had consensual sex, just before he killed her, so the guy must be smooth and charming. The worst kind, 'cause gals will trust him. Trust him to death. Theirs."

"Oh, how awful. Do you know how he's selecting his victims?"

"There's no pattern yet. This babe was very beautiful. A smart, active kid who seemed to know where she was goin' in life. Or thought she did, until the killer short-circuited it. The perp's motivation could be anything at this point. All we know is, in some distorted way, he may think he's on a mission. At least that's what the note indicated. The question is, *what mission?*"

"What did the note say, Al?"

"Shouldn't say." He shook his head. "Already told you more than I shoulda. Enough to know it's scary."

"No leads of any kind, Al?"

"Nothin' yet. Forensics' still sortin' through the stuff Gold collected at the scene. Plenty of prints, but I'm bettin' none of 'em belonged to our man. We've got five guys on the street, followin' up what little we have."

"Geez" she said, her voice colored with concern, "No wonder you're not getting much rest. I'm surprised you can sleep at all, with this being so close to the Leordano case."

"Yeah, well I'd usually be goin' full speed when we get one like this. But I'm so wrung out, the old brain is in a fog half the time. For instance, I know I've seen this gal somewhere. A photo, or somethin'. But I can't pin it down. Never use to be a problem. Before Leordano, anyway." He sighed.

"Even hittin' the hay early doesn't help much. I get enough to keep goin', but I'm not razor sharp. That scares me, 'cause I just might miss something that'll get another gal killed. Shit. I hate these loony bastards worse than anything."

"So, let's have dinner tonight and a quiet evening together. Get those batteries recharged. I should be done with court by Five. You need some major TLC, and I'm just the one to do it."

"Great idea, Sherry. Sometimes gettin' away from a case is the best way to solve it. You're good for me, hon, but I keep wonderin' what you see in a hard-case schlep like me?"

"Well, they say, 'love is blind.' But the truth is, you can't hide that big, tender heart under your crusty exterior."

"Don't broadcast that, babe. Bad for my rep."

"Are you kidding? You're the most compassionate guy I know, and an intellectual equal to anybody I've dated. They may have graduated from fancy schools and have post-grad degrees, but you understand things they never even thought of." A short hesitation and she continued, her voice soft and sweet.

"You're my first guy who really seems to understand love. Always eager to do things to make me happy—and not expecting it the other way around, and that's pretty damned special."

"Yeah, well, it's easy with you. I've never been in love. In lust maybe, but never love. I'm just gonna enjoy this while it lasts."

"You think this is a passing fancy, Al? A fling?" Her words choked. "What have I ever said to make you feel I'm so shallow?"

"Sorry. Didn't mean it that way. It's not you. It's just I'm still not use to—to being loved."

"Cut it out. You *know* I love you. So, tell me what time you're picking me up. We can go to that little Italian place in the Grove."

"How about 7:30? Gives me time to review what we get today."

"Good. We need the break. See you this evening, lover."

"Okay. 'Bye." His mind was already drifting back to the scarce facts he had on the Gannon murder.

"'Bye" she echoed, noting the preoccupation already creeping into his voice as he disconnected the line.

THIRTEEN

At 4:12 that afternoon, Detective Warner fielded what seemed his hundredth call of the day. The young cop screening the telephone traffic was instructed to put through anything remotely sounding serious. That seemed to qualify everything.

51

He wasn't about to be blamed for scotching someone who might have important information.

"Detective Warner," Al muttered. Exhaustion and the tension of the day had wrung him out. A long silence at the other end of the line was punctuated by some quiet throat-clearing and audible breathing.

Terrific. A heavy-breathing weirdo.

"Hey, if ya got something to say, spill it. I don't have all day to sit here and listen to you pant on the phone."

"Sorry." The youthful male voice cracked.

Warner's antennae perked up. This kid sounded scared.

"I'm just uneasy with this," the young man continued. "It's about the murder. Jodi Gannon?" Another nervous pause.

"You knew her? D'ya got some information, or what." Annoyance crowded the detective's voice.

"Yes. No. Oh, Shit. I don't know. I mean, yes, I knew her. Not personally. But most guys on campus knew who she was. We all saw it, you know."

"Saw what? The murder? You saw the murder?" Fatigue shed, he was fully alert.

"Oh, no. Not that. We just saw her. You know, the pictures and stuff."

"Listen buddy, if you know something, spit it out. If not, stop wastin' my time."

"Well, we saw her. With him. You know, that night."

"Him? Who? What night? C'mon, kid, this ain't twenty questions. Just relax and tell me what you know, all at one time." He took a breath. "Sorry I yelled, but we're under some pressure here. Just start at the beginnin' and take it through to the end. Okay?"

"Yeah, sorry, but, like I said, I'm kinda nervous."

"There's nothin' to be afraid of. Just get on with it. I promise I won't bite."

"Well, we were at the lounge that night—the night she was

killed. Mike, Tommy, Jose and me."

"What lounge? It got a name?"

"Yeah, sorry. The Hurricane Bar, on south Dixie. Anyway, we're at a table, drinking beer, and watching Jodi. She was at the bar, looking hot. Some old guy in the back sends her a drink with a note, I think. Anyway, she reads something, and after a minute or so, she throws him a smile good enough to make you come in your pants. She sure was one fantastic looking babe."

"Yeah. Yeah. I know. Go on." Warner grabbed a pen and pulled over a pad of yellow-lined paper

"Sorry. Anyway, she gets up and goes to his table. We're all jealous as hell because no one we know was making any real time with her. Anyway, she sits, and they drink and talk for probably an hour or more. They even danced a little. Then they get up and leave."

"This guy," Warner voice very quiet, "can you describe him?"

"Not really. It was dark there, and even worse where he sat."

"Shit, man, can't you tell me anything?" Warner was struggling to contain his frustration. "Age, height, build, hair and skin color, distinguishin' features? Anything? Close your eyes and try to picture him."

"Yeah, well like I said, he was old. Maybe forty."

Fuck. Warner was forty and didn't think that was so old. At least not until he started this conversation.

"He looked fit," the guy continued, "slim but big shoulders, like he lifted. We couldn't see much, but he looked white, and his hair was dark. He was wearing a ball cap, so I couldn't make out his face at all. We were all sitting, so it was kinda hard to tell how tall he was. We were too busy being jealous."

"Think back, now. Gannon was five-foot-seven. Think. How much taller did he seem than her?"

"Yeah. Okay. Maybe four or five inches taller, I'd say. So maybe six feet, or a little less. That's pretty smart of you, officer. It's only a guess, though, because we were mostly watching her. Couldn't be anywhere Jodi was and not watch her, especially after that *Pla . . .*"

"Okay. That's good." Warner interrupted, having no patience for rambling. "About six-feet. Anything else? Take your time. Try to picture those minutes in your mind."

"No. Not really. Sure going to miss her . . .."

"Yeah, I bet. Listen, I'm turnin' you over to another officer who'll take your name, address and phone number. I want the names of your friends who were with you. Thanks for callin'. This is our first real lead." He scrawled *six-feet, white, forties, dark hair* on his pad.

"If you think of anything else, call me. Detective Alan Warner. We'll need you and your friends to come in as soon as possible. Make a formal statement, look at some mug shots, and maybe work with a sketch artist. Maybe one of your buddies saw something you didn't. Okay?"

"Sure Detective. Anything we can do to help."

"Okay. Hang on a minute." Warner punched "Hold," and signaled the cop at the desk to pick it up.

Then he called Harris's cell phone, but got an "out of service" recording, so he tried his beeper.

FOURTEEN

Jack Harris' pager beeped stridently, just as he entered the Hurricane Bar. The incessant call of the little device brought a growl from the detective. He snatched it from his belt, silencing its squawking, grumbling to himself.

"Nag, nag, nag. How am I gonna get the damned job done if they keep pestering me?"

Newly necessary half-frame glasses were plucked from his breast pocket. His irritation dissolved when he recognized his caller was Al Warner, his friend, ex-partner and immediate superior on this investigation. Al wouldn't bug him if it weren't important.

He approached the bar as he dug out his shield. Only a few customers were scattered around the room at that early hour, college kids drinking beer. The bartender, a balding, beefy man in his early fifties, greeted him with a friendly smile. Harris produced his badge.

"Metro-Dade PD. I'm here about the Jodi Gannon murder, and need to ask you a few questions. But can I use your phone first? Local call. My cell's dead."

"Why not? Everybody else does. These kids must think I'm Southern-fucking-Bell." He reached under the bar, producing an old black, desk-type telephone. Then he drifted down the bar to a pair of new arrivals.

The short, wiry cop glanced after the departing man. The detective's penetrating, coal-black eyes missed very little. Tired and deflated from a so-far fruitless day, he punched out Warner's number. He'd spent a full day on the streets visiting the names and places provided by Gannon's roommate. Each stop proved even less productive than the last. The Hurricane Bar was his seventh of the day. Maybe Warner had something valuable to follow up. He hoped so.

"Warner," a voice answered after the second ring.

"Hi, Boss. It's Jack."

"What's with your cell, buddy? I couldn't reach you."

"Forgot to charge it, and it's been a busy day. What's up?"

"Our first lead, amigo. Get to the Hurricane Bar on South Dixie. A U of M kid says he and some friends saw Gannon drinkin' there with an older guy the night of the murder. Not much of a description. White or Latino, maybe six-feet, dark hair, average build but looked muscular. Late thirties or maybe forty. See if you can get any more from the barkeep, or maybe a waitress. She was a gal they'd remember."

"Great. I'm there now. I'll see what I can dig up. Want me to call it in, or just come back to the office?"

"Call. I'm tryin' to bug out early and take Sharon to dinner. Need to get my mind off things for a few hours. Be terrific if we had a real lead."

"Still having bad dreams, Al?"

"Yeah, and I'm not hittin' on all eight. Still gettin' over that lunatic, I guess. And here we are again, before the dusts even fully settled on the last bastard. I sure ain't gettin' much rest, partner."

"Yeah, well, I can dig that. That sleazy nut drove us crazy before you finally put him away. That was a close one. Anyway, I'll call when I'm done here."

"Good. Dig up something solid. We're goin' nowhere with anything else."

"I'll try. Talk to you later."

Harris hung up, lost in thought. Al Warner was the best. Smart, honest, loaded with integrity, and the man had a conscience. Those last two qualities were pretty damned rare in a lot of cops. Life on the street often dictated what was expedient, but never for Warner. That's why their last major case, the vicious serial killer, Luis Leordano, really beat up his friend.

The last two victims especially plagued Warner. He'd just missed the madman at his sixteenth, double abduction. Fate, and dumb luck, but Warner blamed himself. The memory of two kid's mutilated bodies tied him into a Gordian knot. He needed help—professional help—but someone else would have to tell him. Sharon, or maybe the captain. Now, with a new maniac on the horizon, there just won't be any free time for some needed R & R.

The little detective looked up, shaking his head like a dog after a bath, throwing off the mantle of his thoughts like water droplets.

He waved the bartender over for a little Q & A.

FIFTEEN

"Okay, buddy. I just need a few secs of your valuable time." Harris handed the barkeep his phone. "Like I said, it's about the Gannon murder. Witnesses say she was here the night she was killed. Some kids saw her join an older dude for a drink. You remember anything about that? Night before last?"

"You bet. Couldn't miss a knock out like her. She came in regular. I seen her picture, too."

"Sure, sure. But I'm not interested in school photos. What d'ya remember about that night."

"Well, she sat on that stool, drinking vodka on the rocks. That was her drink. Vodka, rocks."

"Right. Go on, will ya."

"Okay. She sipped her drink, looking gorgeous and happy. This older guy's sitting at that table, all the way in the back."

Harris barely made out a little table and two chairs in the dimmest corner of the badly lit room. A good spot, if you didn't want anybody to make you out.

"You recognize this guy?"

"No. Well, yeah. Sorta."

"Yes or no? Which is it?"

"I don't actually know him, but I seen him here three or four times. Has one scotch and soda. And he always sent a drink to the Gannon chick."

"You mean he was only here when she was?"

"Yeah, now that you mention it. I never seen him around if she wasn't here, too. A coincidence, you think?"

Jack doubted that. This clever bastard had her cased out.

"Can you give me a description? You've seen him three or four times."

"No way, José. It's dark over there. I can tell you he's maybe six-feet, darkish hair. Pretty good build. Maybe forty, but that's a pure guess. Looked fit and moved well. White, I think, but he coulda been Latin. No way to tell for sure from here." He ran a rag over the bar top.

"Someone got close enough to serve drinks. Who was that?"

"True. Let's see. I guess it musta been Fran. Yeah, she was working that evening. She's off today."

"Okay. Gimme her name, address and phone number when we finish talking." Jack sighed. One more stop he'd make that afternoon before quitting for the day. But he was diligent, and wouldn't let this cool overnight. With a crazy perp, every second counted if you wanted to hold the body bags down.

"Okay, Mac. So, what went down that night?" the detective asked.

"Like I said, this was maybe his fourth time here. Always sent her a drink, but until the last time, she never paid him no mind. She took the drink, and I could see her watching him, but that was it.

"But this last time he sends a note or something. She reads whatever, then throws him a smile that coulda lit up all Miami.

She slides off the stool, real pretty-like, and strolls to his table, carrying her vodka. They talked and danced for maybe an hour, hour-and-a-half. Then they leave. Thinking about it, he sorta put her between him and the rest of us, making him harder to see. Then they're gone, and that's it."

Harris studied the man. It was clear he had more than a passing interest in Jodi Gannon.

"You kept an eye on her. Know what they were talking about?"

"Are you kidding? From here? With the music playing? No way, José."

"Didn't think so. Anything else, bub?" Harris extracted his notebook from his pocket.

"Nope. So, you think he's the guy what done her?"

"Don't know yet. Just gathering facts. What do you think?"

"Oh, yeah. He's the guy. Make book on it. I hope you get the bastard. I'm sure going to miss seeing that gorgeous babe around here. I hit on her a couple a times myself, but she wouldn't look twice. Like I was part of the furniture, or something. Then the bitch goes with Mr. Mystery and winds up dead. Don't seem fair."

"Nope." Jack flipped open his notebook, copying the information on the waitress off a three-by-five card that the other man had produced.

And you just hit the suspect list, too, bub. The snubbed suitor. Not likely, but we ain't gonna miss nothing on this one.

* * * *

The waitress seemed more intent on seeing her name spelled right in the newspaper than of being much help. The only new thing was that the guy was definitely white or very light Hispanic. Strictly an American accent. She never saw enough of his face for a description. A peaked cap shadowed his features and he always looking down at his wallet or something every time he ordered. She couldn't add to his description in any way.

59

Jack wasn't too annoyed at her lack of perception. She was just too cute, with a terrific set of boobs and a full, round ass. He'd love to see her again—play her along for a quick fuck or two, but he worshipped Doris too much to chance hurting her.

Enough daydreaming. Gotta call Al with what I've dug up.

Warner would be disappointed. Jack hoped Olvida came up with something more concrete. This guy's no dummy. He may be a loony, but he'd been extremely careful.

Jack hoped they wouldn't have to collect too many bodies before the bastard made a fatal mistake.

SIXTEEN

Michelle McIntyre glanced at her list, then surveyed the contents of her shopping cart.

Better get a head of lettuce and maybe a few Red Delicious apples. Jerry liked a salad with dinner, and a piece of fruit after they'd made love. He certainly was horny for a middle-aged guy. Well, anything within reason for an "A" in Lit.

With a smug half-smile, the tall, dark-haired beauty wheeled her cart toward the vast produce section for which the Publix stores were famous. Lustful eyes, both male and female, followed the voluptuous seraph.

Stopping at the first counter, she selected a package of six shiny red apples, then drifted to a large array of lettuces.

Oh, how nice. A shelf overflowing with corn, still in the husk. A tasty treat when first soaked in water, then microwaved while still encased in the green leaves. They'd go marvelously with the two fat Porterhouse steaks from the gourmet meat counter.

60

Michelle expected Jerry Markham to be a very happy professor when he left her apartment tomorrow evening. A great meal followed by wonderful sex (both things she excelled at) would surely guarantee the top grade she coveted in her English Literature class.

Her erotic photo in the recent *Playboy* pictorial, *The Girls of the Southeast,* proved more useful than she ever imagined, providing the final tease Jerry needed to make an overt move toward seducing her, just as she planned. It was less than three weeks since that first night, but the professor was already hopelessly lost.

Musings about sexual conquests were abruptly interrupted by a strong voice, startlingly close behind her.

"Excuse me, miss."

She turned slowly, her wide-set, emerald eyes glittering under dark, full eyebrows. The man, slightly taller than her, held a large green melon, looking a bit sheepish. She appraised him in the split moment before answering.

He was moderately attractive, probably late thirties—rugged, and leanly muscular. Penetrating, dark eyes peered out from under the bill of a Miami Dolphins ballcap, igniting a delicious chill skipping erotically down her spine. He exuded an overpowering aura of virility. In that fleeting instant, she found him incredibility sexy.

"Yes?" Goosebumps peppered her neck and back. She was deluged by his animal magnetism.

Cut it out, Shelly. You can't get the hots for every mature, virile guy who comes along.

"I'm sorry to bother you," he said, "but do you know about this stuff? How do I tell if this thing's ripe?"

Her soft chuckle tinkled musically, a wind chime in a light breeze.

"Honeydews are tough," she replied, still laughing. "I usually try giving them a good shake. If I hear seeds rattle

61

around inside, it should be ready to cut. Some people knock on them, but I've never discovered what they're listening for. Let me see it."

She took the melon from him and shook it a few times, close to her ear. Then she pressed on one end.

"Well, I don't hear the seeds at all, but it's getting a little soft at the stem end. It ought to be ready to eat in a couple of days. Those cantaloupes over there," pointing to a bin full of small, orange melons, "are ripe now. If you bought one of those, by the time you finished it, the honeydew should be ready."

"Gee, thanks. You've been a big help. Kinda surprising someone so young and beautiful knows so much about food." He smiled, and a new surge of heat flooded her, setting her heart racing. This was stupid. She was supposed to turn him on, not the other way around.

"Glad I could help." She delivered a radiant, breath-snatching smile, sensing desire in his gaze, and felt better. *That's* how it's supposed to work.

Returning to her shopping, the young beauty glanced at her list again. She decided she had all she needed and headed toward checkout. She glanced over her shoulder and noticed him again, openly staring at her.

Where had she seen that guy before? On campus, maybe? She was pretty sure he wasn't a prof. Funny not to place him, because he sure lit her fire. No doubt he was interested in this tall, gorgeous body, from the look he just gave her. What intense eyes.

Michelle McIntyre *expected* to be appraised with lust. At five-foot-ten, she was surprisingly slim, considering large, firm breasts that, despite their size, didn't stoop her elegant carriage. Broad shoulders accented a small waist, below which swelled full, muscular hips and long, tapered legs. She was the epitome of the fabled Amazon.

That evening, she was clad in a short, Navy-blue skirt of tight, stretchy silk, and a robin-egg blue silk blouse. A wide, blue leather belt set off her natural curves—a heart-stopping beauty exuding harnessed animal sexuality. A classic, heart-shaped face, framed by curly black hair, hanging below her shoulders, crowned her physical magnificence.

Young Miss McIntyre, now a sophomore at Florida Atlantic University in Boca Raton, had been longingly revered by older boys and men since she was twelve.

Michelle loved attention and knew exactly how to make the most of her incredible beauty. Clearly, men were put on earth for her use. Fortunately for some, she enjoyed the sex she regularly ventured into. In her mind, everybody was coming out ahead. She just intended to come out more ahead than the guys with whom she shared her passions.

Well, it wasn't a good time to look for a new lover, however much he excited her. If he shopped here regularly, she might bump into him again when she was done with Jerry.

Was he someone to help her career? Someone to open doors to better modeling jobs, or even get her a part in a movie?

All she needed was the right guy to give her the break she deserved.

She was always looking out for Number One.

SEVENTEEN

Michelle made her way to the crowded checkout counters and eyed the long, damned lines. She spotted a guy she thought she could "work."

Approaching the front of the second cue, she stopped next to an average looking, middle-aged guy with a cart full a beverages and snacks. Placing her hand on his arm, she delivered a radiant smile.

"Pardon me," her voice a soft purr. "Do you think you might let me in front of you? I've only got a few things, and I'm in a real rush."

The man swallowed hard twice and licked his lips.

"Sure. Sure. I'm in no real hurry. Glad to aid a damsel in distress." He fidgeted, struggling to tear his gaze from her magnificent cleavage, but finding the task impossible. Michelle, still smiling, squeezed his arm gently, laughing inwardly. The poor dupe was breaking out in a sweat.

"Oh, thank you. I just *love* mature men. You're all such gentlemen." She unloaded the contents of her cart onto the belt, unable to hide a smug little grin. Men were so easy.

As the clerk rang up her purchases, Michelle glanced back, finding that hot guy, buried in a long line, two registers over. Their eyes met and he winked, smiling softly. Would she ever see him again and somehow find their way into bed together? She chuckled.

God, she was some bundle of hormones. She loved sex. Her striking beauty usually brought any man she desired to her bed. It was so easy, she had to keep herself in check. Since *Playboy* hit the stands, though, she was like a nympho, knowing she'd given so many guys hot rocks.

"Forty-seven ninety," the cashier said, breaking her reverie. Michelle plucked a fifty from her wallet. Taking her change, the young goddess followed the little old Haitian bagger, wheeling her purchases out to the parking lot. Looking back, she saw the dark-eyed man, still watching her as he waited in line. She lost sight of him, feeling a strange pang of sadness, as she exited the store behind the slow, steady progress of the little black man

64

pushing her cart.

Her thoughts dissipated as she approached her shiny new Chrysler convertible. Strange. Almost all the high area lights in the vicinity were out. It was dark.

Very dark.

She popped the trunk as she searched the immediate area for danger. Parking lot muggings had been rampant, especially in these up-scale areas. It was late, and few cars remained in the lot. She glanced at the old man, methodically placing her bags into her car. She wished he'd hurry. Agitated, she grabbed the last two bags, tossing them into the trunk and slamming the lid.

"Have a good evening, Miss," he mumbled in a thickly accented voice as he started back toward the store, picking up a few other empty carts en route.

Michelle slipped quickly inside, locking the doors. She ran her hands over the upholstery and the leather covered steering wheel. She loved her new little Chrysler. It was sexy, just like her.

Grinning, no longer nervous, she cranked the engine. But the car didn't start. Pumping the gas pedal, she tried again.

Raa-raa-raa. Raa-raa-raa. The usual starter sounds, but the engine didn't catch. Strange. It always fired up on the first shot. She tried it again and again with the same results, which were no results at all. She shivered, trapped alone in that dark, nearly deserted lot.

Well, I can't just sit here, waiting for a miracle. Releasing the hood, she hurried out of the car and raised the bonnet but had no idea what to look for. She knew nothing about the mechanics of an automobile. Looking under the hood just seemed the thing to do. Was that a guy—a very *large* guy—two rows over, watching her, lurking behind that lamppost? She *had* to get out of there.

"Having a problem?" She jumped, grazing her head on the raised hood. Whirling, she gathered herself for a run to the store, until she saw it was the sexy guy from inside. A shiver sluiced down her spine. Was it excitement, or fear? She studied him for an instant, finally deciding to be happy he was there.

"Yeah, damn it. A brand-new car, and suddenly it's decided not to start. I thought American cars were getting better." The adrenaline rush subsided and she gained control of her thudding heart.

"They are," he said. "But any car can get cranky. Want me to take a look for you?"

"Oh, would you? I don't know a damned thing about these machines, other than how to drive one. That's one of the things we girls have men for. To fix the machines for us." Relaxed now, she laughed.

"Oh? I thought we were good for a few other things, too." He grinned.

"Yeah. Just kidding. I'd sure appreciate some help." God. How did such a slightly better than average guy get to be so damn hot? Her heart took off again like a trip hammer. He was—what? A real man, that's what.

Damn, she was horny.

"Okay. Get in and try the ignition again. I'll see if you're getting any spark."

I'm getting plenty of spark, she thought, climbing back into her car. *My engine sure is running, even if this lousy car isn't.* She turned the key, and the starter sung its futile song.

"Hold it. There's no spark. All these cars have solid state ignitions," he said, leaning against the open door of the convertible, "and while they work better than the old systems, sometimes the ignition module will burn out for no apparent reason. Then there's no juice to the plugs. You'll need to get it towed to the dealer tomorrow. Ought to be in warranty, though, so don't worry. Want me to call a taxi for you?"

"That's okay. I can do it. Thanks for your help." She locked her car and started back toward the store. Damn, it was dark. Was that other big guy still watching her? She wasn't sure.

Fishing in her purse, she realized she left her cell phone home, and Publix was already closed. Her new "friend" stood by her convertible, watching as the darkness blanketed her. She shivered, her skin prickling, and hurried back to her car.

His lips twitched up, eyebrows arching.

She smiled back. "I forgot my phone."

"It's dark out there. Can't blame you for being nervous. Why don't you lock yourself in the car, and I'll call a cab for you?"

"Gee, thanks. I only hope my ice-cream doesn't melt."

"Sit tight. I'll put my stuff in my jalopy, and then call. I got nothing more important to do than see you get out of here safely, with your ice-cream intact." He trotted off toward a battered old Ford, before heading for the lone outside pay phone. No cell phone for him either, apparently.

He returned in five minutes, no longer smiling.

"I called both cab companies. Yellow had nothing for an hour. Checker said they'd send a car in thirty minutes. If you want, I'll hang around. See you don't get stood up. You can't rely on cabbies this time of night."

"That'd be nice." She started to relax, tension peeling away. While Michelle was no soft mark for a mugger, she was happy this rugged-looking guy would be there while she awaited transportation home.

"I guess we should introduce ourselves," he said. "I never expected to do more than just talk to you for a minute in the store. I hope it's not out of line to say you're the most gorgeous gal I've ever seen." She smiled. It was something she heard frequently, but never too often. She liked this guy's direct style.

"Anyway, I'm Angie Dedios." They shook hands.

"Hi, Angie. I'm Michelle McIntyre. To my friends I'm Shelly." She paused, studying his face, seeing no danger there.

67

"You can call me Shelly, too, if you like."

He nodded, patting her hand protectively.

Wow! This guy got her hormones going. He was strong, but still gentle. She was so turned on, she'd likely tear poor, timid Jerry apart tomorrow. Would a lustful Amazonian beauty intimidate this masculine guy? Or would he be a tiger in bed?

That might be for another day. Besides, she knew nothing about him. A gal had to be careful. Look what happened to that U of M kid, Jodi Gannon, murdered just last week. They met at the *Playboy* photo session. Her being killed like that was eerie.

They settled down to wait, each lost in their thoughts.

EIGHTEEN

Forty minutes later, Michelle discarded her melted ice-cream after Angie returned from calling Checker Cab again.

"Sorry, Shelly. They're backed up. Strange they're so busy at this time of night, but nothing for at least another thirty or forty minutes, and that's not guaranteed."

"Shit! I can't spend the whole night in this god-forsaken lot."

"Look," he said, "I'm not doing anything important tonight. Just a movie, and I've missed that. I can drive you home, if you'd like. It's up to you. Don't do anything that makes you nervous." A small smile tweaked his lips.

"Thanks, but you've done enough. I think I'll wait."

You seem like a swell guy, but I just don't know you.

"Suit yourself. Well then, I guess I'll go. Good luck." He patted her arm and strolled off toward his car.

She was checking her groceries when she jerked up at a

small "pop," followed by a loud bang. The already poorly lit lot plunged into utter darkness, as the few remaining mercury vapor lights blinked out. Leaden clouds, heralding an advancing front, obscured the moon and stars, shrouding the night in a velvet mantle of blackness.

Her heart palpitated at the sudden change, and she leaped from her car and ran after her newfound friend, already driving away.

"Angie. Angie. Wait." She waved her arms, framed in the lights of his car. He pulled to the side, stopped, and leaned from the window of an old blue Ford and smiled.

"That was pretty loud, wasn't it? Just a transformer blowing. It did get mighty dark in a hurry though. Change your mind about me driving you home?"

"Yeah, if you're still offering. My apartment's near the FAU campus, if that's not too much out of your way."

"Right on my route, and I'd love the chance to spend more time with you."

"That's so sweet." She chuckled, her tension swept away. "I'll get my stuff."

"Okay. Hope you don't mind riding in my stakeout car. I own an investigations and security company and just came off a job, or I'd have the Mercedes. The seats are comfy, though." He chuckled. "A necessity when you're parked in them for hours at a time."

"No problem. It's not very far, and a girl can't be fussy when she's being rescued, can she?" Michelle smiled with a heart-stopping radiance.

As they gathered her plastic bags of food, his body lightly brushed hers. Little electric bolts danced across her skin, heightening her sense of the immediate probabilities. Arms filled with her bundles, they grinned at each other. His dark, luminous eyes, a fathomless abyss, sucked her breath away.

69

Dammit, he really turned her on.

She entered the car while he deposited her groceries in the trunk. The clean interior surprised her. She'd expected wads of food wrappers and foam drink cups scattered around, like in the movies. So much for creative reality. The custom upholstered bench seat was, indeed, quite comfortable.

He slipped in the driver's side, fishing keys from his pocket. Wafts of Royal Copenhagen after-shave (her very favorite) filled her nostrils. He grinned.

"I can't remember the last time I had a woman in this jalopy. Certainly, never one as gorgeous as you. I work too many hours to have much of a social life."

He edged over, and her heart bolted into a gallop, anticipating the kiss. Instead, he snagged her seat belt, pulling it secure.

"Got to keep precious cargo safely strapped in. It's the law, you know." A mischievous little grin tugged at the corner of his mouth.

"Thanks. I already feel very safe." She placed her hand on his, giving it a gentle little squeeze.

"I'm glad. Where d'ya live? Gotta get your groceries home quick as we can, so nothing spoils. Too bad about your ice-cream."

"Oh, that's okay. I don't need the calories." The crystalline chimes of her laughter filled the car. They each dwelled on separate thoughts of a promising new relationship.

Michelle gave directions. Traffic was light, and the distance short. They arrived in less than twenty minutes, just after midnight, and the streets and sidewalks were empty. Tomorrow was a school day, and the people of the area, mostly university related, had all turned in for the night.

As Angie parked near her building, her heart raced. Her libido, always difficult to contain, was soaring out of control.

Jerry was tomorrow, but tonight was looking better every minute. This sexy guy better not become timid. Many guys had, unsure of beginning a romantic liaison with this beautiful young woman.

Unbuckling her seatbelt, she took his hand in hers, smiling seductively, speaking softly to her new white knight.

"I want to thank you for coming to my rescue. What would I have done without your help, and maybe even protection?"

"My pleasure." His dark eyes appraised her

"So, will you help with these bags, and maybe stop and have a drink with me? I'd like to get to know you better."

"Sure. I've enjoyed this, and I'm definitely not ready for it to end." He stepped on to the street, tugging down the brim of his cap and putting up the collar of his lightweight jacket. He circled the car, opening her door and offering her his hand.

"It's gotten pretty chilly. You got a sweater or something?"

"No. I didn't think this cold front would get here 'til tomorrow. I love cool weather, but I wasn't prepared for this."

"So, maybe it's my job to keep you warm, too?" He folded her into his arms, running his hands slowly up and down her back. She snuggled close, feeling very safe. She leaned back to looked into his dark eyes, her face almost even with his. A hand in her thick hair, he gently pressed her to him. The kiss was soft and lingering, their lips parted, tongues gently fencing. Neither was any longer aware of the brisk evening air. Leaning back, she smiled softly, but her heart trip-hammered in her chest. He gave her a quick, possessive squeeze.

"C'mon. Let's take your things upstairs and get comfortable." As he gathered her bags from the trunk, a tiny smile ticked up the corners of Angie's lips, firing a small shiver down her spine. That look was almost—what? Wicked? How foolish. He's her knight-errant, her rescuer. Everything will be perfect. She knew men, and this guy was special—a real gentleman.

The building was old, but had retained its elegant, Palm Beach-style charm. Management kept it neat and clean, recently repainting it inside and out. Everyone seemed turned in at that hour. The eight units rented entirely to faculty and students, but no rowdiness was allowed.

It was a nice, quiet building.

NINETEEN

They tiptoed softly up the three flights to Michelle's one-bedroom apartment. Angie stood, arms loaded with her packages, as she fumbled for her keys. Stifling giggles, they swept inside, unrestrained laughter erupting as she kicked the door closed. Fumbling in the dark, they bumbled into the kitchen where he set her purchases on the counter, once she flipped on the lights.

Michelle stood in the doorway, smiling happily, incredibly radiant. He moved quickly, gathering her willingly into his arms, her hands resting lightly on his shoulders. Dark eyes met green eyes, each filled with passion. Then they kissed.

The embrace started gently, almost reverently, but quickly flared to a rampant heat. Busy hands explored trembling bodies, searching, stroking, teasing, shifting from gentleness to urgent intensity and back again. His iron-hard physique contrasted sharply to Jerry's soft, flabby body. Her own well-toned figure quivered as his fingers brushed her firm, braless breasts.

Finally separating, breathless, their eyes locked again.

God, she wanted to fuck this hot-blooded stud.

Easy. You don't know him. No need to screw this attractive guy just to prove you can have any man you want.

But before she could put steel into her newly forming resolve, he swept her up, easily lifting her, and headed for the bedroom. Michelle's effort to cool the cauldron of her passions was a losing struggle. Arms around his neck, moving swiftly through her living room, her voice was throaty with ardor.

"Easy, big guy. Let's not rush things. We've got plenty of time to get to know each other. Please."

"No, Shelly. I've waited long enough. I need to have you now. There are things to do, and they just can't wait any longer." Already in the bedroom, he released his left arm, dropping the girl to her feet, trapping her tightly against him.

"Wait. Wait a minute." she panted, a nervous trickle of fear tip-tapping down her spine.

"What d'ya mean, you've 'waited long enough?' We just met. I *have* seen you before, though. The university library?" Her voice cracked, full of the passion she was unable to restrain.

"Yes, I was at the library, looking for you—hoping to meet you. Saw your photo in *Playboy*. Had to find you. Had to have you. You were to be next, or things couldn't go forward."

One hand was inside her blouse, teasing her sensitive breasts, while the other tantalized her buttocks. Now a nipple was in his mouth, ignited by his clever tongue.

Despite the small fear growing in the back of her consciousness, he fueled her ardor so thoroughly, it swamped her ability to reason. He wasn't *forcing* her. He was, instead, skillfully stimulating her. She was swept away by her own highly charged sex drive, something never easily controlled when expertly manipulated—and Angie Dedios was stirring that pot with superb skill.

"You were—looking for me?" She struggled, unable to decide through this sexual miasma, whether that was flattering—or dangerous.

"Yes, I wanted you. Needed you. *Planned* for you. And I hoped you would want me. You *had* to want me. And you do. You do, don't you?" Angie panted. He stripped Michelle to her panties as he talked.

Lost in her own fervor, she snatched away his shirt and was shoving down his trousers, not noticing something, like a little black snake, fall from his pocket. She was more intent on the bulge in his briefs, something there she desperately wanted to get her mouth around before he put it inside her now pulsing and very wet other set of lips.

"Yes. Yes. I want you. But I need to lick and suck on this beautiful thing before we fuck. Oh, how I love the taste." He groaned as she dropped to her knees and freed his rigid organ, wrapping her mouth lovingly around it.

Head thrown back, grunting with the intensity of his pleasure, his hands moved gently through her thick, dark hair and over the silky smoothness of her neck and shoulders.

"Oh, yes." he sighed. "That's so wonderful. Wonderful and wicked. It couldn't be more perfect."

TWENTY

Nearing his orgasm, Angie pulled Michelle up, his lips ravaging hers. Adventurous hands deliciously explored the other's body, seeking new crevices of sensitivity. Laying on the bed, he began exploring her luscious form with his mouth and fingers. She squirmed, groaning and shuddering under his expert caress. He rose above her, preparing for the final act.

"Wait," she hissed, barely able to speak through her unbridled passion.

"A rubber. You need to use a rubber."

"Not necessary," he whispered. "You won't catch any diseases from me, Shelley. God will protect you."

"Pregnant." She squirmed under his weight, struggling for control, but too heavily submerged in her own ardor to make a real effort. "I don't want to get pregnant."

"I won't make you pregnant. I won't give you a disease. I'll bring you to God, and you'll be safe forever."

God? What does God have to do with this? Oh, damn, I just need him in me. To hell with it.

"Oh, take me, Angie. Take me. I don't care. I need you now. Just do it."

Needing no urging, he entered. Her long, powerful legs hooked around his, crushing him to her. Her hands ran across his back, through his hair and clutched his buttocks as they surged against each other. Both were quickly ready to orgasm. The young Amazon bound him so tightly, with such surprising strength, he had difficulty maneuvering his hands into position.

Michelle orgasmed first, heralded by pulsing vaginal muscles and a full-throated shout of ecstasy. She clutched him fiercely and shuddered with her release as he erupted an instant later, sounding a protracted groan.

Finally able to break free from her bands of passion, he leaned back, still encased within her, his dark eyes raking her. A thin film of perspiration glistened both bodies. Catching her breath, a smile lit her face.

"Hey, handsome. That was . . ." she began.

"God, she is gorgeous," he interrupted. "Gorgeous but wicked, immorally parading herself before all who would look. Lord, I pray you redeem her soul."

"Hey, where the hell do you get off . . .?" Michelle blurted, unaware yet of any real danger.

"I? I am Angel de Dios. The Angel of God." He straddled

her, hands resting lightly on her shoulders, near her neck.

"You have sinned. I am here to bring you to Him for redemption." Suddenly his thumbs were pressing against her throat, digging into her esophagus. Michelle uttered one stifled croak, her body quivering and thrashing weakly.

"The Lord calls," he intoned. The girl died quickly, with little struggle for one so young and strong, a look of surprise frozen on her once exquisite but now bloated face.

He withdrew his shrinking organ, wiping off their combined juices on the sheet. They had no DNA matches for an angel. He rummaged around her bathroom drawers, opening several tubes of lipstick until he found one of bright red. Less than a minute was required to print his one-word message.

As he dressed, he saw a sinuous black thing lying on the floor. Smiling, he placed it across her still lovely breast.

He moved around the apartment, wiping off anything on which he may have left fingerprints. Slipping out the door a half-hour later, Angie Dedios, God's Angel of Death, disappeared into the night.

The Lord's work had only just begun.

TWENTY-ONE

Warner flopped into his worn but comfortable swivel chair and took a large swig from his mug. Hopefully the coffee, hot and acrid, would get him started on the day. He tilted back, propping his legs on the desk's scarred surface, knuckling his dry, red eyes.

He was absolutely bushed from a night fraught with

terrifying dreams he couldn't quite remember. He awakened in a cold sweat, shaking, unable to shed a lingering presence of terror.

His hand absently caressed the no longer visible scar above his right ear. The still recent wound throbbed like a kettledrum, conjuring up unwanted visions.

South Florida called him hero, but bravery had nothing to do with what happened that day. He acted stupidly, and was lucky to survive.

Nearly eight months had passed, and physically he was fully recovered. Two months, first in a coma, then physical therapy before he was finally able to get around on his own.

He threw himself into a rigorous strength-training regimen, and at age forty, was in the best physical shape of his life. His cop buddies needled him over his dedication, but only physical exhaustion gave momentary relief from the memory of that too-close brush with death.

Then there was Sherry.

He smiled. Despite their obvious social differences, she truly seemed to love him. Being with her was the only other thing momentarily quelling those fearsome ghosts.

He dropped his feet, scooted closer, and listlessly began shuffling papers scattered across his desk, musing to himself.

Warner was sure this was another one—another homicidal lunatic. He'll kill again, and so far, they had nothing.

Absolutely nothing.

Keep plugging, looking for some little kernel they missed, but the painful truth was, they needed another victim. Maybe then they'd figure out what kind of gal he was after: a college girl; a model; or just a beauty? Or something else they haven't thought of yet? They desperately needed a break.

He picked up a portfolio photo of Jodi Gannon, looking gorgeous in a very skimpy bathing suit.

Why couldn't he place that hot chick? His mind was usually a steel trap, but the lack of rest had rusted its spring. The memory was lurking close by, hiding behind a fatigue-induced wall.

The electronic warble of his phone snatched him back to the present. Groaning, annoyed by his morbid mood, he plucked it up.

"Homicide. Detective Warner speakin'."

"Hey, Al, just the guy I wanted. It's Vinny Fanucci, Boca PD"

"Hey, Vinny. How you doin'? Still roustin' the boiler room cons up there in la-la land." Fanucci had attended an FBI training seminar with him.

"Nah. Those were the good old days. Now I'm in homicide. I guess that's a demotion, huh?" He chuckled.

"Tell me about it," Warner sighed. "What can I do you for, *Paisan*? I doubt ya called just to say, 'Hi'."

"Yeah. Well, we had a murder up here last night. A gorgeous babe from FAU."

A chill coursed through Warner, the hairs on the back of his neck rising. Was this the beginning of the next act? Impatient, he interrupted the Boca detective.

"Let me guess. Strangled, her larynx crushed. Apparently consensual sex. And a message in red lipstick on the bathroom mirror. How am I doing, Vince?"

"Bingo. Only the message was on the wall above the bed. You know this guy, Al? Same MO as that U of M gal from about a week ago?"

"That's my guess."

"Nothing in the papers about a message on the mirror. You holding out on the press, buddy?"

"For now. Had all the signs it's just the first of many, and we didn't need to start a panic, so soon after Leordano. Wasn't sure how he's pickin' his targets until now. Probably all young and beautiful, but his message indicated he's after something more. What did yours say, Vince?" Fanucci repeated the single word printed neatly on the wall.

"Yep." Warner responded. "Same as ours. Sounds like he's got more against these girls than just beauty, though. He's on some kinda mission. And, I know I've seen our vic somewhere. A photo or something, but I just can't place her.

"Anyway, you wanna team up?" Warner drew over a yellow lined pad. "We're goin' nowhere with ours. He sure didn't waste time takin' number two, and that's scary, 'cause these psychos usually escalate as they get a taste of what they're doing."

"Yeah. I was hoping you'd offer. You're the resident expert on these nuts. I'm not looking to be a hero. Look what it got you. But, if this guy's gearing up to be another Leordano, we've got to snag him before his numbers start adding up. When can we get together and compare notes?"

"E-mail me what you've got, and I'll do the same for you on the Gannon case. After we've crosschecked our info, we can meet and do some brainstormin'. Send a 'before' photo, too, if ya got one. I wanna see if this gal looks familiar, too."

"You got it. It'll be out in the next ten minutes. Not much so far because they just found her. Her English professor had a key to her digs. Probably some hanky-panky going on there. We're checking that out. Talk to ya later." They broke the connection, and Warner absently began rubbing his scar again.

Now it would start in earnest. This bastard hadn't waited very long between kills. They'd better not miss something important. He didn't want seventeen more dead kids before they got this guy. He poked his head through his office doorway and called one of his detectives.

"Harry, get the Gannon file together and e-mail it to the Boca PD, attention Vinny Fanucci. Looks like he's got our second vic. Supposed to be another beauty."

Was, anyway. Bet she don't look too terrific now.

Damn this son-of-a-bitch.

Warner began clearing his desk, preparing for a new file of senseless death.

TWENTY-TWO

Al Warner lingered in front of his cluttered desk, the limited file on Michelle McIntyre spread out for review. He studied her photo, standing alongside of a shiny new Chrysler convertible, wearing tennis duds and looked absolutely smashing.

Vinny was sending a car with the original photo, plus everything from the crime scene he could get away from forensics. Al wanted to see it all. What he had, however, was enough to appreciate the beauty of their second victim.

"Damn. What a piece of ass," Jack Harris said, looking over Warner's shoulder. "She looks like one of those hot Amazon broads in the movies."

"Yeah, Jack. A real knock out. And damned if I haven't seen her somewhere, too. How could you forget a dame like this?"

"Don't know, Al. Even the babes in my dreams don't look that good. That bastard's sure having one helluva fun time before he offs these chicks."

"Keep it in your pants, Jack, and get going on the stuff I gave you to cross-check. See if there's something tyin' these girls together, besides beauty and college."

"Sure, Boss. Don't get testy. I'm on it."

Warner peered at the photo again, shaking his head before

adding it to a small stack of growing papers on the right side of his old, battered oak desk. He reread Vinny's notes and the M.E.'s preliminary report for the third time.

The girl was evidently comfortable with the killer. They'd even gone grocery shopping together at a Publix somewhere. Bags full of food were all over the kitchen counters. The wrappers on two steaks were dated that day. They had sex, all right, and there was no struggle to indicate rape.

Two girls in the next apartment heard the lovemaking. Said that they knew McIntyre entertained men occasionally, and the sex always sounded wild and passionate. The noises coming through their wall the night of the murder were pretty much the usual. They never saw the man, nor heard him leave. It was late. They had early classes the next day and were trying to sleep, but it was impossible with the ruckus going on next door.

Both girls agreed that they heard McIntyre yelling, "take me," and then a name. They weren't sure what name, however: Andy, Manny, Angie—something like that.

The students IDed the English professor, one Jerold Markham, as a regular visitor to the girl's apartment. Fanucci would bring him in for questioning, but he seemed an unlikely murderer. Sleeping with a student, though, was sure to get him into trouble with the University.

Fanucci had several uniformed cops canvassing the Publix Supermarkets in the immediate area, hoping to find a witness to Miss McIntyre's activities that night. Maybe, with luck, they'd get a description of her companion.

Al Warner both loved and hated the first days of an investigation. It was stimulating to examine a fresh crime scene, digging for vital pieces of damning evidence, but it always seemed an interminable wait for the new material to be processed and turned into something useful.

Detective Fanucci jumped at Al's suggestion to send Moe

Gold to consult with their Crime Scene team. The Boca Raton PD was good, but little Moe was a legend in South Florida. Warner was quick to convince Captain Santiago of the benefits of loaning out the Hawk. The seventeen gruesome murders committed by Leordano proved incentive enough for a temporary assignment.

"I sure the hell hope we get this damned loony quickly," the detective muttered aloud to no one in particular. "Miami'll be up for grabs if this guy starts pilin' up body bags. All beautiful young gals? Shit, it'll be a national media circus.

"Hey, Harry," he called to the older detective, "Get a murder board set up and do a chart like we did last time. See if we can find out what ties his vics together, so we'll know where to be lookin'. All we got is both were beautiful and in college."

"Good idea, Al. What else d'we got to work with?" Captain Santiago, who had hovered outside his door, entered and perched on the corner of his desk.

"Not much, Cap. I know it's a little early, but we oughta tip the Feds. I hope the Department ain't goin' to wait 'til we're up to our asses in bodies again before askin' for Federal help this time."

Santiago shrugged. "I'll talk to the chief, but it's all politics, and who gets credit when we finally take this nut down."

"I'll get things organized at this end, Al." Harry hurried off.

"Thanks, Harry." Warner looked at his captain. "I don't give a damn who gets this bastard, but it's gotta be quick. He's already turned serial. Can't leave any stones unturned."

Captain Santiago nodded, and headed for his office to make the call.

Warner began handing out assignments to the two other detectives on this case. Another body or two and his staff would quickly grow. He wanted the extra men, but he dreaded the motivation that would provide them.

He sighed again, picked up the phone, and punched the auto-dialer for Sharon Clark's private number. Six weeks had passed since returning to work, and it was just as if he were back in the middle of Leordano. Anything but that again—another homicidal kook on some perverted mission only he understood.

This job was starting to get to him.

TWENTY–THREE

Warner took the steps two at a time. He hated being late, especially with a new murder on his plate, but he couldn't just leave him lying there by the side of the road.

He hurried through the doorway of the Homicide Squad room. A uniformed cop, wearing a Boca Raton shoulder patch, stood by his office, holding a small brown carton.

"Sorry to keep you waitin'," he said, shaking his hand.

"No problem." The young cop's heavily tanned face could have been cut from stone, and even smiling, as he was now, he still exuded an intimidating physical aura. This wasn't a guy to screw with on the streets, Warner thought, noting the restrained power in his grip.

"Yeah, well our killer ain't gonna wait for anybody, but I got hooked into a mini-rescue mission." Nobody needed to know it was a dog he had saved. Why anybody would abuse that beautiful golden retriever was a mystery to him. The poor, skinny pup was pretty lucky. Clipped by a car, he wasn't seriously hurt. Just too weak from malnutrition to get up again.

Warner stopped when he saw him, huddled by the side of

the street. He raised his head, watching with soft trusting, brown eyes as Warner approached. Checking him over, he found a chain collar with no tags. He lifted the dog into his car, getting a thorough face licking in the process. His head rested on Warner's thigh, all the way to the Humane Society, the long, plumed tail sweeping the passenger's seat. Warner half hoped they wouldn't find his owner, because he might kill the bastard.

He left instructions to let him know if no one claimed the animal. If he were lucky, the pup would be his. He reminded him of his retriever, Goldie, when he was a kid. An avid reader of the Terhune books in his youth, he'd call him Buff.

Settling at his desk, he glanced at the Boca cop.

"That for me, officer—Concetti?" Noting his name tag

"Yes, sir. The stuff from the McIntyre crime scene. Fanucci asked me to stay while you go over it. He wants it all back. I was first on the scene, so I saw pretty much everything like it was when that Markham dude found the body. And boy, what a body. That was one gorgeous babe. Used to be, anyway, before some prick tried to squeeze her head off."

"Okay, Concetti. Got a first name?"

"Tony, sir."

"Right, Tony. Grab a chair and give me a few minutes to see if I got any questions."

Warner opened the carton, pulling out a large, manila envelope, which he laid aside for the moment. There were a few other items, all in plastic bags, lying on the bottom. Dumping everything on his desk, he moved them around, much like a hustler, playing the old three-shell game. He picked up the largest bag, holding it out a foot in front of his face, looking quizzically at the young police officer.

"What the heck is this?"

"Looks like an ignition coil wire, sir."

"I know *that*. What I don't know is, what it's doin' here?"

84

"Me either," the officer said, "I just know it was there."

"In the apartment? Exactly where in the apartment did ya find it, Tony?"

"On her tits, sir."

"Where?" The killer was sending them a message with that little black wire.

"On her tits, sir. Lying right across 'em. Oughta be a photo in there somewhere," pointing to the large envelope.

Warner picked up the brown packet and removed the contents, spreading everything out on his desk. There were eight photos from the crime scene, mostly of the dead girl. Sure enough, there was the foot-long black wire, resting across her bosom. He studied the picture briefly, then began digging through the stuff on his desk.

"You guys find the girl's car on the street, Tony?"

"Uh, no, I don't think so. No one was even looking for a car, far as I know. Why?"

"Why? Why not? This is off a car, ain't it? I bet it's off hers. So, where's the car? He didn't leave this by accident. He's tellin' us something. Like maybe he fixed her car so it wouldn't run, so he could offer her a ride home."

Finding what he was looking for, Warner held up the e-mailed photo of the girl, standing next to her new convertible.

"Yeah," the cop responded. "I think the original's in those pics. Man, that was one gorgeous piece. What a damned waste."

"Yeah, but where's her car? This car?" He pushed the items on his desk around, plucking up another small plastic bag.

"Here. Chrysler keys. For that convertible, sittin' in some Publix parking lot, I'll bet. The same Publix where she shopped last night. The same Publix where she probably met the guy who snuffed her. A guy who already had her marked for some kooky reason of his own." He rotated the black key fob in his fingers. "He pulled the coil wire while she was shopping, so her car wouldn't run. So, he could help a lady in distress."

"So, he could offer her a ride home, like a real Samaritan." Concetti nodded

"She's grateful enough to let the clever bastard fuck her. Then he finishes off an evening of fun by killin' her. Savior and executioner, all in the same night. He must be one smooth son of a bitch." Warner dropped the keys on his desk.

"Of course, it's all hypothetical, but that wire was left to tell us something. Call Fanucci so he can have his troops checkin' Publix parkin' lots. I think he'll find the right store easier if he can find that convertible."

The patrolman understood why this guy had so much respect throughout the Gold Coast police forces. Why hadn't their guys tied this together? They were supposed to be pros. This Warner was really something. He punched an auto-dial on his cell phone.

"This is Concetti. Put me through to Detective Fanucci." There was a momentary pause, then the young cop spoke again.

"It's Concetti, Sir. I'm with Detective Warner, and he's come up with something pretty interesting. I'll let him tell you." He offered Warner the phone.

"Vinny, it's Al. I think I can speed up your search for the right Publix . . .."

TWENTY-FOUR

Officer Tim O'Rourke pulled into the Publix parking lot, his third of the afternoon.

"What a pain in the ass. Ah well, orders are orders."

He began cruising back and forth through the lot, looking

86

for Michelle McIntyre's Chrysler convertible. He stopped half-way down the third row and checked the license plate number of the red car to his right.

"Well, I'll be damned."

Picking up his radio, he called his headquarters.

"This is O'Rourke. Patch me through to Fanucci in Homicide." After a moment filled with clicks and static, the connection was made.

"Fanucci."

"Yeah, Detective. This is Officer O'Rourke. I found your missing car. The Publix lot on Military and Linton."

"Good work. You didn't touch anything, did you?"

"No, sir. I ain't some dumb rookie."

"Good. Don't let anybody near that car. I'll be there in a few minutes with Forensics. Maybe we'll get lucky."

"Okay. I'll be . . ." He stopped talking since the line was already dead. The damned detectives were always in such a Goddammed hurry.

* * * *

Fanucci arrived twenty minutes later with Detective Mike Brown, Art something from forensics, and a funny looking, scruffy little guy.

"Okay, O'Rourke. We got it now. This is Moe Gold from Miami. He's gonna help Art go over the car. Me and Brown'll be inside, asking questions. You keep the traffic moving and the gawkers out of here. Got it?"

"Yes sir. Hope you find something useful."

"Yeah. C'mon Mike, let's see who worked last night. You got the girl's photo?"

"Right here, Vinny."

The two detectives were back in twenty minutes with a list of employees working the night before. Four were in the store

87

now, and three remembered the girl.

"Can't miss a doll like that," the meat counter clerk had said. "She comes here all the time for our steaks. Says they're better than the store where she lives."

"Well, she ain't coming anymore," Vinny said. "You remember seeing her with a guy?"

"No. She seemed alone. I was sort of caught up by the view when she leaned over, looking at the meat."

"Think back. About six-foot, white, dark hair, well-built."

"Nope. That gorgeous Amazon usually took all my attention. What a pair of tits."

"Terrific. What a big help."

Back in the lot, Fanucci used his phone to e-mail headquarters the list of other employees who were off that day. They'd assign other detectives to find and question them.

He wasn't going to let things cool until the evening shift showed up.

TWENTY-FIVE

Warner drummed his fingers on the pock-marked edge of his desk. Three days since the McIntyre murder, and even though Boca PD pulled out all the stops, their investigation turned up very little. Several Publix employees (mostly men) remembered the girl quite well. Only one had seen her talking to someone near the produce section. Since the stock clerk, a high school junior, was busy looking at Michelle, he couldn't give the detective much of a description, but what he did remember sounded like the same guy seen with Jodi Gannon. Unfortunately, the kid could not remember a single facial detail. Their artist put together a composite from the little they had— an average guy with shadowy features.

Who knows what evil lurks in the hearts of men? Warner thought. The killer might as well be as invisible as that radio character. While *this* guy sure was no hero, he was just as tough to ID as *The Shadow*. What they did have described half the guys in the tri-counties, including Fanucci, his guy Concetti, Warner, and even the captain. They had a drawing of nobody— and everybody.

Boca's forensics, even with Moe's help, came up with nothing. No prints, even on the hood of the Chrysler from when he boosted the ignition cable. No meaningful description, and no witnesses.

Nothing. Why were these bastards always so clever? There might be more dead women before they dug up anything solid with which to run an investigation.

Shit.

Warner looked up as Jack Harris burst through the door, strutting like a bantam rooster, a big smile on his face.

"What're you so fuckin' happy about. Got a promisin' new lead, I hope?"

"No such luck. But I questioned that waitress, Fran, again. What a lovely little piece."

"Cut it out, Jack. I got enough problems without havin' to pinch the wife of my ex-partner for murder. And you'll sure as hell be dead if Doris suspects you're fuckin' around. Keep your nose in the investigation."

"Just looking, Al. Can't fry a guy for that. And I've run out of things to investigate. What few damned leads we got came to zilch. We're nowhere." He plopped into a chair and massaged his neck.

"Yeah. Stuck waitin' for the bastard to move again, and that's gonna mean another beauty in a body bag. I'm goin' nuts tryin' to remember where I saw those two babes. Photos, TV, or something like that." Warner knuckled bloodshot eyes.

"You still look pretty wasted, Boss. Maybe ya need a day off to recoup."

"Not a chance. I finally did catch a couple night's sleep with no bad dreams, but it didn't help. It's really buggin' me."

"Relax. Don't force it and you'll remember where ya saw 'em. Fanucci's turned up nothing on his vic? No leads at all?" The little detective came out of the chair.

"What little he's got all dead-ended, just like ours. We're probably stymied until another lovely stiff comes along," Warner said.

"Well, you got the conn, Jack." He rose, stretching. "I'm takin' Sharon to dinner, and I need some time to calm down and get presentable. We're celebratin' tonight."

"Celebrating? What? I thought she lost her case. They convicted that baby-fucker, didn't they?"

"Yep. He'll get twenty-five-to-life. She did her best, but we know he got what he deserved. She's relieved it's over.

"Anyway. I gotta go. Text me if you get anything on either of these two kids, however small, okay?" He gathered his gun and shield from a drawer.

"Sure, but don't hold your breath. There's nothing left to follow up. We just gotta hope he screws up somewhere next time. A real pisser, having to wait for him to kill again, hoping he gets sloppy.

"Anyhow, try to have some fun tonight, and say 'Hi' to Sharon for me. That's one terrific gal."

"Damned right, Jack. Don't know how I got so lucky, and luck ain't been my strong suit lately."

"Oh, I dunno. Leordano's slug could have gone right

through the middle of your head, instead of bouncing off that thick skull of yours." He chuckled.

"Yeah, I suppose." He rubbed the hidden scar with his thumb. "Maybe, I'm luckier than I thought.

"Well, gotta run. Tomorrow we'll to go back over everything on both killin's. Hopefully, we missed something somewhere."

Starting for his car, his fingers again tentatively explored the sensitive spot above his right ear, triggering a flood of memories of that frightening day, nearly nine months ago . . ..

He lingered in the cool shade of the live oaks, a wispy southerly breeze stirring a mournful soughing from the branches above. He studied the shadowy wooded area beyond the little dike, crossing the canal in front of him.

Now what? He came out there without Jack, against department policy, and without a shred of good sense. So many useless tips had flooded them, he'd become careless. And a careless cop is often soon a dead cop.

Damn.

Well, this probably wasn't anything significant, either. A secluded access across the canal didn't necessarily lead to anything important.

Although alone, he had to follow it up. And he better step it up, 'cause he didn't want to be late again with Sharon. That was becoming an unhappy habit. Walking to the edge of the earthen bridge, he squatted, studying the ground.

Hmmm. Recent vehicle tracks, probably a pickup or small truck. Had to be something in those woods. If it were the Baby Butcher, he damned well wasn't going to let him get away this time.

He crossed the mud-covered dike, checking his Beretta 9mm and chambering a round. No safety, so all he had to do was squeeze the trigger. Reholstering it under his left arm, he started into the woods.

Before he worked up much of a nervous sweat, he was through the narrow screen of trees and at the edge of a marshy, sawgrass plain. The dirt dike, barely the width of a car, continued into the tall, dense vegetation. Whoever crossed the dike drove down that path.

He stood on his toes, but could see nothing more than the waving, golden grass and cane, looming ten feet high. He groaned and again lamented his decision to venture out alone. He shrugged and shuffled down the path. He was here now, and had to follow through. Someone had recently come this way. Probably an Indian from the village. Whatever, he'd check it out. More likely to run into a gator back here than the Baby Butcher.

Eight minutes later, drenched with sweat, he was wishing that he'd gone back for his car. Where the Hell was this damned path going? If something didn't turn up soon, he would go back. This was ridicu . . ..

He froze and sucked in a sharp breath, not believing his eyes.

A shack! A windowless, clapboard hovel, nestled among the tall grass and a small stand of live oaks. A pungent odor wafted out to him on the water-laden air.

It was a smell he knew too well.

The smell of Death.

The sight of his Dodge broke Warner's reverie. He had to get home, get cleaned up, and not dwell on that miserable day.

He needed thirty minutes at a Publix to shop for Mrs. Gerber. His aged, arthritic neighbor was expecting her bridge-players for a weekend marathon, and he promised to grill steaks and corn for the next evening.

She'd make some sort of delectable dessert—usually

flourless chocolate cake, brownies, or lemon squares. Whatever, it's how she repaid him, and although he always insisted it was unnecessary, he never turned down whatever treats she created. Adele once owned a bakery up in Virginia, and she still turned out scrumptious pastries.

It'd be a pleasant but short break from the case. Maybe Sharon could join them.

He'd invite her that night.

TWENTY-SIX

Warner scanned the brightly lit restaurant. Did she wait for him? This would be the third time this month he'd stood her up, if she'd already left. He was an hour late, goddammit.

"Ah, Detective Warner." A little cherub of a man materialized, his rosy face split by a broad smile. Warner shook the soft, well-manicured hand.

"It's good to see you again after so long. Your recovery from the wound is quite satisfactory, no?" Warner nodded. The barest trace of French accent made Rene LeBlanc seem very debonair.

"Miss Clark, she awaits you in the lounge. I am pleased to have the Hero of Miami as my guest. Your drinks are on the house tonight." With a little bow, he started toward the bar.

"Thanks, Rene. I can find it. I haven't been gone *that* long." He hurried to the dimly lit room. Chez LeBlanc was Sherry's favorite haunt. They visited it twice a month before Leordano. This was his first time back since the shooting. He wouldn't insult Rene by turning down the free drinks, as required by department regs. They'd just have one before having dinner.

He paused at the entrance, eyes adjusting to the lighting,

and saw her perched at a small table near the rear. As he made his way through the growing crowd, she looked up and smiled.

Thank god she's not pissed.

"Sorry I'm so late, Babe. It's these damned murders. I was half out the door when Vinny Fanucci called. You know him?" He settled on a stool next to her. "Boca PD. He updated me on what they got, which is the same as us—nothin'. And I promised Adele I'd do some shoppin' for her. I'm barbequin' for her and her bridge buddies this weekend."

"No problem. It's nice you help her out. I heard about that murdered girl. Not much in the papers. Is it the same guy?"

"No doubt about it. Same MO. Identical message left at the scene. Appeared to have consensual sex—then he killed her."

"You're keeping important facts from the public, Al. Don't you think young women should know what's out there, so they can protect themselves?"

"Yeah, but there's another side to it. Like encouragin' a copycat who likes his style. Plus, avoidin' panic, so soon after Leordano, which could turn this town upside down again." He nodded as the bartender set a tumbler of Dewar's in front of him.

"Damned thing is, we still don't even know who his targets are. These two were beautiful college kids, both doin' some modelin'. So, is it beauty, college, modelin', a combination of one or more—or something we haven't found yet? We ain't got any answers. We're still diggin', but so far we got zilch."

"That's scary. I can see it's taking a toll on you. You sleeping any better?"

"Off and on. I've had a few good nights recently, but I need a solid week. Not too likely between this case and our Inner-City Youth Camp program."

"How's that going?" She sipped her martini. "I heard they made you Activities Chairman."

"Yeah. The Camp's my idea, so I'm expected do the work. Like I got free time. Don't mind, though. Some of these kids are comin' to realize that there's more to life than gangs and drugs."

"How do they respond to working with cops. That's got to be pretty strange for them."

He laughed. "Us, too. We got punks Juvie's busted more'n once. We're all learnin' the other guy's not automatically bad. A few try to take advantage of the relationship, but most are finding it very educational." He rotated the glass of Scotch on the bar top, then took a small taste.

"Last weekend we did an overnight canoe trip down the Kissimmee River—cookout, tents, the works. You shoulda seen those tough teens roastin' marshmallows and singin' around the campfire." He covered her hand with his, squeezing gently.

"You think it will have any lasting effect?"

"For some. A half-dozen have dropped out of the gangs and are workin' harder at school, hopin' for college. And I'm plannin' with three other cops to set up a tough boot camp in the 'Glades for the more hardened kids. Problem is, between the camps, this new killer, and all the bad dreams, I'm bushed."

"Then here's what we should do." She took his hand. "Order dinner, then back to my place where I can work magic on my overworked lover. We haven't spent a night together in ages."

"Sounds good to me, Sher." He smiled mischievously, eyes twinkling. "But how about this instead. We skip dinner and cut out. I'm not that hungry, at least for what I can get here."

She laughed. "Now, that's the Al Warner I used to know." Squeezing his hand, she stood, reaching for her sweater.

"Rene's buyin' the booze," he said, "so we can go. Now that I know what's comin', I'm up for it—really *up* for it." He pulled her into his arms, holding her close, his hardness pressing against her. She shivered in anticipation of what was to come.

This rough-cut cop was a total paradox. Despite his well-earned reputation as a tough, hard-nosed guy on the streets, he was also a wonderful, considerate lover. She never regretted taking the initiative two years ago.

If Charley Sweeny's colitis hadn't flared up, the Rojas case would never have been dropped in her lap.

She tingled at the memory of their first meeting . . ..

TWENTY–SEVEN

"Detective Warner?"

"Yeah. What can I do for ya, ma'am?" One eyebrow arched.

The woman, probably in her early thirties, was the definition of classic beauty. Her exquisitely curved, athletic body was topped by a regal face, framed by a shoulder length mane of chestnut hair, spilling in gentle waves down her cheeks. Liquid, hazel-green eyes regarded him with unveiled interest. Her tailored suit was conservative, and she wore very little makeup. Framed in the light of the window behind her, she glowed like an angel.

Warner swallowed hard.

"I'm Sharon Clark." Her lips ticked up at the corners. "The public defender representing Vitorio Rojas in the Hidalgo murder. I'd like to ask you a few questions, if you've got a minute."

"Glad to help, especially with something as putrid as that one."

"What do you mean, Detective?" She appraised him, trying to suppress her excitement. Did he doubt her client's guilt as much as she? That'd be a fresh breeze, coming from a homicide detective. Not a bad looking guy either, in a rugged, crooked-nose sort of way.

Warner glanced around, then leaned across his desk in a conspiratorial, almost comical manner.

"This is off the record, Counselor. Nothing you can use in court. Strictly an opinion, for now at least. Your word?"

"You've got it. I'm desperate for anything starting in the right direction for a defense."

"Your guy didn't do it."

"I know that. So why are you prosecuting him?"

"*I'm* not prosecutin' him. That's the D.A.'s job. I told 'em they got the wrong guy, but they don't give a shit. Oops, pardon me, Miss." A sheepish grin tickled his lips.

"That's okay. I've heard worse. Go on, Detective. How do you know Rojas is innocent? That's what I need."

She withdrew a yellow lined pad from her briefcase and prepared to take notes, her heart doing a happy jig. Was it due to a possible break in the case, or the man himself?

"Got no evidence to clear him yet, if that's what you mean. But I know he didn't do it. I've been at this job a long time. You get a nose for what smells right—and what doesn't. This one stinks." Warner perched on the corner of his desk.

"The D.A. says he's got an iron-clad case, but I believe Vitorio, and apparently so do you." She sighed. He had nothing to help her but his intuition.

"Anything else, besides your sense of smell, Detective Warner?" Her hazel eyes studied him intently. This was still her first kernel of hope, and it was coming from a very unlikely source. This cop was getting better looking every minute.

"That's what smells—the Iron-Clad Case. It's *too* damned good. I arrested your client, based on a tip. He had to be a moron to leave such a perfect trail of clues, and I don't think Vic Rojas is any kind of a dummy. It's a set-up. It's gotta be."

"Well, that the best news I've heard all week," she said. Her smile was a sunburst, lighting up the room.

Warner blinked several times, gulping for air like a beached trout.

Sharon's heart tripped over itself, recognizing the magic of the moment.

"You making any progress in proving your theory?" She struggled, trying to concentrate.

"Heck, no. The Hidalgo case is considered closed. We got three other murders workin'. Pissin' in the wind tryin' to reopen it now. Sorry." Her elegant shoulders slumped. Then steel came into her yellow-green eyes.

"Well, then I'll have to do it myself. Can you at least point me in the right direction? I'd certainly appreciate your help."

"Look, Miss Clark . . . or is it Mrs.?"

"I'm not married, Detective." She grinned. "Are you?"

He blushed and swallowing twice before answering.

"No, Ma'am. Almost tried it once, but it didn't work out. Anyway, goin' after these guys won't be a picnic. There are some mean mothers in Little Havana. You got a couple of months 'til the trial. Lemme see if I can find something on my own time. The boss won't like it much—unless I get the real killer. That'll make us look good, and the D.A. look like the asses they are sometimes. My captain would like that."

"Gee, that'd be great. I don't know how I'd be able to thank you. I'm getting nowhere on a defense."

"Just wanna see justice done. I hate for some half-assed D.A. to get a gold star over the bones of an innocent guy, just 'cause it's convenient. Helpin' you is just a pleasant bonus."

"That's good enough for me," she said, touching his hand.

He shivered, and a rosy tint again reinvaded his face.

"It's a real pleasure finding a cop doing his job for the right reasons. I haven't met many. Help me get Vitorio acquitted, and I'll owe you the best meal at any restaurant you choose. I mean it." She grinned. This was a real, honest-to-god *man*, the first she'd met during her three years in South Florida.

Three weeks later, she entered the cubby called her "office" and found a large unmarked manila envelope sitting on her desk. Inside was the proof she needed of her client's innocence, plus a well-documented finger pointing to the real perpetrators. There was a short, handwritten note.

You take the credit for digging this up. I'd be in trouble if they thought it was me. Now you owe me a fancy dinner.

Sixteen hours later Vitorio Rojas was back on the street, and two members of the Cuban Mafia were behind bars for the murder of Estevan Hidalgo. They had eliminated some competition, and Stefan Martin pinned it on Rojas for marrying the woman Martín had coveted.

Sharon Clark came to Miami to escape New York, but it wasn't for the weather. Public Defenders were a large step down for a Georgetown Law School magna cum laude. Her father insisted it was no place for the daughter of a New York Congressman and a partner in Clark, Wigham & O'Shea, Buffalo's premier law firm. Helping people was secondary to joining to the *proper* firm and living the *proper* life.

Leaving town was the only way to escape his constant badgering, and South Florida seemed as good a choice as any. Saving an innocent man when no one else (except one very special cop) gave a damn, reaffirmed her purpose in life.

As promised, Sharon bought Warner a wonderful dinner at Joe's Stone Crab. They got a little drunk, and over the next several weeks, fell very much in love. They had been together ever since, Al frequently spending the night at her apartment.

Her love and support were his bulwark during the Leordano killing spree, and afterward, recovering from his wound.

She shook off the memories as they entered her apartment. This was now, and she was about to spend the evening with the man she loved. She hoped it would bring him some peace—at least for the moment.

TWENTY-EIGHT

He was coming, brandishing a chrome-plated semi-automatic. Warner couldn't make out his face. There *was* no face. But it was Leordano. It had to be him, back from the dead. The madman fired the gun, squeezing off shot after shot. Al could see the bullets hurtling toward his own head.

"No," he screamed. "No."

He bolted upright in bed, drenched in sweat, and flinched when a cool hand brushed his arm.

"Al, are you okay?"

Shuddering, he turned his back to her, gulping air, adrenaline fanning flames in his racing heart.

"A bad dream," his voice a hoarse croak. "Leordano again, I guess. I dunno. He was shootin', the bullets comin' right for my head, and I couldn't dodge. I just stood there, watchin'."

"My poor darling." She took his arm. "Come back to bed. It's over now. Try to sleep."

"No, Sherry. After a dream like that, I can never get back to sleep. I gotta go. When I'm like this, it scares me."

"Maybe you should go see Dr. Carlsen. If Captain Santiago knew what you were going through, you know he'd order it."

"No shrink. I gotta work this out myself. It'll just take a little time."

"I didn't realize how tortured you are, Al. Carlsen can help,

100

if you'll let him."

"Look. I know you mean well." He pulled away. "But it's something I gotta do myself. Just leave it be, will ya?" He lurched away from her, swinging his feet to the floor.

"I'm just trying to help." There were tears in her voice. "In case you've forgotten, I love you, and I've got my own stake in this. Look what it's doing to us. We never used to fight."

"Sorry, beautiful. Didn't mean to snap. I know you mean well. Maybe, if I can't get a handle on this soon, I'll go. I like to deal with my own problems." He sat on the edge of the bed, donning his pants.

"What's different is havin' someone else worryin' about me. It feels strange, but kinda good."

Dressed now, he bent over, kissing her gently.

"I'm up now anyway, babe. Might as well go to work."

"It's five a.m., darling. Please don't run off." It was as if he were trying to escape her.

"Homicide never sleeps, hon. I'm not gettin' anymore shut-eye, so I might as well go in. Maybe there'll be something new on these murders. Gonna zip home fist and feed Buff and give him a run. Despite the scary dream, this is the best I've felt in weeks. You're sure good for me. Go back to bed. I'll talk to ya later." He hurried off.

"Al, don't go. Please." Her eyes filled with tears at the sound of the apartment door closing. An ominous wave of despair rolled over her, stifling her breath.

It was all going wrong, and he didn't even know it. He was a good man. She loved him desperately, but nothing was working. They were like strangers. This killer was doing more than just murdering young girls. He was killing their relationship.

She lay in bed, clasping her knees to her chest, keening softly.

It was all going wrong, and she didn't know how to fix it.

TWENTY-NINE

Warner fidgeted, waiting for him to come to the phone.

"Fanucci," he heard, finally.

"Vince, it's Warner. It's been five days. You come up with any leads?"

"Fuck no. Don't ya think I woulda let you know, if we had? It's been two weeks since he snuffed *your* gal. You got any leads on that?"

"Sorry. Sorry. I didn't mean to be a wise guy, but you know things start gettin' cold after 72 hours. Ours turned to ice after the second day. I was hopin' you mighta done better. You got nothin'? No anonymous tips? Nothin'?"

"*Nada*. No prints. No witnesses. Just got a DNA match on the sperm and sent it to your lab. Same guy, all right, but we knew that from his love letter. Even your tech, Gold, couldn't produce anything new. We're still beating the bushes, but I ain't got much hope."

"We gotta find what ties these gals together in this bastard's warped mind, Vince. I doubt it's anything as obvious as college or looks. Anything there?"

"Nope. We ain't got a clue. You got no idea what the connection it is either, huh?"

"Not even a good guess. I just wish I could remember where I saw those dames before, dammit." Warner studied photos of the two girls resting on his desk.

"He nails one more gal and we'll be forced to call in the Feds," he said. "When it's serial, it's their bailiwick."

"Yeah, I hate when they come in and take over. Act like

we're bush leaguers."

"I worked with the BAU before, on Leordano. And I trained down there a couple years ago and got to a behavioral symposium. Those guys aren't so bad. They usually let you run the case, while they give a profile of the perp, and try to help identify him from that."

"Yeah? Well, maybe. We sure need all the help we can get."

"No argument there from me, bro. Talk to ya later."

* * * *

"Al, you got a minute?"

"Sure, Harry. What's up. Any good news for a change?"

"No such luck. It's taken me close to three weeks, but I've finally talked with every name in Jodi Gannon's phone book. Hate to say it, but I got bubkes. At least nothing I think might help. She did some modeling and TV commercials and a few photo spreads in some magazines: Miller Beer, *Elle*, *Pla* . . ."

"Yeah, yeah. So, what does that get us? Anything else?"

"Well, she was trying to be an actress. Had a couple of very small parts in some low budget films. She was testing for a bigger role in a crime film to be shot in Miami. Some coincidence, huh?"

"How about McIntyre? Any tie-in with Gannon?"

"She was modeling, like Gannon. Even a few of the same magazines. In fact, they both . . ."

"I don't need details," Warner knuckled bloodshot eyes and sighed. "Unless you think they'll lead somewhere. That's why I got ya plowin' through the dirty bathwater, lookin' for the baby."

He shook his head, lips compressed into a narrow slit, and ran a hand through his unruly mop, avoiding the pulsing scar. Exhaustion was making him short with people just doing their best.

"Sorry, buddy." He squeezed Harry's shoulder "Didn't mean to snap. So, you got nothin' that might connect the two gals in this nut's mind?"

"Doesn't look like it, Al. It's all pretty simple stuff. I'm at a dead end."

"Okay. Stay at it and keep me posted. Go over your list and revisit anyone you think might have more to tell. You got the best instincts in the department. Use 'em."

"Right," the older man sighed. "I'd like to cut out a little early today. It'll give me a chance to clear my head. I'll get right back on it in the morning."

"Go ahead. We got nothin' to work with until this bastard kills again. My gut tells me it's gonna be pretty soon. I hate relyin' on another vic to make any progress on a case."

"Sometimes that's all we can do. Wait and watch, and hope he slips up next time. It's sure a helpless feeling, isn't it?"

"For sure. Well, have a good evening and get some rest. I hope I can do likewise."

"Thanks," Klein said and picked up his coat on the way out. Warner returned to his desk and studied the photos of two gorgeous, sexy—and very dead young women.

Why couldn't he remember where he'd seen these two babes before? It drove him nuts, because intuition told him it was important. He was just too damned tired.

"Ah, shit." he grumbled. A glance at his calendar reminded him he had a counseling session with four teens from the Youth Camp. All juniors in high school, they were hoping to make it to college. He couldn't give them much help in course selection, but what they really wanted was advice on how to stay out of trouble with friends still in the gangs. There he was a real expert. Getting four more kids out of the ghetto and on course to a productive life was more important than a few extra hours of sleep.

He'd still get home early enough to get some rest. First, he and Buff would go on a good run. The retriever was tireless and needed at least two miles to dispel the restless energy from lying around his townhouse. No one had claimed the golden, so he was officially Warner's. The beautiful dog, now recovered from its injuries and filling out with good food and care, had adopted Warner as much as the other way around. They'd become close pals and sleeping companions. Warner even brushed him twice a day, trying to minimize the fur fallout around his home.

If Warner could just shake the terrifying dreams, he'd be okay. He'd lurch awake, finding Buff licking his face, trying to calm him. He needed solid rest. Needed to be sharp when that bastard struck again.

It'd be soon, if the timing on the first two were any indication of his schedule.

The captain was primed to call the FBI as soon as the next body bag came in. Those guys at the BAU are pretty smart. Maybe they'll spot something Warner missed.

As tired as he was, that seemed likely.

THIRTY

"I've got to go, baby. It's an early shoot tomorrow, and I gotta be bright-eyed and beautiful. I'd like at least six hours sleep, and I'll only get five tonight, even if I leave right now."

"Aww, Kym, honey, you can sleep here with me."

"No way, Mickey. Your forty-year-old hormones must think this gorgeous body is the fountain of youth. Most studs half your age aren't as hot as you.

"Don't think I don't love it, baby." She chuckled. "The orgasms blow my mind. But I gotta make a living. Once I get a serious part in one of your movies, we can spend every night together." She'd finished buttoning her blouse and slipped into her alligator pumps.

"C'mon, Kym. You know I'm trying, but I can only do so much. The rest is up to the director. Stay with me tonight. We'll figure something out."

"Sorry, hon. As much as I love the fucking, I gotta get some shut-eye." She picked up her matching clutch bag and blew him a kiss.

"Call me in the afternoon. Meantime, you got all those lovely pictures of me in *Penthouse* to keep you warm. 'Bye, sweetie."

And she was gone. He never heard the apartment door close behind her.

Bitch. But what a gorgeous bitch. Such magnificent tits. Mickey Porter was sure they were natural. He never had a babe turn him on over and over again like she did. He *had* to have her. If he didn't land her a part in his next flick, she'd probably ditch him.

The bitch.

Problem was, he'd fallen in love.

He picked up the *Penthouse* magazine, flipping the pages until he found the photo feature: *JANET AND JAMES*. Six glorious pages of Kym, wearing an exotic mask, with some muscular stud in numerous sexually explicit poses. The magazine had evolved past suggestive to explicit. It was hot, and so was he–again.

"Kym, baby. Look what I got for you. Come back, baby." But he was alone.

"I'm going to have to do this one myself, I guess."

Bitch. Oh, how he loved that gorgeous bitch.

*　*　*　*

"Asshole." Kym Atkins muttered, as she started her little Nissan sports car.

All he wanted was to fuck, fuck, fuck. You'd think by this time he'd pay off with a sizeable role. Three more months. That's all she'd give him. Two other eager "sponsors" were already lined up, just waiting for her to make a move.

"Well, I'll give him this. He's damned good in the sack. I don't have to fake my orgasms with Mickey. Now I gotta get home and get some sleep."

She slipped the car into gear and pulled away from the curb. One a.m. on a weekday and everyone was in for the night. Accelerating down the street, she passed an old, beat-up blue Ford, parked on the opposite curb.

Boy, that old Fairlane has been through some wars. Two car-crazy older brothers had taught her about automobiles. She glanced in her mirror, surprised to see the old car pull out, making a U-turn behind her. Its headlights did not come on.

"Oh, Oh. Trouble. That joker's tailing me."

Kym Atkins was normally a conservative driver. Too often she'd seen the results of recklessness at the various speedways she'd attended with her brothers. But she'd also raced fast little cars in several small rallies and knew how to do things with a vehicle that would put most guys to shame.

Scared now by the ominous presence of the old Ford close behind her, she downshifted into second gear, and tromped hard on the accelerator. The little car almost leaped off the road. Making a sharp right, then a quick left, she hurtled down a small side street, shifting smoothly as she gained speed. Doing 70, she glanced in her mirror, and saw the old jalopy still coming.

Dixie Highway was just ahead. Making a flying left, she kept the pedal pinned to the floor. Then she saw it. A cop car, cruising in the other direction. Braking hard, she pulled onto the center median, blinking her lights and waving frantically out the window. He slowed and turned on his flashing lights. Kym skidded to a halt and leaped out of her car, running toward safety. The policeman also stopped, stepping out of his car, hand resting on the butt of his weapon.

"Thank god I found you." She panted from tension more than exertion. "Who says I can't find a cop when I need one?"

"What's the problem, Miss? You musta been doing eighty out there." His hand rested on his gun, but he no longer looked wary.

He watched as she slowed to a trot, then a walk as she approached—a tall, slender nymph in a tight mini skirt and a flimsy silk blouse, only half buttoned, barely containing a terrific pair of tits, bobbing enticingly. The waist was small and the legs were long. She smiled, stopping in front of him, her eyes shining with green fire. A chiseled nose and high cheekbones on a heart-shaped face was framed by a mane of thick, copper-colored hair. He got a terrific hard-on just watching her.

"Thanks for one on Miami's finest." She laughed, catching her breath. "I just left a friend's apartment, and this old Ford Fairlane pulls out and starts following me with no lights. I panicked and took off, but I think he was still behind me. I was hoping when I got to Dixie, I'd find one of you guys. And here you are, the answer to my prayers."

"You sure the guy was tailing you, Ma'am?"

"Yeah, I think so. The car was parked when I pulled away. I noticed it 'cause my brothers were into old cars. Anyway, it made a U-turn and started after me, lights off. I thought of that U of M girl that was murdered three or four weeks ago. That was all I needed. I blasted out of there in a flash."

"You have anything else on the car, like color or license number. Did you see the driver?"

"It was blue or gray, about ten years old. Didn't see a face." She looked nervously over her shoulder, then turned back to the young cop. Tension sluicing away, she smiled.

"Any chance I can get you to escort me home, Officer? It's only a couple of miles. I'm pretty shook up."

"Sure. Can't turn down a beautiful maiden in distress. Wait here. I'll make a U-turn at the intersection, then you lead out."

"Thanks Officer Martinez." She read his name off his ID badge. "I just love Latin men."

He licked his lips, probably wishing she'd love him well enough to pay for services rendered with a visit up between those long, lovely legs.

But Carlos Martinez was clearly pissing in the wind. A gal like this wouldn't waste her time or talents on a lowly cop, however handsome.

The ride home was uneventful. The old Fairlane was nowhere in sight.

Officer Martinez returned to his patrol, a burning ache between his legs.

THIRTY-ONE

Kym scrambled up the stairs, fumbling with her keys, taking quick, nervous glances over her shoulder. She burst into her room, quickly slamming the door, snapping the deadbolt home. Dropping her purse on the hall table, she darted to her window, peeking out from behind the shade. Was that the red glow of a taillight disappearing around the corner?

Get a grip, Kym.

The cop came all the way here with her, and she never saw another vehicle anywhere. She got spooked, and now her imagination was running wild.

Calm down. There's nobody out there now.

Entering the bathroom, she stripped in front of the full-length mirror, raising her arms above her head, crossing her wrists. Her skin was smooth and tan from modeling skimpy swimsuits, one of the places well-endowed young women could make a name for themselves in fashion. And Kym Atkins was the epitome of "well stacked."

"God, your gorgeous. No babe in Hollywood's got anything on you, Kymie. You just need that first break." She pivoted and moved to the sink. "That damned Porter better come through with something good pretty soon."

She washed up, too tired for a full shower, then slid between her satin sheets, still nude.

She sighed. Everything will probably work out. Mickey'd produce a part, and she was going to be famous. She probably just imagined that car following her. She could be such a drama queen—and that's why she'd be a terrific actress.

Her thoughts trailed off as she fell asleep.

*   *   *   *

On the corner below, a drably dressed man stood in the shadows, dark eyes peering from beneath the brim of a Miami Dolphins cap. Though the lights in the apartment were now extinguished, still he looked up.

Another day. Another day, my beauty. God longs for you at his side, but his angel is patient. There will be another day.

Soon.

Very soon.

Turning, he strode down the side street, slipping into his

beat-up old blue Ford, and drove off.

THIRTY–TWO

Warner jerked upright, startled by his own scream, still echoing in his ears. Buff sprang onto the bed for another tongue attack on his cheeks. Warner roughly pushed him away, too shaken to appreciate the dog's attempts to soothe him.

Another Goddamned dream. Trembling, soaked with perspiration, Warner's fear slowly oozed away, calming his galloping heart. The LED display of his clock bathed him with a ghostly green glow. It was 5:10 AM. He groaned, dropping his feet to the floor, rubbing sleep-sanded eyes. He absently scratched the dog behind the ears.

It was almost two weeks since Michelle McIntyre died. The bastard was going to kill again, and soon. He could feel it.

And they could do nothing but wait.

"I gotta get some real rest. If the fuckin' dreams would only stop. Sherry's right. Maybe I *should* see the damned shrink."

They hadn't spoken since a tumultuous dinner, four days before. It seemed as if they argued all night—first about abuses of the legal system by obviously guilty defendants who knew how to work it, and finally about politics in general. Calling her a bleeding-heart liberal pretty well finished off the night.

Frustration over these damned murders was grinding him down, making him irritated and short-tempered

Sharon was the best thing to happen to him—too good to be true—and he was driving her away. Amazingly, *she* was the one fighting to keep it together, but if he didn't get a hold of himself, he *would* lose her. Between his nightmarish sleep and self-inflicted pressure to snare this villain, he wasn't fit company for

111

anyone.

Crawling out of bed, he stumbled into the bathroom to relieve his bladder. Back in the sack, drifting off to sleep, he thought, *I gotta get some rest.*

He slept soundly for two hours, awakening fairly refreshed and ready for work. As he fixed a breakfast of shredded wheat and a half grapefruit, a depressing thought crept into his mind.

We got no chance at this sly bastard until he kills again. And that should be any time now. *The son-of-a-bitch had better fuck up the next time, or it's gonna be a long winter.*

He hurried out of his townhouse, Buff on heel, for a quick run. The eager dog loved getting out for some exercise and a chance to relieve himself, and a fast mile jog would get Warner's endorphins fired up and, hopefully, clear his head.

With the retriever settled back in, Warner left his townhouse, musing over his unhappy dilemma. He hated to rely on luck again to catch this murderous bastard. It was only luck that finally brought down Leordano. "Luck" that nearly got him killed.

Driving off, the painful memories of his own reckless stupidity crowded back into his mind . . .

He froze, mouth ajar, enveloped by the sickly smell. What the hell was a windowless, ramshackle hut doing out here in the middle of the Glades? He slipped the Beretta from its holster, holding it unobtrusively at his side. No need to provoke some young Seminole buck smoking pot.

He eased out of the center of the road and into the meager shelter of the tall grass. He swiped his left forearm across his forehead, trying to disrupt rivulets of perspiration stinging his eyes.

This could be dangerous. Really dangerous. And he was there alone.

Careless. Careless and stupid.

Teeth clenched, he inched ahead, closing on the dilapidated building. There were tiny windows, after all—high, perched just under the eaves.

The stench became almost overpowering. An odor, unfortunately, he knew too well.

No vehicle? The road ended there. Oughta be a car or a pickup nearby. Some vehicle made those recent tracks.

He reached the edge of the clearing, maybe fifteen yards from the hut. There—a door, an open padlock dangling from the hasp.

He took a deep breath and stepped forward—and his right foot slid out. He did the splits but managed to catch himself without crashing to the ground.

Shit!

Looking down, he realized that's what he'd stepped in.

Shit. And from a pretty big animal. Didn't look like a dog's.

A panther? Maybe. He didn't know what gator crap looked like. There was some more over there. Damn. It was all around this place. What the hell attracted so many big animals?

The smell, of course. The odor of Death, and it brought out the predators.

Treading carefully now, he approached the opening, head on a constant swivel. Where the hell was the fucking vehicle? Had it left already?

The door, roughly crafted out of oak 2 x 6's, hung ajar. He snatched one final look around, stepped to the threshold, crouched, and gently pushed. It opened inward on surprisingly silent hinges.

The single room was barely lit by the two tiny windows. He could make out nothing amid the thick shadows. Still crouched, he slid inside, his back now to the wall, the Beretta held, two-handed, in front of him. The power of the stench slammed into him, watering his eyes, churning his stomach, sucking up gorge into his throat.

He'd smelled death before.

Old Death.

Ripe Death.

But nothing *like this.*

This was Evil *Death.*

He choked down nausea, drawing his forearm again across his face, blinking sweat from his eyes, slowly acclimating to the gloom.

What was that, in the center of the room? Some sort of low table. Something indistinguishable lay on it.

He scrabbled across the floor, breathing through his mouth, and rose up to see better, his eyes finally accustomed to the gloom. Rising a little higher, he leaned over for a better look.

What the hell . . .?

Oh, fuck.

The contents of his stomach surged up his throat, no longer restrained.

Warner shook his head and swallowed hard, tasting the remembered bitterness.

Damn those memories. He parked his car in the Police lot and headed for his office, wondering when—or *if*—these visions would ever dim.

It would never be too soon.

THIRTY-THREE

Al Warner sat in the Java Spot, a Miami Avenue diner, drinking coffee with four other Dade County cops.

"You got a location staked out, Hector?" he asked the Narco detective who worked Little Havana.

"Yeah," Hector Carrera nodded. "I got two, but I think you'll like the one out north of the Tamiami Trail."

"Way out in the Glades?" asked Darnell Franklin. That was a long haul from his B & E beat in Overtown.

"Yeah, it's gonna be a schlep," Detective Ben Ellison pitched in, "but if it's gonna be effective with these young hard-cases, it's gotta be remote—and miserable." He'd seen too many kids involved with homicides in North Miami.

"I agree," Warner said. "These punks gotta see us sweatin' and swattin' bugs, same as them."

"Right." said Jose Ignacio. "My Hialeah gangbangers ain't gonna be any pushovers. We gotta break 'em to mold 'em, if we're gonna have any kinda success."

"Okay, Hector. Show us the map," Warner said.

The five men crowded around the table as Hector spread out a topographic map of southwestern Dade County. A yellow circle indicated an approximate ten acres area, just off a dirt trail, maybe three miles north of the Tamiami Trail, the only paved highway crossing the entire southern tip of Florida. It was desolate country, igniting deadly memories for Warner. His thumb stroked the suddenly-aflame hidden scar above his right ear.

"You okay with this, Al?" Hector asked. "I can find another spot not so close to . . .."

"It's okay, buddy. I ain't the kinda guy haunted by ghosts," he lied. "Looks like a fine spot. Is it available?"

"Yep. Owned by the sugar company, but they aren't using it and were happy to give us a dollar a year rent for 'such a good cause,' they said." Hector chuckled. "I 'spect they're gonna make a public relations to-do about how they're helping the community."

"With their rep, they need all the help they can get," Darnell growled.

"Looks good to me," Ben said. "We're gonna have to make maps for the kids' parents, if they're gonna find our little Eden."

"I already drew something up, figuring you guys would go for this spot." Hector slid a drawing onto the table. "Had a preliminary talk with a guy I know at Florida Highway Commission, and they'll let us erect permanent signs, pointing the way. The *Al Warner Teen Boot Camp for Troubled Kids* is officially under way."

"Hey, how did I get to be the headliner?"

"Your idea, Al," Jorge said, "and you organized us. Only seemed right is should be named for the *Hero of Miami*."

Everyone chuckled—except Warner.

"Let's make it Dade County Boot Camp, instead. Couldn't do it without you guys, ya know. Better acronym, too: DCBC." Warner scanned his four comrades faces.

"Everybody okay with DCBC?" Darnel asked. They all nodded.

"Good," Warner said, slapping the table and standing. "I gotta get to work. We got a serial loony out there, killin' honeys. If it's okay with you, Hector, parcel out the set-up jobs and make assignments. For me, too. I ain't too busy to pitch in gettin' this organized."

"Will do, Al. Seems to me, getting the kids assigned should be your job. Got any ideas."

"Yeah, I know a judge in Juvie who I think will jump at the chance to try to make a difference. He's told me, more'n once, he's tired of sentencin' the same kids, over and over. I'll make time to see him this week.

"First, you contact Big Sugar, Hector, and get that lease

signed before they change their mind. Try to get ten years, with an option for another ten."

"I got some guys," Jose said, pushing back from the table, "who I think I can get to donate some used camping gear and tents and stuff. We gotta set 'enrollment' limits, so I'll know what we need."

"Right," Warner said, and scanned their faces. "What d'ya think of thirty kids, max?"

The four cops grunted and nod agreement.

"We gotta organize a complete game plan," Warner continued, "with all the require logistics. A lotta people are gonna be lookin' for us to fail. They think these kids are lost forever. I wanna prove 'em wrong."

"Amen to that," said in ragged chorus, as they rose. "Here's to the DCBC," Ben said, raising his coffee cup.

"The DCBC," said in unison, the cups clinking.

A minute later, they were all in cars, heading back to their jobs, trying to keep Dade County safe.

Five good cops, trying to do something other than make arrests. At that moment, the arrest Al Warner craved seemed pretty unlikely. They were still without a single lead as to their killer.

He headed for his department, hoping for some sort of break before the appearance of a third victim.

Something he expected to occur too soon.

THIRTY-FOUR

Kym Atkins was in the midst of her morning's photo shoot.

The Italian swimsuit manufacturer was trying to break into the lucrative American market, and cost seemed no issue.

Kym did all sorts of modeling, but swimsuits were her bread and butter. She seemed selectively bred to enhance the sexiest outfits. Firm, full breasts, rounded hips, a tiny waist, all anchored by long, gracefully tapered legs. The burnished copper hair didn't hurt, either. By any standards, she was dynamite to look at. The camera unequivocally appreciated her natural sensuality.

Like many others in her profession, Kym lusted for stardom on the silver screen. Free time was spent on acting classes to refine her natural talents into a considerable skill. Looking for "the break" to get that new career in gear, she'd spent weeks researching possible benefactors. Once Kym selected producer Mickey Porter, hoping he'd be the one to supply that push, she set out to seduce him. Few men could resist Kym's beauty and erotic charm. Why would any normal man even want to?

Six-months had passed, but so far Mickey was a dud. If he didn't come through soon, she'd dump him. It was never a problem finding men to jump in bed with her. The trick was finding the one who could do her career some good.

That morning, however, career advancement wasn't her primary concern. She'd spent fifteen minutes peering first from her window, then from the building's doorway before girding herself for the sixty-foot run to her car. She jumped in and locked the doors, fumbling with the ignition keys while hyperventilating.

She tore away from the curb and drove wildly for a few blocks before forcing herself to pull over and take command of her emotions. No Fairlane followed her. Was she being paranoid?

No. Someone dogged her last night. She was sure of it.

Or was she?

She shook her head, coppery curls swirling, a rue smile

creeping out. Oh, how she loved dramatics. She was working herself up over nothing, and she was going to be late to work.

She was *never* late.

*   *   *   *

Jorell Kingsly strolled up to the scantily robed redhead.

"You okay, Kym? You look a little beat this morning."

"Yeah, I'm fine. Had a bad night. It doesn't show in my work, though, Jory. You can see that."

"Sure. It's going swimmingly."

She burst out laughing. "Oh, you *are* a card, aren't you," still chuckling

"Just worried about you, that's all," he said, grinning. "Partying late, were you?"

"No. I just had a scare coming home." She tightened the sash of her robe. "An old jalopy started following me, but nothing happened. I found a cop to escort me home. He was *so* dejected I didn't invite him up to protect this perfect body more closely. Poor darling had a terrible hard-on."

"You give those to most any guy, kid, especially if you're dressed to kill. I got one now, as hot as you're looking in that little nothing you're wearing."

"Poor baby. You'll have to find someone else to relieve you, though. I'm committed, you know."

"Yeah. Mickey's got clout in the flicks. It's so refreshing to see you pick a guy just for love, huh?"

Mozart tinkled in the melody of her laugh, her emerald eyes twinkling merrily. She had worked with Jory several times and enjoyed his straightforward honesty. Their banter dispelled the mist of her earlier apprehensions. She was less and less sure anything ominous had occurred last night.

"Well, looks like the set's ready again. Go knock 'em dead.

I'm not gonna watch, though. My libido can't take any more unrequited lust. Gotta find a lesser star to hit on. Good luck, kid."

"Thanks, Jory. And keep a lamp lit. You never know when I might get sentimental."

"Swell. I'm a patient guy, Kym." He sauntered off, a handsome tiger, searching for fresh prey.

THIRTY-FIVE

"Hi. You've reached Sharon Clark. Leave a message. I'll get back to you as soon as I can." A moment later came the telltale beep.

"It's me, Sherry. We keep missin' each other, and we gotta talk about the other night. How about dinner? I need to get away from this case for a while. Pick you up around 7:30, if that's okay? No need to call back, unless you can't make it."

Warner hung up the phone and sighed. He had to get things straight with Sharon. The unfathomable mystery of her love was too important to let it slide away unchallenged.

He surveyed the organized clutter of his desk, feeling better. After the bad dream that morning, those two hours of real sleep had done a world of good. But the investigation still loomed, totally stalled. Plenty of evidence and genetic proof it was the same perp, but not a single clue to point them to the right guy, or even to throw some light on how he selected his targets. No fingerprints to match in the system. DNA, but no matches there. Either he's new to this, or has never been caught before.

Discouraged, he remembered his earlier thoughts: awaiting his next victim, hoping he finally proved careless.

He talked with Fanucci that morning, but Boca was coming

up just as empty. The waiting was the toughest.

Meanwhile, three new, there were unrelated murders to keep him busy. They had already secured a confession on one, a jealous lover, and there was an abundance of evidence on the other two. Warner expected to have all those perps in custody very soon. With a groan, he attacked the tottering pile of paperwork accumulating on the corner of his desk. The scourge of being Chief of Homicide Detectives was definitely a downside.

THIRTY-SIX

The morning arrived perfectly. A bright, cloudless sky allowed them to shoot clear through to 11:30. The president of the American office for the swimsuit manufacturer watched Kym's last two sessions. Very Italian and very horny, he drooled when she emerged clad in a black, backless one-piece suit with leg openings cut to the hip and the front V plunging to her belly button. Not enough material to hide all she had to show.

She loved it.

He loved it.

The camera definitely loved it.

He approached her as they finished.

"I, Giovanni Multi, would seek the pleasure of your company for lunch."

God, he's so—so Italian. She smiled and tilted her head.

"Where did you have in mind, Mr. Multi? A girl has to watch her figure, you know."

"Don't you worry. Where I take you, you will be happy. And it will be my pleasure to watch your figure for you. It is a figure I have enjoyed watching for the past ninety minutes." He winked.

He was handsome and fit, despite pushing sixty.

"How can a girl refuse such a gallant offer," Kym laughed. "Give me ten minutes to change and shed some of this makeup."

"Do you mind if I watch?" A sly leer in his smile.

"As long as that's *all* you do. No touching the merchandise."

"Ah, such restrictions. But merchandise would indicate something for sale. Is there a price on touching?"

"God. Italian men." she chuckled. "My dressing room's over there." Men like him were easy marks, and often very profitable.

THIRTY–SEVEN

Warner bulled through the door, rattling its hinges, causing it to kick back. Only a quickly raised hand saved him from a broken nose. A furtive glance over his shoulder and he was inside, closing it quietly. He sagged against the jamb, tossing his keys on the hall table.

Shit. Nine o'clock and all's not well.

He went to his wall bar and poured a stiff shot of scotch, too tired to bother with ice. Buff sidled up for an ear-scratching.

"I never learn. You're an idiot," he mumbled, sinking into a worn overstuffed chair, the dog's head parked on his lap. Absently stroking his soft fur, Warner kicked off his shoes and stretched, wiggling his toes. He took a long swig of his drink.

Things had not gone well. Sharon had been a little cool, right from the beginning. A discussion of crime and punishment began again over drinks. She was defending a Cuban kid who had confessed to killing his girlfriend. The D.A. had pressed for

First Degree Murder and the death penalty. Sharon's complaint about a lack of compassion fell on unsympathetic ears.

"The death penalty for a basically good kid who acted out in a moment of passion? C'mon, punish him, yes. But not to death. It's second-degree at worst."

"First of all, the death penalty's the D.A.'s call. Second, this 'good kid' got a rap sheet three-feet long, includin' four other violent crimes that, luckily, didn't end anybody's lives. You think he brought that big switchblade with him to pare his nails?" He looked at her with a restrained belligerence.

Here we go again.

How did they get into these philosophical discussions? Being on opposite sides of the fence promoted the to-be-expected differences in opinions. It was unique they were in love in spite of the gaping schism on this issue. Guilt and punishment were the bastions of their professions. He dropped his eyes and sipped his scotch.

"I don't think the needle is cruel and unusual punishment for someone who purposefully takes another's life. Your client went to that girl's house armed. You know the law better'n me. That's grounds for premeditation—First Degree Murder." He found her eyes and shrugged.

"What *is* cruel and unusual is lawyers draggin' things out for eight, ten, even twenty years with appeals, hookin' the taxpayers with a huge bill, and givin' the miserable bastards hope when there probably ain't any. Justice is supposed to be swift, but it sure can drag its ass."

"You'd just execute them all, Al? No chance to fight for their lives?" She sat back, her eyes flared.

"You bet. Give 'em a year, two max, for appeals. Then do it. It'd make room in our prisons and help balance the budget. Maybe some of these guys would think twice before cappin' someone." He swirled the ice in his Scotch.

"Well, if you're looking to free up cell space, why not execute the drug smugglers and rapists, while you're at it?"

"A helluva an idea, Sherry. Make a second conviction for rape or pushin' hard drugs a mandatory death penalty. You'd probably see much less crime around here, and fewer kids hooked on opiates."

"You can't be serious." Her arms folded across her breasts.

"Why not? I was raised to believe in morals. The Bible says an eye for an eye and severe punishment for sinners. We got a crisis in our cities, and we need tougher action to quell it."

He sat back, stubborn challenge creasing his face. He'd gone over the line again, but couldn't take any of it back now.

"Wow. I can't believe you. You're the most humane man I know, under that crusty exterior. You even run programs to rehabilitate troubled kids. How does that fit with what you've just said?"

He shook his head and sagged back in his chair.

"Tryin' to make a difference when they're young enough to change. But you see what I do, day after day, it'll sour you. Like two young women snuffed out without a real reason, or all the other crap we gotta wade through in this cesspool. Maybe you'd see it different if you spent some time in my shoes. I dunno. I guess I just got my fill."

He stared moodily out over the crowd as the woman shook her head in wonder. There wasn't much left to say.

Home now, he wished he'd said less. The rest of the evening was a quiet formality. Two strangers sharing a table out of necessity.

"Well, what's done is done. I'd better hit the sack. Gotta be sharp, 'cause that fucker's comin' visitin' again soon."

He headed toward his bedroom, unbuttoning his shirt as he went.

THIRTY-EIGHT

Kym closed her door and leaned against the jamb, a smile tweaking her lips.

"God, Italian men sure know how to treat a gal. What a stud for fifty-nine."

Opening her purse, she withdrew a thick roll of bills, fanning them in front of her eyes and giggled.

"Two-grand, plus two thousand more for the day's shoot. Not a bad day's work." She stretched, and then ran her hands down her body.

Things had started out fine, and then got better. Despite her warning, Multi couldn't keep his hands off her while she changed. He buried his face between her luscious breasts, moaning. He had a very talented tongue.

"Now, be a good boy," she said with a laugh. "I've got to change, and you promised me a lovely lunch. We'll see how things go before I decide to offer you any dessert."

Despite her admonishments, forty minutes passed before they left her dressing room. After a sumptuous lunch and many flutes of champagne at the Plum Room, he begged her to return to his hotel with him.

"Well, I don't know, Giovanni. I'm seeing someone, you know. It wouldn't be right."

"Ah, Madonna, it would bring me so much pleasure, as I promise it will also bring you. If you come, I guarantee you an appearance in the *Sports Illustrated Swim Suit Edition* next spring. They are featuring our new line. It pays very well."

"*Sports Illustrated*, huh? Well, then that makes it business, so it might be okay. But how do I know that you'll keep your word. We girls are such easy marks for handsome, mature men."

That's when he offered her a two-thousand dollar "advance" as a show of good faith. She accepted coyly, already quite aroused by his obvious lust. Kym wasn't surprised that, in spite of his age, he was a wonderful lover. She had two lovely orgasms.

Still glowing with the warmth of his touch, she pushed away from the door, starting for the bedroom, when she noticed the blinking light on her answering machine. She perched on the edge of the couch and retrieved the message.

"Hi, Kym. It's Mickey. I've got big news, doll, but I can't be there before one a.m. Wait up for me. It'll be definitely worth it."

She leaped to her feet, pumping her fist.

"Finally! A part in his new flick."

She glanced at the clock. Three hours. Plenty of time for a warm soothing bubble bath and some beauty sleep. If she were finally going to be in movies, she wanted Mickey to be properly rewarded.

She strolled into her bedroom, whistling merrily.

THIRTY-NINE

Where the hell is he?

She prowled her living room, glancing at her watch. Already 1:30, and Mickey was never late when it came to Kym.

This better be a good part in a movie. Not a shitty one-liner. He'll leave horny if I got all dolled up for nothing.

There was a light rap at the door.

Finally. Kym hurried over and looked through the peephole. She recoiled and sucked in a sharp breath.

It wasn't Mickey.

Visions of an old blue Ford popped into her head.

"Who are you? I got a gun here."

"Take it easy, Miss Atkins. Mr. Porter sent me. He's delayed and didn't want you to worry."

"Yeah? I've never seen you before."

"I'm Angie Dedios. I work for the director on Mr. Porter's film. An errand boy today. I got something Mickey sent over for you."

"Just a minute." She scurried to the window. No blue Ford in sight.

Just like Porter. She was all turned on and ready to party, and he sends over a runner. Not bad, if you like them rugged looking. Not soft like Mickey. But she wasn't letting someone in she didn't know.

"Hang on a minute. I'm gonna call Mickey."

"Take your time. Don't blame you for being cautious. They're in some kind of pitch meeting, though. Cell phones might be off."

"Yeah? We'll see." The phone rang but no one answered, and it went to voice mail. They did put them on "silent" when in the middle of brainstorming. Didn't want to break the mood.

She canceled the call and peered through the peephole again.

"No answer. Just drop it outside. I'm nervous about strangers."

"Sure, if that's what you want. I'll just sit out here until Mr. Porter turns up, if that's okay."

"What for? Can't you just leave whatever it is and go?"

"Nope. Mr. Porter told me to stick around until he shows.

Heard you got spooked last night and wants to be sure you're safe. My main job is security, but when there's nothing going on, sometimes I run errands for the execs. I don't mind waiting out here, if you're nervous."

Through the fisheye in the door, she saw him start for the stairwell.

Damn.

"Hey, wait. It's okay. I'll let you in. It's sweet of Mickey to worry."

Releasing the dead bolt and opening the door, she peeked around its edge. Him seeing her decked out in her sexiest black silk lace teddy and a transparent negligee didn't concern her. Her body was her living.

The guy picked up a small box he'd placed at her threshold and entered the apartment. Looking at his sun-darkened face, she found herself drowning in dark, bottomless eyes. He wolf-whistled softly, breaking her almost hypnotic stupor, as he handed her the package.

"Here. These are for you." His eyes envelop her, and a delicious tingle raced down her spine.

Kym smiled. He was pretty damned sexy. Very masculine and quite strong looking. Her heart skipped a beat, and a moist stirring surged between her legs. The prospect of finally being in one of Mickey's movies had fired up her hormones. And this guy was a stud. She went up on her toes, doing a pirouette.

"Like how I look?" She grinned. "Well, that's my job, ya know."

"Yeah, but you're more beautiful in person than you were in the magazine."

"The magazine?"

"Yeah, the spread in Penthouse. Wish it was me you filmed it with. Guys like me only dream about making love to gals like you." He leaned against the door jamb, hands in his pockets.

"That's sweet. You liked the pics, huh?" Kym chuckled. "The sex scenes were faked, ya know."

"I guessed. Still, you looked hot, but this is different. It's hard staying cool, being this close to you."

Her laugh was friendly. Being openly admired always stirred her sensuality and was still on a high from the afternoon's fun and games.

What a nice guy. And what a chiseled, hard body. So different from soft little Mickey and old Giovanni. It might be fun to make it with all three in the same day, each so different.

Damn, she's so reckless when her hormones are pumped up. She tore the wrappings off her gift and giggled.

"Chocolate truffles. My weakness. How sweet of Mickey to know."

"Actually, it was me. I remembered it from the *Penthouse* sidebar. Mickey didn't have a clue what to send."

"Very clever. Mickey's lucky having a quality guy like you around."

"I'm the lucky one, Miss Atkins . . .."

"Call me Kym. Everyone does, even people I don't know."

"The price of fame and being so damned gorgeous. Geez, it's tough being here. I'm aching to kiss you. And," he glanced at his watch, "Mr. Porter won't be here for at least another hour. Don't know how I'll stand it. I may have to wait outside after all."

Geez, his sweet, open adoration was so sexy—and so damned exciting. Another whole hour before Mickey arrived? Enough time to give this guy a once in a lifetime memory? She never had three different men in the same day before.

What a kick. She smiled and stretched, her glory plainly visible through the gossamer material. Taking his hands, she tugged gently. His dark, intense eyes glittered with passion.

"I need you here to protect me, Angie. Actually, I think I need more from you than that. You're so sweet and considerate,

I'm gonna reward you with something you'll never forget."

Kym wrapped her long arms around his neck, tilting her head, one hand lightly stroking his neck. Her pink-tipped tongue caressed slightly parted cherry lips, her pelvis undulating softly against his, and the hardness growing there.

"What about Mickey?"

"What Mickey doesn't know won't hurt him. I'll make him *very* happy later. But right now, I need *you* to make love to me. I'm so damned hot."

"Just what I thought," he murmured, molding her against him, their mouths consuming the other's. Erotic explosions rocked their senses. The moaning and groaning over the next fifteen minutes plotted their progress toward Nirvana.

"Oh, fuck me. Fuck me!"

"Yes, whore. Yes."

"Oh, I'm coming. I'm coming now." Growling, panting, groaning—a noisy tale of their passionate journey.

The only thing to confuse a voyeur, if one listened in the hallway, was sudden silence, followed by a small cough, a little whimper, and a rough voice, reverently sing-songing those final, fatal words—

"The Lord calls."

FORTY

The man moaned, rolled over, and struggled to sit up. With almost comic determination, he shimmied his back to lean against a nearby wall.

"Oh, shit. My head. What the fuck happened?" Mickey

Porter fingered the egg-size lump at the back of his skull and the stickiness oozing from it.

"I was fucking mugged, that's what. Oww. Crap. I bet I got a concussion." He reached for his back pocket and he found his wallet, still in place.

"Shit." He pulled out his billfold and blearily peered inside. All his money, over $400.00, was still there. Why was he sapped, if not for his cash? No credit cards missing either, and his Rolex still circled his wrist.

He struggled to his knees, but the first effort to stand was an abject failure, as was his second. He turned and using the wall for balance, finally made it shakily to his feet.

Kymie. If he could make it there, she'd take care of him. Call a doctor, if necessary.

Mickey struggled on newborn colt's legs out of the little alleyway and onto the sidewalk. Braced against the building for support, he staggered up the street toward the safety of Kym Atkins' apartment. By the time he entered her building, his head was clearing, and he had regained some strength. He shuffled up the stairs with minimal difficulty and stopped at the top. He struggled to clear his aching head with a shake and plodded toward solace in the tender arms of his lover.

Dismayed, he found her door ajar. Kym was very security conscious, and the incident of the previous evening would make her even more careful. He crept in and looked around.

"Kymie. Kym. It's me. Where are you, babe?" He elbowed the door closed.

Maybe she'd fallen asleep. He peered bleary-eyed at his watch. After 2:30. He quietly tottered toward the bedroom. He'd awaken her with kisses and a wet tongue on those lovely tits.

At the door, he leaned heavily against the wall, caught his breath, and peeked in. Kym sprawled across the bed, probably asleep while awaiting him.

Something strange about how she lay there, skewed diagonally across the mattress. He slipped in and softly called again as he shuffled toward her.

"Kym. It's me, baby. Kym." He smiled. She was already naked for him. Finally, at the bedside, he could see her plainly.

"What the hell . . .?"

His eyes bulged as he staggered backward, collapsing to the floor.

"KYYYMMMIEEEE!"

FORTY-ONE

He staggered up the rough, stone stairs, as if churning through molasses. Python-crushing panic clutched his chest more tightly with each frantic step.

It's coming!

The clatter of its claws echoed sharply in the narrow stairwell, just around the curve. The hot, fetid stench of burned sulfur and rotted meat saturated the air and stifled his breath.

The smell of Death.

Immense, flesh-rending fangs gnashed together over a deep, rumbling growl.

The Beast.

It was going to get him this time. Thick chains around its three massive necks clanked together, an insistent chiming. It was here, about to pounce.

Clang, clang, clang . . ..

Warner lurched bolt upright, peering wildly around the darkened room, his own scream echoing in his ears. The creature was *there*, its green, luminous eyes shining. He trembled and blinked, his pajamas drenched with panic-laden sweat before he realized the glow was only the LED of his clock: 3:40 AM.

Another terrifying dream, and a ringing phone instead of the clang of chains.

Fumbling in the dark for the receiver, more alert now, he had a premonition.

He's killed again.

"Warner," he croaked, his voice still choked by dreamed terror.

"Al? This is Santiago. We just got number three. Another beauty. Same M.O. Same message."

"I knew this wasn't gonna be good news." He knuckled gritty eyes, still filled with sleep. "I just hope the bastard made a mistake this time, Captain. When and where?"

The information copied onto a small pad on his nightstand, he dragged his still trembling body into a cold shower to clear his head and to wash away the odor of fear. He fed Buff and got a soulful glare when the golden retriever was only allowed enough time for a quick pee and poop.

"We'll get in a good run later," he said, scratching the silky furred head behind his ears.

Ten minutes later, balancing a chocolate donut on a mug of strong instant coffee, he was in his car, tunneling through predawn gloom. Few other vehicles were on the road.

He turned off Biscayne Boulevard and spotted the scene. No address needed. Three cruisers, lights flashing, marked it well. He skidded to the curb just short of the modern concrete and glass building. A dozen people milled around the walk. What the hell were all the civilians doing up so early? What a mess. He flashed his shield to the cop on the sidewalk.

"Who's in charge here, officer?"

"Uh, no one, sir. Just us three patrol cars responded to the call. You're the first detective to show. The other guys are

133

inside."

"Okay, disperse this crowd and keep traffic movin'. No unauthorized personnel allowed inside."

"Yessir. Uh, but . . .."

"What? Spit it out. I got an investigation to run."

"There's a reporter from the Herald . . .."

"Yeah?" Warner moved toward the doorway. "Well, just keep him out of the buildin'."

"He's—uh—already in the apartment."

"Wha-a-t?" Warner spun around and glared at the cop, who tried to avoid his stare. "Shit. Now it's really hit the fuckin' fan."

Warner burst through the door, taking the steps three at a time. He spotted the apartment, another cop standing just outside. Flashing his shield, he entered the room, searching for its occupants. A guy wearing a rumpled sport jacked was sitting on the edge of a sofa, comforting another man, stretched out, his face wet with a mixture of tears and blood. He blubbered softly to himself.

"Oh Kymie, Kymie. My beautiful Kymie."

Warner glowered at the seated man.

"Who the fuck are you, and what the hell are you doin' here?"

"Eddy Roush, *Miami Herald.*" He stood, his proffered hand pointedly ignored. He shrugged.

"You're Al Warner, huh? Well, I'm, glad they got their best on this one."

"Get the fuck out of here, Roush. This is a crime scene, and it's not open to the public, hot-shot crime reporter or not."

"Yeah, I know, but I picked it up on my scanner and got here right with the first patrol car. I've already . . .."

"Out, I said. Now. Or I'll run you in for obstruction of justice. You're taintin' the evidence. Out."

"But, Detective, I . . .."

"Out, I said."

". . . saw the mirror. There's something written on the mirror."

Warner sucked in a deep, shuddering breath. So that secret was out. A flood of relief tempered his anger. He'd been filled with doubts over hiding the real nature of these brutal, senseless crimes. Now it was time for damage control. He sighed, and fingers found his now fiercely itching hidden scar.

"Look, I gotta go over the scene for evidence. Get outta here, and I'll talk to you when I'm done. You gonna stick?"

"Yeah, if you promise to give me some time. Say, is this connected to the Gannon murder?"

"How the hell should I know?" He glared at the man. "I just got here. We'll talk later, I promise."

The reporter shrugged, leaned over, and patted the blubbering man's hand.

"I'll talk to you later, Mickey, when you're stronger."

"Who's that," the detective queried.

"Mickey Porter. He's a local film producer. The girl's boyfriend, I guess. He found the body. Seems he was mugged just downstairs. When he eventually made it up here and found her, he passed out. Poor bastard."

"All right. Thanks. See ya later." Warner turned to the cop at the door.

"No one else in here but authorized police personnel."

"Yessir. I got it covered."

Not fuckin' soon enough. What the hell would he tell that damned reporter? Gotta come up with something good. The poor bastard on the couch was a complete wreck. He wasn't going to get much from him for a while.

He groaned. *The Cap's gonna want to bring in the Feds and their BAU after this one. How are we gonna keep a lid on panic after that?* He shrugged and headed for the bedroom, glancing around as he went.

Nice digs, tastefully decorated with expensive furnishings.

135

This gal made some good bucks.

He strode through the doorway and saw the third street cop in a chair, looking at an issue of *Penthouse*.

"You're lookin' comfortable. Who're you?"

"Officer Martinez, sir," he said, jumping to his feet, recognizing Warner.

"Well Officer Martinez, take your magazine and get your ass out on the street and keep unauthorized people away from the crime scene. That includes the press, Goddammit."

"Yessir. But—uh—this ain't my magazine. It was on the floor. She's in it."

"What? Where the fuck did you get your badge, in a Cracker Jack box? How'd you know that ain't a piece of critical evidence. The perp's prints coulda been all over it. Give your badge number to Detective Olvida when he arrives so we can pull your prints for forensics. Now get the fuck out of here." The young officer, his face bright red, turned to leave.

"Hey, wait a minute. She's in what?" Warner asked.

"Huh?"

"You said 'She's in it.' In what?"

"Oh, the magazine. *Penthouse*. In one of those photo features. Pretty sure it's her, even with the mask. She looked damned hot."

"Humpf. Okay. You can go," Warner donned latex gloves and leafed through its pages. Martinez paused at the door, then resolutely turned to face the detective.

"I knew her, ya know."

"Who? The victim?"

"Yeah. Well, I didn't *really* know her, but I met her night before last. She flagged me down on Dixie Highway about 1:15 a.m. Said someone was following her in an old blue Ford Fairlane and asked me to escort her home. I filed a report. I never saw nothing, but looks like she might have been right."

"Yeah. That might be a lead. Get me a copy of your report, ASAP. Thanks."

"Yessir." Martinez left, clearly feeling a little better that he may have helped.

FORTY-TWO

Warner found the six pages of sexually suggestive photos. The girl was incredibly gorgeous. He closed the magazine and turned to the bed for his first close look at the corpse, something he had unaccountably delayed. He felt a strange reluctance about everything to do with this case lately. He didn't know why.

He surveyed the waxen-looking body. The bastard had killed another real looker all right. No signs of struggle. Her larynx appeared crushed, same the others. The Horseman of Death had swooped down on this young beauty unexpected and unheard, and he was swift and merciless. Semen stains covered the sheet beneath her pelvis.

He shuddered and turned away, and tears of rage and frustration filled the corners of his eyes. Moe Gold was due any minute, and so was one of his own crew, Rafael Olvida.

Warner glanced at the open bathroom door. Rauch said he saw a message on the mirror. The detective knew he had to go in there, but he couldn't get moving. He finally steeled himself, and edged to the doorway and peeked inside.

Nausea swept over him in a hot flash. He began to shake, as he read the now familiar call to death, emblazoned in red on the reflective glass. That reporter, Roush, saw it too, and that was trouble.

The clatter of new people arriving drew him away from the message of death. This case was getting personal. He desperately wanted this guy dead.

He found Detective Olvida sitting with the still sobbing wreck on the sofa. Ralph was trying to get him to down a shot of whiskey as he comforted the man. He did those kinds of things much better than Warner, who tended to be direct, and occasionally impatient in his eager search for truth.

The Hawk and one of his assistants were next to arrive, carting in a bunch of equipment to aid in their search for clues. Moe's face looked as rumpled as his pants.

"You look like something the cat wouldn't even bother dragging in, Moe. We disturb your beauty sleep?" Olvida was always quick with a quip.

"Yeah, and I was having one terrific dream, too. We've got to stop meeting like this, guys."

Warner grunted and nodded.

"That's the job, Moe. Find something to show me who's doing these dames, and we can stop. The girl is on the bed and the handwritin's on the mirror. Work some magic, buddy."

"Another looker, I suppose."

"Oh, you bet. Good enough to have made *Penthouse*."

The little man sighed and headed for the other room, black bag in hand. His assistant began examining the entranceway.

Warner joined his partner and his disheveled companion, who had finally managed to sit up, glazed eyes momentarily dry. He was in a state of shock but was trying to get control of himself. The right side of his head was matted with dried blood.

"You Mickey Porter?" Warner asked, hunkering down in front of the pallid face.

"Yeah. Michael Porter," he sighed and his eyes flooded again.

138

"I know this is hard for you, Mr. Porter, but can you tell us what happened? Right from the beginning."

"I'll—I'll try. It's just such a shock. She was so young. So beautiful. So alive, just last night. I loved her, you know. I really loved her. Who would do such a terrible thing? What am I gonna do now?" Tears rolled silently down his bloodless cheeks.

It was a thing to which Warner was never inured, someone utterly destroyed by another's mindless cruelty.

Warner took the man's hand and spoke softly.

"I know it's a terrible loss. We need you to tell us everything that happened so we can catch this bastard."

"Her—her name is—was—Kym Atkins. She's a model and wants—wanted—to be in an actress. I can't believe she's dead." He was sobbing again but continued resolutely on, determined to finish.

"She was my girl. I was trying to find her something in a movie, and a part had just come up today in something we're going to shoot next year. Anyway, I left a message on her machine. She was at a shoot today and . . . ."

"A shoot?"

"Yeah. Modeling swimwear. No one looked better in a sexy suit than Kymie. My poor Kymie." He sniffed. "It was for some Italian manufacturer." He dragged a hanky from his rear pocket and blew his nose, then sighed.

"She was tied up most of the day. I told her—her machine, anyhow—that I'd be over around one a.m. with a great surprise. You know—the movie part. So, I park and I'm hurrying to her place when someone grabs me from behind and hits me on the head." He reached up, rubbing the bloodstained knot on right side of the back of his skull and grimaced.

He paused, trying to collect himself, the tears flowing again as he fought for control.

"Anyway, I wake up in a little alley," his voice now a tired drone, as he slid deeper and deeper into shock, "and I get up and try to make it to Kym's apartment. I was real wobbly so it was slow going. I remember thinking she's gonna be really mad I'm so late. But when I get to her door, I see it's open a little. Kinda strange, because she's always so careful about security, especially after that *Penthouse* spread. She did a sexy feature in *Penthouse*. Did you see it?"

"Yeah, we saw it. She was dynamite, wasn't she Ralph?" Warner looked at his partner and give a sad little shrug. This guy's life would be in the crapper for a long time before he got over this, if ever.

"Dynamite." He spoke in a listless monotone. "I never met anybody like her. Anyhow, I go in sort of careful like, calling her, but there's no answer. I peek in the bedroom and see her on the bed, naked and so beautiful, and I think, she's just waiting there for me." Warner saw this shattered soul's vision turn inward to that terrifying memory, his face distorted by the horror of it, as he struggled to continue.

"So, I went over, happy with my surprise. Then I see her face and her *eyes*, bulging out like that, and—well, I guess I fainted." He sniffled and dabbed his eyes with the hanky.

"I woke up on the floor, thinking it was all a dream. But then, I see her foot, hanging over the side, and I was afraid. I didn't have the nerve or the strength to get up and look, but her foot was so cold. I knew it was no dream." Tears flowed again.

"So, I crawled out of the room—I couldn't stand—and called 911. But I was crying so hard I couldn't talk. Finally, I told them she was dead. Then I think I fainted again." The last of his strength gone, Mickey Porter dissolved into himself, a broken heap, rocking back and forth, keening quietly.

"Shit. Poor bastard," Olvida whispered, as he rejoined Warner at the sofa. "He'll be a lifetime getting over this.

"I've been prowling around while you were getting his

140

statement, Boss. I found a few kinda interesting things."

"Yeah? Like what?"

"I found this in her nightstand." He held up a rubber-banded wad of hundred-dollar bills. Warner whistled softly.

"You count it?"

"Yeah. I had to wait for Moe to lift some prints off it first. Two grand. And this business card with what looks like a hotel room number written on it."

Giovanni Multi, President
American Division
Swimwear Milano Corp.

"Must be who she was workin' for yesterday. Do models get paid cash? I thought they're paid through their agents."

"Yeah. Me too," Olvida said. "This smacks of 'Personal Services,' with the hotel room and all. I'll call Harris. Get him to check out Mr. Multi. Jealousy could be a motive here."

"Could be, but that don't fit with our psycho profile and the two other deaths, does it?"

"You sure it's the same guy, Al?"

"Take a peek in the bathroom. It's our guy, all right. But this time maybe we got a little something to go on."

"Oh? What?"

Warner related Officer Martinez's story about the blue Ford Fairlane. It wasn't much, but so far, it was the only thing they had after three murders. They called in their limited description of the vehicle. A top priority search was issued to all patrol officers with strict instructions to report and observe possible matching cars, but under no circumstances was any action to be taken if such a vehicle was discovered. They didn't want to spook their prey.

Meanwhile, the two detectives continued their detailed

search of the crime scene, frequently bringing Moe Gold to look at something or other they found interesting.

Nothing—absolutely nothing—was going to be left undone.

FORTY-THREE

Golden shafts of light streaked the eastern horizon, fragmented by the tall buildings of Miami's dramatic skyline that stood between Eddy Roush and the actual sunrise. He'd dozed off and on while awaiting the most revered cop in South Florida.

Al Warner—the Hero. The dedicated detective who'd finally brought down the Baby Butcher of Miami, Luis Leordano, almost losing his own life in the process. Roush had covered that story.

Here he was again, at the start of something smacking of more than just another murder. Eddy saw the writing, screaming in blood red from the mirror. Certainly not the trappings of a simple crime of passion. Something much more ominous was afoot.

The reporter was simultaneously ecstatic and repelled at the possibility of another mass murderer, so soon after Leordano. It would make riveting copy and advance his career, but it would also fill him with revulsion. That beautiful girl, killed so brutally.

God, the eyes! The tongue! Bile rose in his throat, acrid and bitter.

"Well, whatever the Hell it is," he mumbled, rubbing his bleary, red-rimmed eyes, "I'm in at the start, like always. What the fuck's keeping him, anyhow?"

Warner appeared five minutes later, as if conjured by the genie of Eddy's thoughts. He stood, gazing east at the glorious sunrise, now in full bloom, absent-mindedly rubbing the hidden scar from Leordano's 9mm slug.

Roush climbed from his car and stretched cramped muscles before walking to meet the haggard-looking detective, as he hurried down the stairs.

"Detective Warner. Hang on a minute. You promised me an interview if I waited."

"Huh? Oh, Roush. You still here?"

"Yeah. You said you'd talk to me about this murder if I'd wait. I waited. Over two hours I waited. So, please, talk."

"What d'ya want to know. You ask, I'll answer, if I can."

"Is this the same guy who killed that Gannon girl?" His pen was poised over a small notepad in his hand.

"How would I know? We just got here. We've got to go over the evidence, whatever that amounts to."

"C'mon, Detective. I saw the mirror." He held up his cell phone, displaying the damning photo. "I've done enough of these to know a 'signature' when I see one."

"I don't know what you're talkin' about. We got a dead girl, possibly the result of a jealous lover, that's all."

"Who? Mickey Porter? He couldn't squeeze a grape, much less strangle that beautiful kid. You saw him. He's all torn up." His eyes held Warner's. "Nah. This has all the markings of another serial killer. So, is this the first, or was it Gannon?"

Warner studied the reporter. Eddy Roush had covered violent crime in Miami for over five years. Unlike many of his breed, he was usually fair in his treatment of cops, both good and bad. He operated with reasonable integrity for a newsman, not writing for sensationalism alone. But how much could Warner trust him? He decided to take a chance.

"Look, Eddy. We got a situation here. I'm gonna trust you if you promise to only print, for now, what I authorize. In return, you'll get all the facts as we get 'em. Verifiable facts. In the end, you'll have the complete story. An exclusive (the magic words). Might even be a book in it for ya. What d'ya say?"

"I'm supposed to print what you want until you catch this guy? After that, I got Carte Blanche. Is that it?" He frowned.

"Yeah." Warner shrugged. "Pretty much. So?"

"Hell, I'm not your propaganda puppet. You should know that. You're denying the public a right to the facts."

"Trouble is, there are damned few facts. What we got will only inflame that public, not serve it. Best I can do, for now. Take it and be on the inside, or leave it and be on the outside. Your choice."

"And if I say 'no'?"

"I'll arrest you for obstruction of justice and interferin' with an investigation, and anything else I can think of. I plan on keepin' what you saw quiet for now."

"Damn, Warner. That's pretty harsh." He tugged at the lobe of his ear and eyed the detective. He sighed, then shrugged.

"So, if I print the party line, you'll feed me the real skinny as it happens, and I get the exclusive when it's over. Right?"

"Right. You get all the details. Everybody else'll just be guessin'."

Roush wondered if he could really trust him. His rep was of a fair and honest cop, and he *was* the Hero of Miami. Eddie shrugged again and readied his notebook and ballpoint.

"Okay. I guess I got no choice, and I'm betting I can trust you. This really *could* be a book, if it's what it looked like. So, what's the poop?"

"One more time. This ain't for publication now. Your story is on a simple murder. No suspects yet. Right?" Roush nodded, notebook in hand, an expectant look on his face.

"You were right," Warner said, exasperation in his voice.

144

"Gannon was the first. But this ain't the second, it's the third."

"What? The third?" The reporter's eyes flared, his tongue darting across dried lips. "I haven't heard of any others."

"Boca Raton. Another gorgeous gal, a FAU kid named Michelle McIntyre."

"Oh, I remember that one. Not on my beat, so I never . . ."

"Same guy, though. All three had willin' sex with the perp. We got a DNA match on the first two, and we'll get it on this one, too. The same message each time. First time I saw it at Gannon's apartment, I knew we had another psycho."

"Any leads, Detective?"

"Very little. He's about six feet, slim but muscular, dark-complexion. Could be suntan, Latino or light black. There're thousands around here that fit that description.

"He's probably charmin' and certainly attractive to these girls. Looks like they're fuckin' him right outta the box. We got a possible make on his car. The Atkins girl told a patrol cop she was being followed the previous night by a blue Ford. That's it. Maybe we'll have more when CSU's done up there."

"Shit. That's not much. What about the message?"

"It tells us he's on a mission. We ain't sure what that is just yet. More than just gorgeous women, though. If we turn up anything, I'll let you know. You're a good guy, Eddy. You were fair with us when we were stymied on Leordano, so I'm trustin' ya. Right now, I wanna avoid panic."

"Okay, Detective, you got my word, and it's always been good. I hope you get this guy quick. I'll call you later."

Roush headed for his car and peered east. The sun had snuck above the building tops. He wanted to get to the office and consolidate his notes. He glanced at his cell phone, open to the message sprawled across the mirror.

A shiver slithered down his spine, at the word, indelibly branded on his memory.

FORTY-FOUR

"Si. Si. I know Miss Atkins. She models my bathing suits, looking exquisite. Other women hope the suits will make them looks so beautiful. Why do you ask, Detective Harris?"

"Because, Mr. Multi, she had your card with this room number written on it, along with two thousand dollars in cash."

"She is in trouble because of this? We spend the afternoon together, celebrating an excellent shoot. Successful work with a camera makes me very excited. *She* makes me very excited. I promise her to model for *Sports Illustrated* Swimsuit issue. The money is proof of my intent to honor this promise. And for this she is in trouble?"

"No. Not anymore," Jack Harris sighed. "She'll never be in trouble again."

"Good. That is good. She is so sweet . . . .."

"And very dead."

". . . to be—What? What did you say? Dead?"

"Yes. Quite dead. Murdered last night in her apartment."

"*Mio Dio.* Kym Atkins? Murdered? How could this be?" He dropped onto the sofa like a bag of sand, his hands coming to rest on his knees. He stared at Harris, eyes big as quarters.

"That's what we're trying to find out. I need you to tell me everything that happened between you two yesterday. We already know plenty from others we've talked with, so make it the truth." He glanced at his tablet, scrolling the screen. "Lying would only cause you trouble."

"Lie? Why should Giovanni Multi lie? You suspect me in this tragedy? Ridiculous."

"I'm just trying to collect the facts. We suspect no one—and everyone. She had a boyfriend, ya know. You did bang her, didn't you? Jealousy is a frequent motive for murder, especially over a dame like that." The detective perched on the couch next to him.

"Bang her?" He shook his head. "You mean make love? How crude you are. Yes, we made the love. Several times, in fact. Exquisitely. She is—was—every man's dream. I know of no boyfriend. She is the best model for my products. And I would only wish to love her again, not kill her. What a waste of beauty and talent."

"Okay. Okay. No one's accusing you—yet. Just tell me everything that happened yesterday. Everything."

"Si. Si. What a pity. I have no luck at all."

"More than Kym Atkins, it seems." This guy was taking everything pretty calmly. Harris wondered if he were hiding something.

"Si. That is true." He sighed. "So, to the events of the day. I arrive at the set at ten, and they are shooting. She is something to see in our lovely suits. I watch and I get, how you say, horny. I take her to lunch and hope for good luck in the afternoon. She invites me into her dressing room while she changes, and I cannot keep my hands off her magnificent body. She seems to enjoy me, so . . .."

Detective Harris left the Italian's room thirty minutes later, his recorder filled with the intimate details of the willing seduction of Kym Atkins at the hands of her new benefactor.

If this guy killed her, Harris was the Wizard of Oz. Multi promised her the golden ring, and she paid with sex. *Sports Illustrated* yet. He supposed that could be a big step for a model. He'd heard some of those girls made it into films.

Harris took a sample of Multi's DNA, but they didn't need it to prove he slept with her. He freely admitted that. Multi could be the killer, but it didn't seem likely.

Harris stepped out of the elevator and hurried to his car. Al wanted whatever he got from the Italian ASAP, but Jack was going to stop at the donut shop for a muffin and some black Java. It was nine a.m. and he hadn't even had breakfast. Olvida's call had dragged him out of bed and got him going in a rush.

The third victim. They finally had a little something to work with. The whole force was looking for an old blue Ford Fairlane. They had Multi and the boyfriend, Mickey Porter, but they just didn't wash with the other two homicides.

He hoped The Hawk and his boys would find something else. What they had so far was pretty damned slim.

He slid into his car, still parked in the hotel drive, and headed for the office, with a short detour at Dunkin' Donut to assuage his grumbling gut.

FORTY-FIVE

Al Warner slouched at his desk, listlessly shuffling photos of three beautiful, dead young women. Kym Atkins' addition to the list hadn't brought them much closer to finding their killer.

He scanned the Medical Examiner's report for the twentieth time. Death due to asphyxiation caused by a crushed larynx, coming so swiftly that she had no chance to defend herself. Same as the other two. No tissue under her nails that might indicate she fought for her life. Just a few foreign hairs, and sperm. Lots of sperm. From two different men. What happened to safe sex? Kym had been a busy little girl that day. The older specimens were Giovanni Multi's. The more recent was surely the killer's. They awaited the results of lab tests for confirmation, but Warner already knew it was the same guy.

Procedure required they sample the DNA of Mickey Porter, but no one expected a match. He was in the midst of drowning in the depths of a complete breakdown.

The poor little guy. He really did love that dame, even though she probably was just using him to get into the flicks.

"Hey, Boss, anything new today?" Jack Harris plopped wearily on the edge of Warner's desk.

"Not much. This careful bastard didn't leave us much to work with. We're still scramblin' for the car. The two we found so far were clean of his DNA. If we find his, it should have hair or something from him or one of the girls—I hope."

Both men jumped as the phone rang. Every call lighted a little candle of hope that, so far, always flickered out. The detective snatched it up.

"Warner."

"Hey Al, it's Eddy Roush. You got anything for me yet?"

"Nope. Not a fuckin' thing, Eddy." Warner glanced at Harris and shrugged.

"You're not holding out on me, are you, Detective? We got a deal, and I'm holding up my end."

"Look, if I had something, I'd cough it up. You ain't gonna print it anyhow. But this son-of-a-bitch is smart and careful. When we get him, we'll know it from his DNA, but he's not worried, 'cause he doesn't expect to get caught. Not alive, anyway. I'll call when I got something worth tellin' you, Okay?"

"Yeah. I'm just a little anxious, is all."

"So are we, pal. We'll get him. It's just gonna take some

time. You'll be the first to know."

Warner hung up the phone, shaking his head.

"What're things comin' to when I got to admit that to a reporter? We ain't doin' too well, are we, Jack?"

The smaller man shrugged.

"You and Ralph review your notes on these three girls again. Something makes 'em special in this creep's mind. Something they had in common, besides being so damned gorgeous. He's eliminated college for us."

Warner snapped closed the battered briefcase into which he had been jamming papers. Harris glanced at the wall clock.

"Got a date with Sharon tonight?"

"Nope. Mrs. Gerber."

"Mrs. Gerber?"

"Yeah, Adele Gerber. You know, the widow next door to me."

"Oh, yeah. That nice old dame. What's with her?"

"I usually give her a hand with chores around her house. At 87 and no family here, she needs all the help she can get. Now she sprained her ankle, so I'm doing some shoppin' for her. Told her I'd fix her an early dinner. Roast chicken and stuff."

"Feisty old biddy, ain't she, Al."

"You got that right. Don't take shit from nobody. But she's kinda adopted me as a substitute son. Hers was killed in Viet Nam just before we pulled out."

"Boy, that's a long time ago. Had to be tough, though."

"Yeah, but no tougher than the parents of these dead girls. So, get back to work, and let's find what ties these gals together."

"On it, Boss. Once more around the patch."

Jack Harris rose with a grunt, stretched, then plodded toward his desk, stacked high with files.

The two detectives dug into their piles of papers, hoping to find some small thing they missed.

But they were looking in the wrong places.

FORTY-SIX

The man hunkered quietly in a shadowy corner of the noisy club, a Miami Dolphins cap shadowing his eyes. A parade of young women took to the brightly-lit stage, one after another, undulating to the blare of pop music, thundering many decibels above the level of comfortable listening. There were thin girls, voluptuous girls, and even some heavy girls. Most were plain, women that would not be noticed strolling on the street. Some were attractive, and a few almost beautiful.

Their attractiveness seemed to matter little to the crowd of rowdy men. They leered and pawed, eagerly stuffed dollar bills into colorful garters, as the dancers peeled away scant layers of flimsy togs to the hoots and whistles of their admirers.

These were local girls, barely skillful at portraying sensuality. Some were clumsy. A few were reasonably erotic.

But he was not there for this mostly pitiful lot of misguided waifs with little talent and less future. Not worthy of attention from the Angel of God.

The star would perform her third show at midnight. She was a past *Penthouse Pet of the Month*, and later *Pet of the Year*, flaunting her gorgeous body for the whole world to see, first in that sinful rag, and now in these halls of Sodom.

Naked. Shameless. Sinning before God, earning succor with lewd displays of her splendor in clubs all over the South. She was Danielle Sutton, and he was there for her.

Not tonight, but soon. Very soon. The Lord called for her, eager to redeem her from wickedness.

FORTY-SEVEN

Warner edged around Harris and peeked over the Dumpster, trying to breathe through his mouth. The malodorous stench of decaying Cuban food assaulted his senses.

"That it, Jack?" A battered, blue Ford Fairlane squatted tiredly at the curb.

"Yeah. That's our baby all right."

"We got a positive ID?" He swept it through his binoculars.

"Yep. One of the vice detectives got in and stole the radio. He cleaned the seat with a little sterile hand vac. Moe got a preliminary ID on some hair. It's the perp's car all right. We got a three-man stakeout on it, twenty-four/seven. If he shows, we'll get him, one way or the other. I'd love to be here, if it goes down." He caressed the butt of the 9mm Beretta at his hip.

"Don't get your hopes up," Warner said. "These sons-a-bitches are smart. It's like they can smell us when we're near."

Warner squinted at the car through a cloud of flies swarming around the waste bin. "Anybody dust for prints?"

"Can't do it and keep the car looking safe, but there were no prints on the radio."

"He must know Atkins made him when she took off like a scared rabbit. My guess is he won't show, but keep up the watch. It's all we got." He stepped over piles of trash on the way to his car, sensing this was a waste of time and men.

Meantime, he had a meet with Hector and the rest of DCBC squad to set up their first group of young toughs. Didn't know how to fit it in, but he'd work it out. Nothing good was happening on this case, so he could probably scrape out some time. He wasn't going to let this killer interfere with trying to get some of these kids on a track out of trouble.

FORTY-EIGHT

Sharon flipped the pink sticky-note onto her desk, flicking it away with a snap of her finger. She sighed, plucking it up gingerly by one corner, staring at the scribbled message. Al Warner again, his fourth call this week. She hadn't yet steeled herself to respond. She groaned softly.

What's *wrong* with her? She loved him, in spite of their recent blow up. He's an intelligent guy and a wonderful, sensitive lover, despite his rough-hewn exterior. So, what's she afraid of? Not the heated infighting about crime and punishment. She can slug it out with the best of them. It's more about tension, and the recent lack of tenderness between them.

He had no substantive leads on this new series of murders, racking him with helpless rage, as if it were up to him alone to snag this new psycho. As if he *needed* to get this guy to finally expunge the last vestiges of Leordano, and all those recurring nightmares.

That they were nowhere near catching this new killer made him sullen and argumentative—not such pleasant company.

Except in bed. He was still wonderful in the sack. Their time together—their lovemaking—seemed to bring him some inner peace.

"I can't keep ducking him," she muttered. "Either see him or call everything off."

You're some piece of work, Sherry. Can't even support the man you love when he needs you.

She punched the auto dialer on her phone, singing the little tune of beeps bringing her to the man whom, in spite of her reluctance, she still cherished.

"Homicide. Detective Warner." He sounded so weary. Tears spilled from the corners of her eyes. It was like a belt cinched tight across her breast, trapping her breath. Biting her lower lip, all selfish doubts evaporated.

"Hi, handsome. How're you doing?"

"Ahh, Sherry. You're a sound for sore ears, to coin a phrase. Where've you been? I miss you."

"Uh—I've just been—very busy. Really understaffed here. I should have called sooner." *Boy, is that lame.*

"Oh, hell," she blurted. "Honestly, our last date wasn't exactly a pleasant experience. We had some serious differences of opinion, and I guess I've been ducking a new confrontation. I've always been such a coward. But I miss you, and I *do* love you. Can you forgive me?"

"Ain't nothin' to forgive. I haven't been the best company lately. We're nowhere on this investigation. Three vics and only one new lead that's already stale."

She leaned back and ran a hand through her hair.

"I read about it, but there was no mention of any tie-in to the other murders. Don't you have *anything* to work on, Al?"

"Keep it to yourself, but we found his car and staked it out, but it's gonna be another dead end. I'm bettin' he knows we made it. The last girl IDed it two nights before she died. Said it was followin' her. He ain't goin' anywhere near it. This bastard's real smart, and goddammed careful. We'll tow her in after a few more days, but I doubt we'll find much."

"Wow, that's frightening. Got any idea yet how he picks his victims? You can't just wait for him to kill again, hoping to get lucky next time."

"We got no choice. We don't know what ties these girls together in his warped mind. They're all beautiful, and do

154

modelin', but that don't account for him seekin' 'VENGEANCE ....' Those four dots at the end really bother me, like there's more comin'." Warner voice dripped with frustration.

"Well, something's got to turn up soon. I wish you luck, lover. Now that I've bared my guilty soul, how about dinner, so I can make my apologies in person."

"Dinner? Tonight?"

"Yes. And cocktails later at my place." She laughed, giddy and relieved. She missed him more than she knew, until that very moment.

"Sounds good, Counselor. Is eight too late? I'm speakin' to a bunch of local Florida police organizations at 6:30."

"Oh? About these killings?"

"No. We're still treatin' those as unconnected, except for the Tri-County police forces. These guys heard about the Dade County Boot Camp four other cops and I just started. Other departments are considerin' establishin' chapters. We might create a statewide organization and share fundraisin'. Despite what some of the public thinks, most cops like to get the ghetto kids off the street *before* they get in trouble. We're tryin' to give these teenagers role models and positive goals."

"That's terrific, Al. We need more concerned guys like you. Eight is fine. You're worth waiting for. I'm so happy I called."

"Me, too. See you then, lover."

She hung up, smiling. She'd keep her opinions to herself tonight. She loved this man and intended this to be a different evening from their last two.

FORTY-NINE

Warner poured skimmed milk on his cereal and settled at the kitchen table, cradling a steaming mug of black coffee.

A wet, black nose and golden furred muzzle furrowed under his hand, flipping it back to the drooping ears. His fingers took Buff's suggestion, contented with the companionship. The dog, healthy again except for a small limp, craved affection Warner was happy to provide. Goldens are smart dogs, eager learners and easily trained.

He continued scratching behind the ears, savoring the warmth and weight of the dog's head on his thigh, as he flicked on the TV, finding one of the myriad talk shows crowding the morning time slots. He was usually at work by the time they aired, but a rarity had occurred. He'd overslept. He attacked the bowl of spoon-size shredded wheat and dried cranberries as he watched, but his thoughts were elsewhere.

The previous evening had ended wonderfully. They returned to his townhouse after dinner and twice made intense yet tender love, followed by the best sleep he'd had in weeks— peaceful, dreamless rest. Sharon still slumbering, a gentle smile tickling her lips, when he shimmied out from under her over-draped arm and slipped into the kitchen to make breakfast.

His wandering mind focused on the TV host's guests, three attractive dancers from local topless clubs, sexily decked out in short skirts and thin blouses, revealing considerable cleavage. The show's host was asking if they felt demeaned by their jobs, but the women agreed, while it had some downsides, it was quite lucrative. One was using it to pay her way through college.

Two new guests were introduced as Warner finished his coffee: a staunch female woman's libber, and a good-looking guy who quickly usurped the show. Warner was fascinated by his surprisingly uptight intensity.

"What you're doing is nothing more than prostitution," the man railed. "You're selling your bodies for cash."

"All we're providing is a fantasy," Danielle, a past *Penthouse Pet of the Year*, answered. "They aren't allowed to touch me."

"I've seen your act. You take bills between your breasts, right out of the guys' hands. There's lots of touching going on."

"So, how did you like the show?" Danielle quipped, winking seductively. "You sound pretty anal for a hot-looking guy. It's innocent fun. Doesn't bother me, and guys love it. What's the harm? I don't cat around. I've got a full-time boyfriend."

"You're whores. Sinners. God will punish you." He lurched to his feet, stalking off the stage and out of the studio.

"Geez, what a nut," Danielle said, slowly uncrossing and re-crossing her legs. Whistles erupted in the audience. She smiled.

"All I'm looking for is a boost to get into the movies. I'm a very good actress. And everything on me is original," she added, thrusting forward her ample bosom.

She gazed into the camera. "Come see my act and judge for yourselves. I'll be at the Top Hat Club through Saturday and Diamond Jack's in Lauderdale next week. My shows are at Eight, Ten and Twelve." She smiled provocatively and re-crossed her legs, accompanied by loud whistles and applause. The other dancers giggled.

"Christ." Warner mumbled as he put his dishes in Sharon's sink. "What's the world comin' to?" He stopped in to kiss Sharon good-bye. She rolled over and mumbled. Lucky stiff. No court this morning. He hurried off, thinking about the talk show.

That guy sounded like someone who could be killing these girls. He'd have Olvida check him out.

FIFTY

She spun with a provocative pirouette, posed, then strutted toward the front of the stage, four spotlights illuminating her naked glory. Jutting breasts jiggled as she danced and swayed to the music. The neatly trimmed brown pubic hair proclaimed the lie of her golden tresses, hanging enticingly over one shoulder.

A disparate gaggle of men crowded eagerly around the platform, brandishing dollar bills, vying for her attention.

Danielle Sutton was a consummate tease. Every dollar, snatched up between naked breasts, made each guy feel *he* was the one. Extra bills held between lips, found those guys faces nestled deep between those two soft, fragrant mounds, an erotic exchange pleasing everyone. It was a noisy, raucous crowd. Dani's nimble feet nudged the rain of bills into fluttering green puddles, as she moved from one admirer to another.

Dark, intense eyes pierced the smoky gloom of the room, unwaveringly locked on her glistening form. Her dance made unkeepable promises, bringing hungry smiles and nervously moistened lips from each hopeful suitor.

A sly whore, selling herself as if for sex. But so beautiful. They were the worst—the beauties—luring men to forsake honor and pride, enslaving them with hollow promises of paradise. His duty is to bring her to the Lord, to kneel at his throne, to be absolved of her sins, the only way she'd ever be cleansed.

He would call her. Soon, but not tonight. First there must be a lesson in humility. He rose, staring at the foolish men, capering like children, showering money on the glistening naked body.

Turning, with a small shake of his head, he stalked into the night, Miami Dolphins cap pulled low over his face.

FIFTY-ONE

"No-o-o!" Warner shot upright in bed, eyes flared, darting frantically across the gloomy room, his trembling, naked body drenched with sweat. He moaned softly.

"No. Oh, shit. Please, no. Not again." Where was he?

He started at the cool touch of a hand on his arm.

"Al? Are you all right? Was it another dream?"

Sharon. It was only Sharon. A convulsive shudder racked him as he slowly became fully aware of his surroundings. He was with Sherry. In her apartment. Definitely not on the pathway from Hell.

"Yeah, a real doozy," he panted, still shaken.

"The damned dream. Like before. I'm runnin' up narrow, windin' stairs, sort of in slow motion, and this beast is after me. Some giant dog-like critter, like the one guardin' the gates of Hell."

"Cerberus? The three-headed dog."

"Yeah. That's him. A nasty, ugly critter. I felt so helpless."

This was the third night that week they had spent at her place. His townhouse, a typical bachelor pad, was a mess just then. The resurrection of their love affair had revitalized Warner and brought him generally more restful sleep, but this was the second night the dreams had returned, as intense as ever.

Sharon cradled him, snuggling close, his body still damp with fear. Bathed in the warmth of her tender empathy, he relaxed, the tension oozing slowly away. He rested his head on her lovely, firm bosom, marveling, as he often did, at her natural beauty.

Although not quite as voluptuous as each of their three victims, she was still well-endowed and equally as lovely, with a

159

curvaceously athletic shape. Her tummy was flat, her hips full but proportionately shaped, and she had round, tight buns and elegantly curved legs. A confident, regal carriage and tastefully conservative clothing highlighted her class and beauty. She was certainly striking enough to be in *Playboy* or *Penthouse*. Of course, she'd never demean herself that way. How was it even remotely possible that someone so terrific, warm and tender could really love *him*?

Playboy or *Penthouse*? Stupid thought. Funny though— Kym Atkins was in *Penthouse*. Something to consider, later.

He wound down finally from the adrenaline-fueled terror of his dream. Sharon stroked his head and back, calming him. One nipple hovered tantalizingly close-by.

His recent panic discarded, his tongue flicked out, tweaking it instantly erect. He sucked the little nodule gently into his mouth, caressing it with his tongue. Her hands pressed him more urgently to her.

"Oh, Al. Ohhh. That feels so good. Ohh, my darling."

Sharon Clark might seem cool and reserved, but Al Warner knew her as a passionate, hot-blooded woman who unabashedly reveled in their lovemaking.

The cauldron of their arousal quickly boiled to a peak, and as he entered her, he had a fleeting thought of the three victims. This act, bringing them such wondrous joy, had surprised those girls with death.

What a crazy world.

Then his own intense arousal blanketed all thought.

FIFTY–TWO

160

"They towed the Ford in this morning, Boss. No use waiting any longer." Jack Harris shrugged and sighed.

"Yeah, I figured he wasn't goin' anywhere near that heap again." Warner leaned against his desk.

"Right, as usual. The Hawk's going over it personally, but he isn't finding much."

"That surprise you, Jack? I didn't expect him to discover anything. This guy's too careful. I figured the stakeout on the car was a waste of time, but we had to try. Tell Moe I want his report on whatever he does get, ASAP. Maybe we'll get lucky."

"How's Ralph coming on the guy from the TV show?" Warner asked. "Anything interestin' there?"

"Lester Jarrett? He's working on it. Dug up lots of little things confirming the guy's a weirdo." Harris flipped screens on his Android, scanning the pages. "He belongs to some ultraconservative Born Again Christian sect, or something like that. You know the type—against anything that might be even a little bit of fun. We should have a profile in a couple of days."

"You know, I was brought up by conservative Christian parents. That ain't necessarily bad."

"No. I didn't mean it that way. But he's shifted way right of mainstream Christianity. People can become overzealous for a new cause, can't they? You're the expert on kooks."

"Yeah. Converts are frequently the most rigid members of any group. Anyway, we got people on Mr. Jarrett? Just in case he's our guy."

"Yep. Three teams from Plain Clothes are running shifts on him twenty-four/seven. I do listen to orders, Boss. Anyway, we don't have anything else to work on. Ralph and me are taking a few of the rotations, just to get familiar with the guy."

"Okay. Lemme know if you come up with anything. Something's gotta break soon."

"You'll be at Sharon tonight, Al?"

"Nope. She's got a new case, and we tend to—ahh—distract each other when we're together." Warner produced a lopsided grin. Harris chuckled.

"She's got the Cuban kid they picked up for those two rapes, doesn't she?"

"Yeah. Thinks it's a bum rap."

"Yeah, right."

"Don't sell Sherry short, Jack. She's got real good instincts about things like this. She might be right." He rose from his perch on the corner of his desk.

"So, I'm havin' pizza alone tonight, and I'll try to get to bed early. I'll be here 'til at least seven. You know where to reach me if anything happens after that."

"Okay. I'm gonna hit the streets. I got a few witnesses I wanna talk to again."

The little man tossed off a half salute as he left. They were both wondering when the next victim would show up. Six days had passed since the Atkins girl died, and the killer seemed to be working more or less on a weekly schedule. He'd take another very soon.

All they could do was wait and hope he finally makes a mistake. One hell of a way to run an investigation. Clever serial killer rarely screwed up.

Sitting alone in the growing gloom of winter darkness, mental videos of his only encounter with Leordano downloaded, unbidden, spooling relentlessly through Warner's head. Despite angry reluctance, he couldn't stem the floodtide of those memories . . . .

His eyes finally accustomed to the dim, shadowed-streaked light of the hut, he rose from his crouch. The table in the center of the room was nothing more than a wood door, resting on sawhorses. Swiping a sleeve across tearing eyes, he peered down, trying to concentrate in the cave-like gloom.

He gagged at the sickly stench and poor lighting delayed for a moment recognition of what lay there. The small, mangled body drifted into focus, quivering to the jaws of busy maggots.

Oh, fuck!

For the first time since his rookie years, his stomach heaved out of control, hurling his lovely Italian lunch. Turning away, bits of sausage and pasta spewed over the earthen floor. He sprinted to the doorway, his intestines knotting in a second assault, stumbling to one knee by the threshold, painfully retching again.

He remained down, panting for a clean breath, his head a spinning inferno. In shocked surprise, he realized this was it— the Baby Butcher's workshop. The place where, at his leisure, he did all those terrible things to his sixteen victims. Seventeen now.

Head hanging, struggling to deal with the aftershocks assailing his gut, he gathered his wits.

Damn. He should never have come alone. What if . . .?

The sigh of rustling grass caught his ear. There, standing close to the wall, a short, plump man, smiling deceptively—and holding a pistol.

The smile stretched into a deadly sneer, as the gun came up.

"Die, pig," he said softly, squeezing the trigger.

Holy shit. Warner lurched to one side, doing a football roll.

He'd found him.

The Baby Butcher.

"See you tomorrow, Boss."

Warner's head snapped up, roughly jerked back from the

past. The older, heavyset man stood in the doorway, a small frown wrinkling his brow.

"You okay, Al?" Harry Klein asked.

"Yeah, Harry. You just startled me. I thought everyone left."

"Just finishing up some paperwork. See you in the morning."

Warner nodded and sighed. He might as well go, too. He was glad to have something else to think about.

Memories of Leordano were the last thing he needed.

FIFTY–THREE

"And now, here's what you've been waiting for gents, Danielle Sutton, last year's *Penthouse Pet of the Year*. Only a few more nights at the Top Hat Club, so let's give her a big welcome.

"Miss Danielle Sutton."

The disk jockey queued up a popular hit song that resounded through the club with the intensity of a jet fighter breaking the sound barrier. A door at the rear of the stage opened and the tall blonde stalked out wearing a short faux-leopard-skin huntress wrap, leather sandals and carrying a large bullwhip. Writhing in a slow, sensual dance, she repeatedly cracked the whip, centering a steamy look on one man after another as they crowded around the raised platform.

I am for you, only you, her gaze promised each admirer. The men knew this was just a lovely, seductive act. But their thumping hearts and pulsating dicks were hoping, just this one time . . ..

A solitary man sat in the back of the club, dark eyes gleaming brightly with a different kind of passion. Soon he would bring her humbly to the Lord. It would be easy. It was *always* easy. His master made him irresistible to these wanton wretches.

The second song of her set finishing, Dani Sutton discarded her final garment and struck a sensual, lewd pose, bringing cheers and whistles from the crowd.

The last of her act began with a new tune. The voluptuous blonde strutted along the stage's perimeter—dancing, teasing, creating personal by-play with every guy, and in the process, building a tidy pile of dollar bills on the stage. The men pressed close to the raised platform, each seeking real contact with her magnificent body.

One man patiently worked his way through the three-deep crowd until he stood directly in front of her, his handsome face twisting into a mask of rage.

"Whore," he shouted. "You're nothing but a cheap whore." The crowd turned, yelling angrily. A burly bouncer materialized, but Dani waived him off.

"Well, if it isn't the prude from the talk show." Her laugh rife with contempt. "What's wrong, honey? Couldn't stay away, huh? Want to come up and dance, up close and personal?" Still laughing, she bent over, dangling her breasts in his face.

"You filthy slut. I'll show you what I want." He lunged, a switchblade flashing open in his hand.

The blonde sprang nimbly backward. Before anyone else could move, a plainclothes cop had one arm around Lester Jarrett's neck, pinioning the arm with the knife. The bouncer bulled through the crowd, leveling the attacker with a well-placed blow from a blackjack.

The room was in an uproar. Dani Sutton's manager/boyfriend draped her in a cloak and rushed her from the stage.

Another cop quickly cuffed the attacker's hands behind his back. Jarrett emitted a small moan as he was hauled to his feet and hustled out to an unmarked squad car. Their surveillance had paid off.

Had the killer of three young beauties finally made a mistake?

FIFTY-FOUR

"Jack, what're you doin' here so early?" Warner headed toward his office as the sky bloomed with a predawn glow. Harris was a night person. He'd rather not sleep at all than get up early.

"I could ask you the same question, Al." The little man looked smug, sitting on the corner of his desk, fanning himself with the report he had been studying.

"Ah, more bad dreams. Once I'm up, I usually can't get back to sleep." He noted his friend's exaggerated casual bearing. His heart skipped a beat with sudden premonition.

"Did I miss something last night? Not another ...."

"Almost Boss, but not quite. Looks like we mighta snagged our perp. I didn't call you 'cause we had him nailed, and he wasn't going anywhere. I thought I'd let you get some sleep."

"Yeah? Who? What? Give. Give."

"That guy, Jarrett. He tried to kill that *Penthouse* beauty, right on-stage last night at the Top Hat. Went after her with a switchblade, but the plainclothes boys snagged him. The detectives had him first, but Ralph's got him now for Q and A."

"He tried to knife her? In public? That don't sound like our guy at all. You think it might be a coincidence?"

"Maybe. It doesn't smell right to me, either. But Sutton seems to fit his kind of victim. Harry's already got a search warrant. I guess you want to be there when we toss his joint."

"You bet. Right MO or not, he can't go around tryin' to stick people. Maybe we'll turn up something interestin'."

"Harry should be back anytime now," Harris said. "Ralph and me are ready to boogie, soon as he gets here."

"Great. I'll be in my office."

FIFTY-FIVE

"Wake up, Boss. We're here." Harris pulled up to the curb.

"Huh? Oh, yeah. Thanks for turnin' off the radio, Jack. That little nap's the best sleep I've had in three days."

"You oughta see a doctor, Al. Not a shrink. Some guy who specializes in sleep disorders or something. Maybe there's something physically wrong. Could be the head wound causing trouble."

"You know, you may be right. All this time I figured it was nerves or something, but it coulda been physical right along. I'm gonna make an appointment as soon as we get done here. Thanks for the idea, buddy." He unbuckled his seat belt.

"Sure. So, let's hit this guy's digs and hope we discover something useful. Pretty fancy building, huh."

"Yeah, I guess." A cream-colored Dodge parked behind them.

"Here's Harry and Ralph now," he said, climbing out of Harris' car.

The four detectives entered the up-scale Coconut Grove apartment building. The first door on their right displayed a brass sign, MANAGER, emblazoned in black. Warner's persistent knock finally produced a hastily robed, attractive fortyish Latina woman. After the officers identified themselves and showed her their warrant, she reluctantly handed over her spare key to Lester Jarrett's apartment.

"She can manage my apartment anytime," Olvida quipped.

"Little old for ya, ain't she Ralph?" Harris stuck a friendly elbow into his partner's ribs.

"You kidding? That's like good wine—better with age. Especially a classy Latin dame."

"Me, I like 'em fresh off the tree. Young and firm."

"Knock it off, you two. Here's the apartment." Warner unlocked the door and cautiously shoved it open.

Number 3C, a spacious, one bedroom with a full living room, dining room and kitchen, was immaculate. Every piece of furniture and each accessory seemed precisely placed. Warner shook his head. This was a new car showroom, compared with his own cluttered digs which was more like an auto junkyard. Hard to believe anybody actually lived here.

Lester Jarrett might be a kook, but he was a well-heeled loony and compulsively neat. Serial-killers often suffered from obsessive-compulsive disorder.

The detectives split up, each working over a different room, not knowing exactly what they were looking for, but searching for it carefully, nevertheless. Twenty minutes produced very little of interest before Harry Klein called from the bedroom.

"Hey, Boss. Come look at this."

Warner found the older man sitting on the bed next to an open carton, filled with men's magazines: *Playboy, Penthouse, Hustler,* and others. From their wrinkled, dog-eared condition, they seemed well read.

"Well, what d'ya know. Looks like Mister Neat is really a horny little bastard, obsessed with the beautiful, naked women he professes to despise. I wonder what his mom would think of this stuff?"

Drawn to the room by their conversation, Jack Harris was leafing through the magazines, making soft, appreciative sounds under his breath.

"Something's not right," Warner mused.

"All this has the right feel for our guy. He's ambivalent toward these girls, he's a compulsive personality, and he fits the stereotype."

"Looks like he lusted for some of the finer things in life, after all," said Jack Harris. "Wow, look at this one. Now that's worth lusting after. Mama Mia."

"Easy, Jack. Geez, for a middle age guy, you sure got busy hormones. But, that's the point. They're all gorgeous, and he apparently *did* lust for 'em and probably hated himself—and them—for it. Just what serial killers are made of. But, tryin' to knife that gal in public? It just doesn't fit. I saw Sutton on TV, and lemme tell you, she's just as hot as any of these chicks. It's only looks."

"Yeah, easy for you to say. You're making it with a dame who could get into *Playboy* or *Penthouse* whenever she wanted. We get the leftovers."

"Should I tell Doris you said that, Jack?" Warner chuckled as he dropped the *Penthouse* on the bed. "Okay, let's finish the toss. Box these up, Harry, and take 'em back to the office. We'll proceed for now with Jarrett as our prime suspect. If that washes out, at least we'll have some entertainment for the squad room. And Jarrett'll be goin' away for a while, regardless."

Twenty minutes later they departed the building, having learned little more than they started with. The only thing worth bringing in was the case full of magazines.

Warner collapsed into his chair. He was bushed, as if someone pulled a plug, sucking all his energy down the drain. He *had* to get more sleep.

Grunting with disgust at himself, he called Dr. Kent. Ivan was there with him day and night after he took Leordano's slug off the head. His concern for Warner's recovery transcended normal medical care. They became fast friends, sharing some instinctive bond they both felt but couldn't verbalize. The nurse made room in the next morning's schedule for the troubled detective.

He stood and stretched. He was meeting Sharon for lunch, but the warmth thoughts of her usually brought him were cruelly overshadowed by the dark mantle cast by this killer—this careful, clever lunatic.

Despite the evidence mounting against Jarrett, Warner's intuition told him the man was the wrong lunatic. A lunatic, yes, but not their special, very deadly psychopath, who was due to kill again very soon. It would take several more days before they had a comparison of Jarrett's DNA with the killer's.

As he left the office, Warner feared they might get an answer of a different sort before those tests came back from the lab.

FIFTY–SIX

He pushed through the doorway and was assaulted by the metronome beat of the music. A corner of his mouth twitched upward, his tongue darting across his lips, as the jungle-like rhythm quickened his heart.

Time to begin his little play.

The stage, made surreal by flickering strobe lights, was surrounded by a small horde of men, whistling and cheering, and waiving dollar bills. His Miami Dolphins ball cap pulled low, he eased through the crowd to get a better view of the platform.

Dani Sutton writhed on her back, nude, her hands roaming between her considerable breasts and the partially shaved area between her thighs. Sensual moans paced her arched, thrusting pelvis, fucking an invisible lover to the raucous cheers of the onlookers.

Tugging on the bill of his cap, he groaned. Even *he* was not immune to such wicked lust, but his plan was perfect. God will reward him.

The music ended coincidentally with a feral shriek, as the sweat-glistened woman collapsed on the stage. Rolling onto all fours, she prowled the edge of the platform amid a shower of greenbacks, slitted aqua eyes roaming from face to face, making impossible promises. Nimble feet shuffled the bills into a tidy pile as she rose. Her manager arrived with a flowered silk kimono, and scooping up her rewards, ushered her from the stage amid a chorus of whistles and cheers.

"There she goes, gents." The DJ's voice boomed over the speakers. "Dani Sutton. Her last show at the Top Hat. Give her a few minutes, and Dani will pose for and sign photos in the lounge. Ten bucks will get you a print together with this sexy gal. Twenty will buy you one with a kiss you'll remember forever. Queue up and get your money ready. This is your last chance to get up close and personal with the *Penthouse Pet of the Year*."

The man watched several guys file back to the rear lounge. The Lord had provided a perfect opportunity.

Thirty-five minutes later, the next-to-last guy's twenty dollars rewarded him with a lingering French kiss, his hand venturing happily across warm skin. Dani locked one of hers in his hair while the other teased his crotch. The flash from the digital camera ended their embrace.

"That was nice," she said. "You're a real stud, handsome." She caressed his cheek. "Paul'll have your autographed photo for you in about ten minutes. Enjoy the rest of your evening, baby." She planted a tiny kiss on his lips and patting his butt, sending him off. She turned to her final admirer.

"Last, but not least, I hope. What can I do for you, cutie?" He raised his head, intense raven eyes, shaded by the lid of his cap, sent a delicious trill down her spine. His rugged face was somehow immensely erotic.

"A chance to talk. Maybe discuss some business." His lips twitched into a gentle smile.

"Business, huh? Maybe monkey business? I'm here to please." She grinned, placing her had on his arm.

"That's nice, Miss Sutton . . .."

"Call me Dani."

"Okay, Dani. You're a stunning woman, hinting at promises that'll never be kept and that's all very tempting . . .."

"Hey, I can't exactly screw every guy at the show . . .."

"Of course not. You're a superb performer, and I've got a proposition for you to use those talents to our mutual benefit."

"A proposition, huh? I get lots of those, don't I Paul?" She turned to her manager, who'd just arrived, a sheaf of photos in hand. She began autographing them with a fine-tipped felt marker. The man stood patiently until she finished.

"So, what d'ya have in mind, Mister . . .?"

"Dedios. Angie Dedios. I'm offering you a chance to read for a featured part in a movie we'll be shooting in Miami."

"Yeah? What's the catch? I gotta hump you to get the part?"

"No catch. And while 'humping me,' as you put it, might be quite delightful, it won't guarantee you the role. Other girls are reading, and it'll go to the one with the most *acting* talent, not who gives the most sexual favors."

"Really?" Her eyebrows arched. "That's refreshing. I'd love to be in a real movie. What's the character?"

"Something you seem ideally suited for—a manipulative beauty, using sex and passion to get ahead. Some of it will probably be fairly graphic, with some on-screen nudity. I don't imagine any of that would bother you?" He grinned.

"Of course not." She chuckled as she appraised him and wondered if this were legit? She'd been trying for two years to get into mainstream flicks, but she'd been typecast, and what most producers or directors really wanted was to fuck her. At least this guy *seemed* different.

"So, what's the deal? You got a script for me to look at?"

"Not with me. I came here on a whim, when I heard you were performing. I'm having auditions for the part Thursday evening at Vanity Studios, on Southeast Second Avenue. If you want to read . . . .."

"What's going on, Babe?" Her manager returned from passing out the photos.

"Something exciting. Paul, this is Angie . . .?"

"Dedios." He held out a strong, darkly tanned hand.

"Yeah. Angie Dedios, with . . .?" She glanced at him, eyebrows raised.

"Sorry about that." He grinned and patted his pocket. "I'm with TriStar Studios. Musta left my card case in the car. Like I said, I came her on a whim."

"Angie's offering me a part in his movie." It was Paul's turn for arched eyebrows.

"A chance to *read* for a part, Dani. No guarantees, although if you can really act—and watching you tonight, I suspect you can—well, you're perfect for the role."

"You might as well cancel the other girls, hon." She smiled, squeezing his biceps. Hard muscle there. "That part's as good as mine." Her eyes, filled with new promise, found his.

173

His answering smirk stabbed her with a momentary chill.

"We'll see," Angie said. He produced a slip of paper. "Here's the address for Vanity Studios. I'll meet you there at eight." Paul took it, glancing at the neatly printed note.

"I don't like this, Dani. You don't know Mr. Dedios." He looked at the other man. "You mind if I check this out?"

"Feel free. Come along. I want you to feel comfortable."

"Thanks, Angie." She blistered Paul with a searing look. "We'll be there. I'm sure it's legit. Paul's just being cautious."

"Hey, I understand. That's his job—looking after you. Nice work, too, I might add."

The only one not chuckling was Paul. He watched this stranger leave, his Dolphins Cap pulled low over his eyes.

Something smelled bad here. He had a busy two days coming up, but he'd have to make time to check Angie Dedios out with TriStar Studios. He loved Dani, and he sure as hell intended to keep her out of trouble, if he could.

But some things were just out of his control.

FIFTY–SEVEN

"So, what's the scoop, doc? Am I goin' loony, or is there a medical reason for this shit?"

"Frankly Al, I can't find anything physically wrong. There's still much we don't really know about the brain, but you didn't appear to have sustained any permanent damage. There was a concussion and considerable swelling from the bullet ricocheting off your hard head and cracking your skull, but everything seems back to normal for months now. Let's see—

your last exam was just over three months ago. You've never been in better physical condition since I've known you." He dropped the test results on his desk, found the detective's eyes, and gave a little shrug.

"I believe you're suffering from Post-Traumatic-Stress Disorder." Seeing his patient bristle, Dr. Kent hurried on.

"Now, don't get your hackles up. It can happen to anyone, even tough guys like you. You were under loads of pressure during the Leordano thing. Only quick reactions saved you that day. Another centimeter over and you're dead." He reached over, gripped Warner's shoulder, and squeezed gently.

"This needs to be treated, same as your head-wound, by a competent physician: a psychiatrist. You guys got one of the best, right at the U of M. Sven Carlsen's had plenty of experience with PTSD. It's pretty common among cops."

"Ah, c'mon, Doc. A shrink? I know Carlsen's good. We've worked together on a couple of important convictions. But hell, all I need is some solid rest. Wouldn't the fuckin' nightmares stop if I weren't so damned tired all the time?"

"I don't know, Al. It's the chicken or the egg dilemma."

"Huh?"

"What came first? The nightmares because you're tired, or are the dreams why you're not getting any rest? A psychiatrist can help you sort that out."

"I'm just not ready for a shrink. How about something to help me sleep?"

"Sure, but that won't solve your problems. You're going to eventually find yourself on Sven's couch. That's my bet."

Warner left Dr. Kent's office a few minutes later, a bottle of barbiturates in his pocket. Maybe Ivan was right: the pills were just a small bandage on a gaping wound. He only hoped they'd help him get some badly needed rest.

Gotta be at peak form, the next time this bastard kills.

*   *   *   *

"What the fuck . . .?" Warner lurched up, rubbing his eyes.

"Jeee-sus. Eight-thirty. Those damned pills really knocked me out last night. Probably shouldn't have taken two. At least there weren't any fuckin' dreams."

He groggily staggered into the bathroom. Fifteen minutes later, he was out of his door, hurrying to work. The lingering effects of the barbiturates hung over him like a London fog, permeating every part of his body.

How to do the job, feeling like this? If he didn't perk up, he might need a nap. He'd been bushed and restless for so damned long, he couldn't expect to catch up in one night.

The day was outstanding by being remarkably uneventful. No new murders, no new clues, no new anything. Warner talked with Detective Fanucci in Boca Raton. They were dead in the water on the McIntyre murder and were pinning their hopes, for the moment, on Dade County.

And his team had nothing new on either the Gannon or Atkins killings, so they were stymied and in a corner. No surprise that Jarrett's DNA wasn't a match. So, they would keep plugging, but they'd pretty much run out of leads to chase. It was likely they'd have to await another homicide and hope this time he would slip up.

The crime lull was like the eye of a hurricane—calm for the moment, but with fierce winds swirling nearby, threatening to wreak havoc.

The upside was, he finally had a much-needed afternoon off. He'd try to get to bed early—get a full twelve hours sleep. Try to catch up.

It was the last break he'd see for a long, long time.

FIFTY-EIGHT

"Aren't you ready yet?" Dani stood, arms akimbo, scowling. "I don't want to blow this role by being late." Paul shook his head, taking her hand.

"Look, Hon, I just got a call from the Crystal Garter chain. They're in town for one evening and want to see us about doing a tour of their clubs. A guaranteed ten grand per four-day stint, plus tips, at all seventeen locations. But if we don't meet tonight, they're gonna sign someone else. They got some kind of promotional deadline."

"That's exciting, baby." She stroked his cheek. "Go make that deal while I'm doing the audition. Once I get the movie part, we can use that to push up the guarantee. Neat, huh?"

"I don't know. I'm nervous about you meeting this guy alone, especially at night. I wasn't able to check him out with TriStar, but it doesn't smell right. Can't you reschedule?"

"Can't chance it. There are other girls after the part. If I don't show today, they may cast someone else. This is my break. I can feel it. Don't worry. Angie seems like a good guy."

"Maybe I should cancel with Crystal Garter? I don't think you should go alone."

"No way. That's a major booking. We're not gonna blow it 'cause you're a Nervous Nellie. Get that contract. Tell 'em about the movie and try to push up the ante. I'm gonna be a big star."

Five minutes of arguing with the brick wall Dani Sutton erected proved useless, so they went their separate ways—Paul to a meeting where, strangely, no one else showed up, and Danielle Sutton to a destiny far different than she expected.

FIFTY–NINE

Dani paced restlessly in front of the locked door, hugging herself. Not only wasn't Variety Studios a jumping joint, it seemed deserted. Scary. Those windows not broken were covered with dust and dirt, and the old stucco building was shedding its pink skin. Graffiti littered the walls, and the rest of the neighborhood was equally seedy.

This wasn't what she expected.

Stopping her agitated patrol, she squinted down the poorly lit street. Where the hell was Angie Dedios? And why wasn't anybody else at this dump, if they're really shooting a movie here? Maybe Paul was right. She'd give this guy five more minutes, then she was outta there. No movie career was worth her life.

A powerful hand closed suddenly on her arm. Shrieking, she whirled, dropping reflexively into a defensive karate position. Dani Sutton was a long time Black Belt and practiced assiduously.

"Easy, kid, easy," Angie said, backing away and holding his hands up. An attractive grin pushed up the corners of his mouth.

"Sorry I startled you. Thought you heard me coming."

"Well, I didn't. You gave me a hell of a scare. I was getting nervous you stood me up. We still on for this?" She nodded at the building. "You haven't cast someone else, have you?"

"Nope. You still got the inside track, if you're any kind of an actress. We'll get an idea about that, soon as the camera crew shows up. They've been shooting some preliminary background shots in the area, but their damned van broke down. They're gonna be at least an hour late." He grasped her arm and guided her toward the entrance.

"Meantime, we can go inside and review your part. Give you a chance to get used to the set and stuff."

He turned to the steel door and started fiddling with the lock. His body blocked her view, but she heard the latch snap open. The door swung in with an eerie creak. Her nostrils twitched at the dank, musty order wafting out.

Tingling little rivers spiraled down her spine, raising the hairs on the back of her neck. This was surreal. She looked at her companion, filled with renewed doubt.

"This place is a dump, Angie. You aren't seriously considering shooting a film here, are you? I'd expect more from a big company like Tri-Star."

"Variety's been closed for nearly a year," Dedios said. "The guys were supposed to get over here yesterday and air it out. We've hired a crew to spiff it up." He glanced around. "Just something else that didn't get done, I guess. We're scheduled to shoot the outdoor stuff first, anyhow. C'mon, let's look around. I haven't seen this place yet, but there oughta be some props here."

He took her in tow and poked his head through the doorway, discovering the light switch. Industrial floods lit the building, casting a crazy quilt of broken shadows. He eased through the door, an ambivalent Dani trailing behind.

This was really weird. She wished now Paul *had* come. What did she really know about this guy?

Ah, shit. She's no stupid wimp. Everything would be fine. *Just relax and do whatever it takes to get the part.* She tugged on his hand.

"Hey, where are the other girls who're gonna audition?"

"They both had other commitments for the day. They'll read tomorrow, unless I've already given the role to you. Like I said, you're a natural for it."

"Great." Her confidence reasserted itself. She knew precisely what she had to do to get this part.

"Give me a feel about my character. I want to get into the mood. You know, into her mind, if I can."

"Sure. I can warm you up while were waiting for the camera crew." He pulled her deeper inside the building, her nose wrinkling at the sour, musty smell. Dust motes floated aimlessly in scattered shafts of light spearing the darkness through small breaks in the windows.

"Okay, here's how it goes. You're a manipulative bitch, out for number one, using men to get to where you are. It's always sex and a pretense of love with whatever guy you're stringing along." His voice echoed in the cavernous studio.

"Today, we'll be shooting one of your last scenes, one that creates the most drama for your character. You've finally met the guy who's going to give you what you've felt you deserved." He cast her a chilling, almost wicked smile.

A ridge of goose bumps scooted down her neck and back. He *was* a little strange. But *nothing* was going to get in the way of her getting this part.

"He's your ticket to fame and fortune," he continued. "This is gonna be your last move for a long time, because he's got it all. You've gone to his office late in the day, and the two of you are alone. You seduce him, fucking him on the desk. He's completely possessed by you. It's gotta be a really hot scene."

"Terrific. That's right up my alley. Sorta like you and me together here today." Her smile dripped with sexual innuendo, and she was in control again. "You make me rich and famous, and you'll never regret it. I promise. So, where's the script?"

"The camera crew's got it, but there's not really much dialogue. You can probably improvise better than we wrote it. Wanna give it a shot."

She grinned as the tip of her pink tongue swept across her lips, and nodded.

There was a large oak executive desk and a couple of chairs on the stage. He found a tattered rag and wiped the top, then settled on a chair behind its scarred surface and smiled.

"Come in from over there. Sorta stalk me in a sensual way. We've known each other for a while, and now you've come to make me yours. The power of this scene is in the action. Do it."

Dani nodded and moved offstage, pausing to gather herself. All she had to do was be herself. She'd used men all her life, and would enjoy doing exactly that with Angie Dedios. He was in for more than make-believe today. This role was hers.

She strolled back on stage, every bit a hungry lioness out for a kill. Her short Lycra skirt molded her hips like skin, her easily aroused nipples clearly visible through a silk and lace blouse. She paused, looking him up and down with smoldering heat. Perching on the edge of the desk, her skirt inched higher. Leaning forward, she caressed the side of his face with long, red-nailed fingers, two lovely mounds of flesh, dangling a foot from his face. His pants bulged as he stroked her silky-smooth thigh.

Cupping his face in her hands, she brought him out of the chair, kissing him, first teasingly on the lips and neck, then with an exploding ardor.

It was going so well. This guy was a terrific hunk. She'd make him totally hers. Him and this role. And she'd love the fucking just as much as he would.

They were quickly locked in a heated embrace. She teased and tantalized with epicurean skill, and soon they both spun out of control.

Her blouse and his shirt magically evaporated. She struggled with his belt as he peeled down her skirt.

'Oh, baby. Take me. Take me for real. Oh, Angie, fuck me.

Fuck me."

In a blink, they were naked, and he was entering her. His hands and mouth were all over her, driving their lust. Their orgasms surged on like a speeding train, massive and unstoppable. Locked in the grip of her long legs, Dani crushed him to her, her eruption triggering his.

"Oh, you hunk. Your mine, Angie, mine. I'll never let you go." Slick with sweat, she shuddered and quivered, while his roaming hands settled at her neck.

"No, my beautiful whore," he panted, his thumbs pressing into the soft flesh of her throat. "My master's, not mine. I bring you to him now, to beg redemption for your harlot ways."

Her eyes flared wide, first in surprise, then fear, and finally, bulging grotesquely in death. Her arms flailed helplessly as he crushed the life from her.

The last fleeting sounds she would hear on earth, rang solemnly . . ..

"The Lord calls."

SIXTY

Warner arrived at Variety Studios simultaneously with Jack Harris and Rafael Olvida. He had been dragged groggily from the depths of drug-like sleep fraught with nightmares he couldn't remember. It was 3:30 AM and another beautiful young woman had fallen to the hands of their madman.

Six squad cars cordoned off the entire block, their pulsing blue and red lights ricocheting surreally off dingy stucco walls. A bit of overkill. Warner smiled ruefully at the unintended pun. Increased activity with each death reflected mounting pressure from the top.

Find this bastard.

Heading for the yellow-ribboned door, he paused. A young man slouched in one of the patrol cars, glassy, vacant eyes fastened inward on a world of his own, fraught with visions he would struggle to forget, but probably never succeed.

The detective shook his head in tired frustration. He knew the dark corridors that man's mind patrolled. He knew them well. This clever maniac destroyed the living as well as the dead. All were his victims, one way or another.

Already surfeit with the agony of survivors, he motioned for Harris to question the guy while he and Olvida entered the crime scene. A cloak of breath-stealing dread enveloped him. He scanned the vacant old building, assailed by a cloying, musty odor—and something else. He sniffed, testing the air.

The smell of Evil—the stifling, sulfuric scent of the beast, Cerberus, from his dreams. He shivered, chilled by the memory, knowing that vitriolic stink was an illusion. He shrugged and strode inside.

The starkly empty studio was poorly lit, rafters and overhead railings casting ominous patterns of shadows. The two detectives approached a crowd of uniformed cops on the stage, their footsteps echoing hollowly.

The old building seemed to whisper to Warner, "I'm empty. There's no life here. Those who linger will soon be as devoid of life as I am." He shivered again. An icy tremor raised hair on the back of his neck, filling him with sudden apprehension.

"Who discovered the body?" Olvida asked, as they mounted the steps.

"I did, Detective." A tall, bull of a man half-raised his hand. "I was just down the street when the call came in. Found that guy out there wandering around in a daze. The door was ajar, so I came in and found the victim lying there."

"Has anyone touched anything?" Warner asked, shaking off

the moribund cloak of dark dreams. The patrol cop shook his head.

"I used a tissue when I opened the door, but you could see where the dirt was wiped away. An open padlock was hanging on the hasp, wiped clean, too. Somebody disposing of fingerprints, I guess."

Warner grunted while circling the desk for a better look. Dani Sutton, naked, sprawled across its scarred surface, long legs dangling over the edge, not quite reaching the floor. An apparent puddle of semen stained one thigh. Her once beautiful, now grotesquely vacant eyes, registered utter surprise.

How the hell did this crafty bastard get these magnificent women so willingly into the sack? Some Don Juan. None of them showed any signs of resisting. It all happened too quickly. Warner cupped her chin, rotating her face. He grunted.

"Shit. This is the stripper Jarrett was harassin'. Further proof we got the wrong loony in jail, Ralph. The bastard's still out there, stalkin' his own special breed of prey."

"Yeah. Well, the MO was wrong, but it was a shot. We still got him for Assault with a Deadly Weapon, though. You think the D.A.'s gonna prosecute Jarrett?"

"Why not? He's a certifiable nut. He attacked her with a knife. Can't pull that shit and expect to walk free." He turned to the uniformed cops.

"Okay, I want two of you outside watchin' the door. Nobody in but authorized personnel. O'Banyon, you help Detective Harris question that guy outside. What's his name, anyhow?"

"Tazwell. Paul Tazwell. He was her boyfriend."

"Swell. Nobody gets near them except people on The Job. Got it?" He looked again at the dead beauty and pursed his lips.

"So, Ralph. Let's get started. The Hawk oughta be along soon. Damn. I hope we find something this time. I'm gettin' tired of pissin' in the wind."

"Say, Al, I was just thinking. Where's the message?"

"Huh?"

"You know, the lipstick on the mirror. Don't these guys always leave their signature? God forbid anybody else should get credit for their gristly work." He glanced around, lips pursed.

"Yeah. Must be around here, somewhere. Maybe not on a mirror, but somewhere." He sighed.

"Let's get busy. We got loads to cover in this spooky old joint."

SIXTY-ONE

Jack Harris joined his partners thirty minutes later, looking bemused. The warble of Fire Rescue had come and gone. Paul Tazwell, wallowing in deep shock, was en route to Jackson Memorial Hospital.

"Get anything outta that guy, Jack? A description? Anything? He's gotta know something." They desperately needed some kind of break.

"Shit. The poor bastard was sinking into shock. It was like pulling teeth." The little detective flipped open his Android.

"She was meeting this guy, Angie Dedios. Supposed to audition for a movie. Met him at the club where she was dancing. Tazwell was gonna come along, 'cause he didn't trust this Dedios, but at the last minute he gets a call from some big chain of titty clubs, dangling a juicy contract. Had to be last night, 'cause they were leaving town. Except nobody showed." He flipped pages on his Android.

"After waiting an hour, he boogied over here. The door was open, and the girl was dead. He goes bonkers. That's all folks. He just dug a hole and crawled inside his head."

"A con to split him from the girl?" Olvida was looking at Warner.

"That's how it plays to me," Warner said. "But if this Tazwell was with the dame when they met Dedios, he's seen him, too. At least we can finally get a description. You get to Jackson Memorial, Jack. As soon as this guy gets a hold of himself, get a sketch artist down there. Let's put a face on this bastard."

"On my way," Harris said, "but don't get too hopeful. This dude was taking a nosedive into a deep, black hole while we talked. Kept blaming himself, as if he coulda saved her. Doesn't realize he'd probably be dead, too, if he'd been here." He pocketed his electronic notebook.

"Then he just froze up, still as a mouse. When the paramedics took him away, he was like the living dead. Kinda spooky. Anyway, I'll let you know what's going on, soon as I talk to his doc." The diminutive detective hurried away.

"Shit." Warner slammed his right fist into an open palm. "Our first real witness, and he goes schizoid on us."

"Hmmm." Olvida was scribbling on a note pad.

"You got something, Ralphy?"

"Maybe. Tazwell said the guy's name is Angie Dedios?"

"Yeah," Warner said.

"I bet he's Latino."

"Why? Dedios sounds more Greek to me. Shit. This whole fuckin' case is gettin' to be Greek to me."

"Ain't that the truth? But look. If it's Spanish, then Angie's probably short for Angel. It's pronounced 'An-Hel,' and means 'angel.' If we break up his last name into 'de Dios,' we got Angel de Dios—the Angel of God." He looked at Warner.

"Could this guy think he's on some kinda holy mission, maybe delivering sinners to God—you know—maybe for redemption?"

"Wow. Could be you're right. But what kinda sinners? I can see it for this one, maybe. She was a stripper and a Penthouse babe. But the other three were two college students and a model. The coeds did some modelin', too, but is that sinful, even in skimpy bathin' suits?"

"Does what we think count?" Olvida asked. "We know he's got some loose screws. Maybe he sees 'em differently than we do."

"Yeah, that's likely." Warner stroked his chin. "But he's too clever to be fully delusional. These nuts usually have an agenda, and from their point of view, it's always very logical. Go back over everything. There's gotta be a better connection than this."

"Okay. We'll pull the charts on the other three and see if anything matches up with this one. We gotta be missing something." Olvida flipped open his notebook and scribbled a reminder.

"Right. I'll get Fanucci down from Boca. Do some brainstormin'. Stick with it 'til we find something. Order in pizza if we have to."

"Yeah. Maybe Harris'll get something out of the boyfriend."

The Crime Scene Unit had arrived, and a tech was making a video record of the entire scene before anything was moved. The two detectives left for the office. Everything now in the capable hands of the Hawk. The little man was examining the corpse, making small clucking sounds under his breath.

"Such a waste. A beauty like this. The mamzer."

Warner hoped their little genius would find something worthwhile this time. Bodies were mounting up. No longer possible to keep this under their hats. The women of South Florida had a right to know. It was time to go public—and bring in the BAU. Maybe they can dig up something his sleep-deprived brain was missing.

As Warner slid behind the wheel of his Dodge, he wondered where the message was. It had to be there, somewhere.

SIXTY-TWO

Sharon Clark staggered into her cubicle, arms overflowing with files, barely making it to her desk as everything spilled from her grasp, scattering across its already cluttered surface.

"Whew. So damned many reports. Just hope there's something I can use. No way he committed that rape."

She slumped into her chair, kicking off her shoes. Wriggling her toes, she sighed. Blasted heels were so impractical. Stupid dress code. She stretched and massaged a crick at the base of her neck.

Finally, dinner tonight with Al. Four long days since they'd been together. The psycho had taken another girl, so Warner was out scratching for a new lead. She hoped he wouldn't be too busy to come.

Boy, that's selfish. If he's tied up, maybe they're hot on the bastard's trail. Are they ever going public about this? They can't cover it up forever. And wow. He thinks he's the Angel of God.

She stretched again, arching her slim, graceful figure, and

sighed. A stack of mail crowded her inbox. Sorting through the letters, separating a few interesting pieces from the usual junk, she found a large envelope, colorfully decorated with a sexy female face, from *Playboy Publications*. Sharon smiled, slitting it open, a small tremor in her hand.

On a whim, she had responded to the magazine's advertisement in the *Miami Herald*, seeking South Florida women attorneys for a new photo feature.

She was uncertain if she were more nervous about getting a "yes" than a "no" What if . . .? Oh, hell, it's no big thing. She grinned, as she read the opening line of the letter:

Congratulations. You are invited to appear in our new photo feature: Luscious Lawyers. Shooting will begin on January 10. You will be contacted several days . . ..

"Wow!" The laugh had a nervous edge to it. "That's only two weeks away. I can't believe they picked me from those swimsuit photos."

Playboy? Should she really do this? Her hands were suddenly sweaty, her face flushed. It would sure turn a few heads at the office, where she was labeled a straitlaced New England prude. Boy, would *they* be surprised.

She sighed and shrugged. This was more about challenging The Establishment, and especially the Public Defender's Office, over exercising her privilege to make a choice. A staunch female rights advocate, she relished the coming conflict when she submitted her portfolio. Now she wasn't so sure.

She groaned and hoped Al, a pretty conservative guy, wouldn't be too upset with her posing partially nude in a men's magazine.

Sharon made a note on her calendar, then went to work on the stack of files overflowing her desk, deciding to be as happy as the proverbial kid in a candy store.

It would be a joy short-lived.

SIXTY-THREE

Detective Fanucci sped south on I-95, en route to a brainstorming session with Metro-Dade Homicide. His mind was elsewhere, however, and he focused just enough attention on traffic to stay out of trouble.

Something was going on. Twice that week she hadn't been there when he got home early. Could Anna be stupid enough to have an affair, knowing he'd beat the shit out of her if he ever found her with another guy? That the bastard would never fuck around again with *anyone* was a given.

What's her deal, anyway? So, he slapped her down once in a while when she got out of line. She deserved it—and liked it, too. They did their best fucking after he'd given her a little lesson on proper behavior. What did she expect from a guy buried in all this mayhem, day after day?

"Bitch. There'll be hell to pay if there's another guy." He turned off the Interstate, heading for downtown Miami.

* * * *

"Well, I guess that does it," Warner said looking from the murder-board to his small audience. He glanced at Captain Santiago, who had joined the group for an update, and he grunted, shaking his head.

"Any questions, Boss?" Warner perched on the corner of his desk. "At least any I might have an answer to?"

"What's the latest on the last vic's boyfriend? He give us

190

anything?"

"Wouldn't hold out too much hope there, Boss." Harris said. "He's in total catatonic-like stupor, the medico said. Can't seem to handle she willingly fucked the guy, I guess. Doc Carlsen's medicating him, but he doesn't see much hope for change soon, if at all. Our first chance at an ID, and the guy's gone bonkers."

"Terrific. Everything leads to a dead end. You're sure it's the same guy, Al? You find a message?"

"Oh, it's him, all right. They're doin' the DNA, for the record, but it's him. Same MO. Gold found the message on the inside of her thigh. He's expanded it." He nodded a Olvida.

"Ralph's guess on the name may be right on target. The nut probably thinks he's the Angel of God." He pushed a photo of the dead woman's once lovely leg across the desk. The words were neatly printed in red on the pale skin.

VENGEANCE IS MINE

Santiago's skin crawled.

Damned fucking loony.

"But you're still not sure what ties these girls together for this guy? Don't think it's just 'cause they're young, beautiful models?"

"That may be part of it," Warner said, "but that doesn't seem reason enough to sic the 'Angel of God' on them. There's something else—something more important to him that we're still missin'."

Warner stood, stretching. "It's time we come clean, and publicly connect the four murders. It ain't fair to the potential victims, whoever they are." He glanced at Santiago.

"You've asked for help from the Feds, haven't ya, Cap?"

Warner's boss nodded. "Couldn't put it off any longer, Al."

"Yeah, I know. So, when the guys from BAU show up, the

little old black cat'll be outta the bag, anyhow. The press may already be tyin' it together, and Eddy Roush at the Herald knows. He's been holdin' back for the promise of an inside exclusive, but time's runnin' out."

"Trying to avoid another panic was your idea, Al. I'm not passing the buck. I agreed to the temporary blackout. Now I think you're right again, and we should break it to the media. I'll do it, if you want."

"Thanks, Cap. That's something I can do without. But hold off until tomorrow. I owe Roush the scoop. You can schedule a news conference for the mornin'. I just hope when the Feds get here, they unearth something we've missed. I ain't gonna be too proud not to get some help." He turned to the dark-complexed detective from Boca Raton.

"Vinny, thanks for comin' down. I don't know if we made any progress, but we gotta keep workin' together. E-mail anything, every detail, back and forth. We gotta catch his nut. After tomorrow, the tri-counties are gonna be in a panic again. You can bet the newsies will dredge up Leordano and start makin' comparisons."

"So, let 'em. You iced that butcher. People oughta be more confident, knowing you're on the case."

They shook hands and Fanucci hurried off, hoping to beat the evening traffic. The Miami detectives scattered back to their desks, and Warner was alone in his office with his thoughts.

Yeah, I stopped the murderin' lunatic, all right, but not until he snuffed out seventeen kids. The trouble with these nuts is they're never who you'd suspect.

That certainly had been the case with the Baby Butcher.

He closed his eyes, unable to stem the surreal flow of those final moments, swirling back from his subconscious . . ..

"Die, pig," the short man whispered. *The 9mm, spitting death*

at him like an angry serpent, was not at all innocuous, however, as Warner rolled sideways out of the doorway, scrambling for cover. Strange, that in this moment of ultimate danger, he felt disgust at landing in the pool of his own vomit.

The Baby Butcher, the insane beast he had tracked for so many months, was coming after him. Warner tried to come out of his roll on one knee, ready to return fire. Instead, he lost his balance, falling backward, landing squarely on his butt. As he raised his own gun, squeezing off two rounds, something, like a baseball bat, cracked him on the side of the head. In the microseconds before oblivion, a thought flash through is mind.

An accomplice.

The bastard's got an accomplice, and he's killed me!

SIXTY-FOUR

Warner grunted as he stacked some papers on his desk. His thumb found the hidden scar, still a definite furrow under his hair. He barked a short, humorless laugh.

The Baby Butcher had no accomplice, and he had failed to kill Warner by the measure of a single centimeter, the slug careening off the side of his skull, cracking the bone and causing severe bleeding.

Warner's two instinctive shots were better placed. The first ripped through the maniac's throat, severing his spine. The second took him squarely in the breastbone. Either proved instantly fatal.

Warner lay in a growing pool of his own blood for forty minutes, before Jack Harris arrived. Finding his partner's note on his desk, he'd hurried after him and quickly located the path, clearly marked by Warner's parked car. After he stemmed the flow of blood, the adrenaline-charged 145-pound ex-Army Ranger tossed his much larger friend over his shoulder, carrying him to his car and a high-speed run back to Miami, a race against death. Warner owed his friend the ultimate debt—his life. Harris insisted anyone would have done the same, but there was a rooster's strut to his step after that day.

The Baby Butcher, known by his shocked friends to be Luis Leordano, was dead. The mild-mannered, seemingly compassionate little man was a well-loved guidance counselor to students at South Miami High. He was also the worst serial killer in South Florida's history, preying at night on the very kids he helped during the day.

No plausible motive was ever established for his rampage of death, nor for the particularly gruesome form it took. The Baby Butcher, labeled thus by the press, took his unsuspecting victims by surprise force, his small, pudgy body hiding iron hard muscles. His victims were trussed and transported to the remote hut, where they were injected with scopolamine, kept semiconscious as the madman slowly dissected them.

The detectives could find no evidence of any Satanic or other rituals. No one, not even the FBI's fabled BAU, ever developed a plausible reason why that little man dealt such pain and horror to the children he professed to love.

He just did it.

And now, there's a new lunatic out there, killing for reasons no more fathomable. Leordano, and Warner's own brush with death, had crowded his sleep with nightmares and filled his days with anxiety. He suspected it would take the capture—no, the *death*—of this Angel of God, before he would finally find peace.

Now the FBI's BAU team was coming. Maybe they'd find

something new—some way to identify this deadly "angel." He just wanted to be there when it all came down.

He shivered, realizing he hoped it would be he, once again, delivering the final act.

SIXTY-FIVE

Warner jerked back in his chair, his head popping up, momentarily dissociated to his whereabouts. He'd dozed off while poring over his scanty notes on the case.

Been so damned bushed, I fell asleep on the job.

A commotion and unfamiliar voices in the bullpen snatched him from momentary oblivion. Groaning, he reared up, stretching, as he sidled up to the window, peeking through the blinds. Six newcomers, four men and two women, all smartly dressed in suits—even the women—were swirling around the room, making introductions.

The BAU had wasted little time in arriving. The usual compliment of six agents for profiling during a serial murder investigation. Warner recognized Special Agent Ed Dalwin from the training symposium he attended three years before. He was a senior guy, and probably the Special Agent in Charge.

Warner yawned, knuckling bloodshot eyes, and ran fingers through disheveled locks before striding into the open office. Time to meet the Feds and put those sharp minds to work. In his limited experience, the BAU agents were the least likely guys to try to hijack an investigation—a major complaint of cops everywhere. As a rule, the FBI treated local cops like minor leaguers, with them as the All Stars, but Warner sensed, from his previous association, Ed Dalwin was different.

"Hey Boss, the Feds are here." Jack was the master of the obvious.

"So, I see," Warner said, strolling into the milling pod of people.

"Special Agent Dalwin. Good to see you—and your team, I presume."

Warner grasped the man's hand. Fit, with auburn hair graying at the temples, and wearing a tailored suit, he'd easily pass for a corporate VIP—until you took in his sharp-featured face and hard hazel eyes. His six-foot-two leanly muscled frame made for an imposing presence, and Warner knew Dalwin had used his athletic prowess more than once in the apprehending of the worst of the worst killers. Despite the BAU's mission as profilers, they were frequently involved in the actual apprehension of the baddies.

"Detective Warner. Good to see you, too. Wish it were under easier circumstances." He took Warner's hand in both of his.

"And of course, this *is* my team. Guys, this is Chief of Detectives, Al Warner." The other five agents crowded around, in various poses of welcome.

"I helped indoctrinate Al to the basics of serial killers," Dalwin said. "Must have done a good job, too, because he brought down the infamous Baby Butcher, all by himself. The BAU was never able to present a single helpful profile for Miami. Didn't even come close to describing Luis Leordano."

"So, you're the Hero of Miami." The tall, Teutonic blond woman held out her long-fingered hand, the nails short, well-kept, but devoid of any polish.

"I'm Special Agent Ina Yeager. These guys do the profiling. I do the shooting, if necessary. And help with tech research, just to prove I can." She winked.

"Don't listen to her BS," a thin little dark-haired guy, with a prominent Semitic beak, said, patting Warner on the shoulder.

"Besides being an ex-Army Ranger Overwatch Sniper, Ina's a whiz at digging background out of the Net. I'm Special Agent Harry Ashkin. But it's true. You don't want to get in Ina's way, if there's a fight." The four other agents chuckled, and the tall blonde blushed.

"My specialties are crime scenes and backgrounds. Seeing what hooks our vics together in our delusional puppy's mind."

"Okay," Dalwin said. "Let me make the rest of the introductions, or we might be here all afternoon." He gestured to a black man, about Warner's six-foot height, but with 25 pounds more muscle.

"This is Ansel Whitehead. Despite his linebacker build, he's a Doctor of Psychology, spearheading our profiling." They shook hands.

"Our research whiz here is Anita Solto. She can find anything, anywhere on the Net. You can run but you can't hide from 'Nita–and she speaks five languages, so she doubles up for interviews. Might be a help, if we gotta go into Little Havana."

"Cuban?" Warner asked, as the bumped knuckles. She was no more than 5'4" and "generously curved." Not fat though.

"Yep. Born in South Miami, not far from Calle Ocho."

"And last, but we don't have a "least," is Lon Pauletti. Another Psyche doctorate, and the BAU's other top marksman, three years running. Handguns, long guns, doesn't matter. Lon's our ace." Wiry, dark Mediterranean skin, with curly black hair and intense dark eyes, they nodded to each other.

"Seems like a fine crew, Ed," Warner said. "Got all the bases covered. I just hope you guys can dig up something we've missed. Our very deadly Angel of God seems to be on a week to ten-day cycle. We got four used-to-be-gorgeous bodies in the morgue and are expectin' number five any day now." His gaze swept across the six Feds.

"We got no clue who he really is, or what links our vics together in his warped mind. Gotta be something to do with them being beautiful and maybe their modelin', but it ain't clear why he seems to think God wants 'em dead."

"Yeah, well, we're eager to get started," Dalwin said. "Ina, Harry, and I would like to visit the last two crime scenes. The rest of the team will go over whatever evidence you have."

"Sure. Detective Harris'll take you guys to the scenes, and we've set up some desks for your team in the conference room. Hope it's not too crowded. We got a murder board workin' in my office." He pointed the way.

"Ya know, we've been keepin' the lid on this bein' serial. Didn't want to start a panic, so soon after Leordano. But with you here, the Cap's gonna break it tomorrow." He led the BAU team toward their temporary digs.

"Let's catch this sick puppy before we fill too many more body bags. I wouldn't be disappointed if we planted him, either. Save everyone pain and money."

"Our job's to help you snag him, not kill him," Agent Whitehead said. "If it happens, it happens. Let's get to work."

"Right. And I've got a phone call I gotta make," Warner said, pointing to the conference room door and then heading for his office. "Just keep us in the loop. I plan on bein' there when this bastard finally goes down."

SIXTY-SIX

"Eddy Roush, please." Warner slumped back in his chair, feet hooked over the corner of his desk, ambivalent about making this call. He saw no other reasonable option. With the BAU prowling the streets, the word will be out, anyhow. They'll get plenty of static from the press for holding back the things connecting these four murders.

"Roush here," Eddy's voice jerked Warner out of his thoughts.

"Hey, Eddy. It's Al Warner. We missed you yesterday."

"I took my kid fishing for specks to Lake Okeechobee. Just got in an hour ago." His voice dropped conspiratorially. "Did he kill another beauty?"

"Yeah, you missed all the fun. The latest was a honey named Danielle Sutton."

"Sutton, huh? Yeah, I see it on the computer. Fuck. The rookie's making the boyfriend sound guilty. So, what's the spin, Detective?"

"The truth, Eddy. The truth."

"What? Really? You're tearing down the Wall of Silence?"

"Too many bodies and not enough clues. I hate to start a new panic, but we can't stall any longer. We've called in the Feds to help. Women gotta know to be careful. Captain Santiago's gonna break it to the press tomorrow. I owed you early notice."

"Boy, that's a relief. I've been shaping the story for weeks."

"I got a packet on all four girls and a recap of what little we know about how he's selectin' his victims. Juicy stuff. The fuckin' lunatic may think he's the Angel of God, maybe out to redeem lost souls, or something. We really don't know yet." He dropped his feet to the floor and pushed back into his seat.

"The Angel of God? How d'ya think *VENGEANCE* .... fits in?"

"He's expanded it to *VENGEANCE IS MINE*. You know, from the *Bible*. It's all in there for you. But don't print nothin' until the morning edition. It's your scoop, but I don't want your media brethren all over my ass for havin' a favorite reporter."

"Okay, I'll send a runner over for the file while I bring the story up to date. I knew I could trust you, Warner."

"Yeah, and thanks for keepin' the lid on 'til now."

Warner hung up and glowered at his scuffed shoe tops.

Now the shit will really hit the fan, with the press all over the place, getting in their way, looking for leads. Loads of dud calls pouring in, and Dalwin's guys will dig into those, too.

Nobody's following up any leads alone *this* time, however stupid they may sound. Nobody. It's not gonna be just Leordano and him again. Not if he could help it.

And the emotional pressure. They're going to expect the *Hero of Miami* to catch this psycho, not the FBI. But he wasn't any hero—just lucky, and there wasn't a single, active lead on this deadly bastard.

He knuckled watery, red-rimmed eyes and yawned. He was so pooped. It was the goddammed dreams. Maybe Sherry was right. A shrink might help, but the idea made him uneasy.

Nothing was simple anymore.

Sitting up, Warner shoved papers around his cluttered desk. Let the Feds deal with it. Warner had a new, unrelated murder, an obvious family squabble. He had to go through the preliminary report before assigning a man to work the case.

SIXTY-SEVEN

"Whew. Hot stuff."

Warner just returned from organizing a place for the BAU

team to work from and distributed what paltry evidence they'd manage to acquire so far. He grunted at the narc detective Jack Harris was working with on a drug killing. He was sitting on the corner of Jack's desk, leafing through a magazine.

"Boy, look at the knockers on this one. We got some hot-looking babes in college down here in the sunshine."

"Hey buddy, keep it down. I don't know 'bout Narco, but we're busy in Homicide. What the hell's got you so hopped up, anyhow." Warner was more amused than angry.

"It's a *Playboy* from the box under Jack's desk. Always knew he was a horny bugger. This one's full of lovely young poon from the U of M and FAU. Geez, this one even looks familiar."

"Yeah, any dame with her clothes off looks familiar to you, Chick. Your horns are showin'."

"Seriously, Al, I know I seen her somewhere. Look."

Warner plucked the *Playboy* from the detective's hand, throwing it down on his desk with a resounding splat. There were photos of four lovely young girls in various stages of undress, all dazzling, voluptuous and exciting, but none tickled his memory.

"Unbelievable. College girls posin' nude in men's magazines. Don't see anybody here that rings a bell though."

"Turn the page, Al. Turn to the next page."

Shaking his head at the promiscuity of modern youth, Warner flipped over the glossy page. How sinfully beautiful and unselfconscious these girls were. Glancing at the three new photos, he jerked upright, eyes bright, his heart breaking into a gallop.

"Shit. That's Michelle McIntyre. In fuckin' *Playboy?* Lemme see this thing." He quickly flipped through the eight-page spread, finding what he was looking for, gracing the entire last page of the photo feature, *College Girls of the Southeast.*

An incredibly beautiful blonde, natural from the look of her pubic hair, smiled seductively out at him. The last time he saw those eyes, they were distended and glassy in death.

"Damn. Jodi Gannon. How in the hell did we miss this? Shit, I think Harry started tellin' me about this and I cut him off. And that kid that called in about Gannon. He said something about seein' the pictures."

This is what no sleep gets ya. Fuckin' careless.

"Jack. Where's Jack Harris?"

"Here, Boss." The little man trotted into the squad room "What's up?"

"Jack, wasn't Sutton a *Penthouse* Pet or something?"

"Yeah. *Pet of the Year*, a year or two ago, I think."

"See if you can find her feature in these mags. Look for Kym Atkins, too. I think she was in *Penthouse*." Rummaging around his desk, he found a photo of the luscious Ms. Atkins in a scanty swimsuit.

"Give a hand, Chick, if you ain't got nothin' else to do. We're lookin' for this dame. Just try not to linger too long over the other photos."

Jack Harris had the case of Jarrett's magazines up on his desk and the three men started skimming the photo features so popular with their male readers.

Fifteen minutes later, Harris let out a happy grunt.

"You find something, Jack, or is the excitement just too much for you?"

"It's Dani Sutton. Shit, this prick sure killed off some of the most beautiful women on earth. Here, look at this."

Warner glanced at the centerfold feature of their fourth victim, then placed it, almost reverently, on his desk with the first one. They continued leafing through the dwindled stack of periodicals.

A few minutes later, Warner picked up another *Penthouse*,

and suddenly his search was over. Kym Atkins stared provocatively out at him from the cover. Opening the magazine, there was their third victim, wrapped around a muscular stud, filling six sexually-suggestive pages.

Damn. Had they finally found what tied these victims together in this lunatic's mind?

"This is it. I'm sure of it." Warner stretched his arms over his head, flexing his shoulders, then jumped up, pacing around the room like a restless panther. Now they had something to work with.

"He's the Angel of God. He sees these gals as wanton sinners, exposin' their bodies for financial gain. He's on a mission to redeem 'em—bring 'em to God to be purified, I guess. They gotta die to do that.'"

"But why fuck 'em, Al? Not that I'd blame him, but it just doesn't seem consistent with what you said."

"Don't know, Jack. Maybe the guys from the BAU can tell us. Could be to verify their sins, to justify killin' them. It sure fits the mold. Now all we gotta do is figure out how it'll help us catch him." He scooped up the magazines.

"I gotta show these to the Captain, and get Dalwin's team on this. I'm not sure the Captain should tell the public about this link just yet. Don't wanna give a copycat any ideas."

"We may not have to," Harris said. "Roush is pretty sharp. He may tie it together himself."

"Maybe so. I'll leave it up to the Boss. The Feds'll work up a profile and brief all local law enforcement, so there'll be no keepin' secrets after that. The Cap'll be the one on the firin' line, once we're ready. Agent Dalwin's one of the rare Feds not eager to usurp the local cops. At least we got something to work with now. Harry, get Special Agent Dalwin to the Captain's office, ASAP." Warner hurried toward Santiago's office, his lethargy evaporating.

Finally, something to sink their teeth into. With some luck, they might catch this wayward "angel" and put him where he belonged. Warner hoped that meant the death penalty, not the loony bin. Or better yet, in the ground.

This guy doesn't deserve to live.

SIXTY-EIGHT

Sharon mewed softly, her body shuddering with orgasm. He had released into her a few seconds earlier but continued on, igniting her climax. She slumped against his chest, letting herself go luxuriously limp, each elegant swell and curve fitting comfortably against him, like perfect pieces of a puzzle.

Kisses peppered his neck and ear while his skillful hands ventured knowingly into secret places, gently triggering wavelets of aftershocks, lapping against her body in ever widening circles.

How surprising different sex with Al Warner was than any other man she had ever known. Her family position, abetted by her Georgetown law degree and classic beauty, propelled her into the company of much of the financial upper class of Southeastern Florida.

She had dated prominent young physicians (two), a high-powered corporate attorney, a rich local yuppie businessman, and a state senator. All had family backgrounds and education far surpassing Warner's rural, Midwestern roots, but she doubted any matched his intelligence. Warner was as bright as anybody she knew. His crusty nature hid an amazingly gentle side, apparently reserved solely for her.

What really amazed Sharon was none of the so-called high class, educated men she dated could even walk in Al Warner's shadow as a lover. At the age of forty, seven years her senior, his ardor was still considerable, his gentle, unassuming worship of her an incredible aphrodisiac. His tenderness, compassion, and understanding of her sexual needs—and his uncanny ability to fulfill them—made all other men she'd known pale by comparison. There had been some good sex, but with Warner it was so much more. It was wonderful lovemaking.

Sharon slowly rolled off her lover, snuggling close to his side. The relatively hairless skin of his chest rippled with hard muscles. Strong arms cradled her and held her possessively close. Knowing he needed her as much as she did him infused her with a heated glow that seeped into every nook and cranny of her being. She slowly traced a slender finger across his face, outlining his nose, eyes, and lips. Their passion slaked, he seemed pensive.

"A quarter for your thoughts, lover. I'm paying top rates."

"You don't really want to know." He sounded forlorn. She ached, knowing the huge burden this new maniac had heaped upon him.

"What's wrong, Al? Talk to me, darling."

He sighed, kissed her, and settling back, holding her close. Shadows, caused by a windblown tree dancing with a streetlight, scurried back and forth across the white textured ceiling.

"I'm just so aggravated with myself. You consume me when we're makin' love. But, after we're done and begin to relax, I can't help but think about that bastard erasing all these beautiful young women. The fuckin' Angel of God. Where do they get this shit? How do such dangerous loonies roam so freely out there? I just can't figure it."

"We don't create these people, like Frankenstein," she said. "Aberrant creatures have always been there, throughout the centuries."

"Yeah, but it scares me, because in some ways, we're kinda alike, him and me."

"That's ridiculous." She scooted back against the headboard. "You're a kind and gentle guy behind that crusty facade. This Angel of God is a vicious animal. He may be insane, and maybe he doesn't even realize what he's doing, but he's nothing like you. Nothing."

"Oh, sure. I didn't mean it like that. But I was raised by conservative Baptists who believe what these girls did—you know, pose in the magazines—is a sin. The most 'righteous' of our church, my father definitely included, woulda sought these girls out for redemption—redemption even through their deaths. If those Fundamentalists were here, they might *celebrate* these killin's. They might really believe this nut *is* an Angel of God."

"You're kidding." A flurry of uncertainty peppered her. What would they think of *her*, after she posed for *Playboy*?

"Nope," Warner said. "You had a liberal upbringin', taught to accept people like they are. The body's not sinful to you. My parents never even saw each other naked. Pop told me once that Mom waited until all the lights were out before she'd even leave the bathroom. He considered that proper modesty."

Shit. He'll never understand. She'd always known it. So why was she so compelled to pose partially nude for the whole world to see? It *was* ridiculous. But she's independent, a *liberated* woman, and not her father's puppet, driven to prove that, even if it might alienate the only man she ever really loved. She could be so self-destructive when it came to her pride. Was she testing him—testing his love?

Somehow, it would work out. Luckily for her, his apple had fallen far from the parental tree. She'd make him understand.

"Well, thank god none of that rubbish rubbed off on you,

darling," she said. "They don't make lovers any better than you. At least, not in my limited experience." She wrapped her arms around him, pulling him willingly against her.

"So, if you're basically this great guy, nothing like your parents, how are you anything like this killer? Tell me that, Buster." Sharon laughed, gently patting his butt.

He snuggled closer, resting his head on the firm pillow of her breasts.

"Ah, I guess you're right, Sher. I don't like much of what my dad stood for. The righteous bastard beat us until I was big enough to chase him away. I just feel there's too much nudity and sex goin' around, especially in the face of AIDS and other STDs. How did we get on this morbid subject, anyhow?"

"I know." She giggled. The lobe of his ear was in her mouth as her hands sliding down his body in a tantalizing, erotic dance.

"You're trying to distract me from finishing what we're in this bed for, aren't you? Well, you can't. I'm due an encore, aren't I, lover? Aren't I?" Her tongue began a slow, wet exploration.

His fingers fluttered to life, becoming busy little adventurers. Soon they were lost in the heat of their passion, each giving and receiving electric excitement.

Sharon's encore performance was already well into the second act.

SIXTY–NINE

ANGEL OF DEATH TAKES FOURTH VICTIM

The *Miami Herald* headline shouted it to the world. Eddy Roush's two-column article ran on the front page, tying the three murders in Dade County and the McIntyre homicide in Boca Raton all to the same perpetrator. He exonerated the police from not coming forth sooner through innuendo, inferring they were working on a lead that hadn't panned out.

The latest death finally forced the summoning of the fabled BAU, and the announced presence of a new serial killer, less than a year after the black terror of Luis Leordano finally ended with two bullets from Al Warner's gun.

Captain Robert Santiago would hold a formal news conference today.

* * * *

Bob Santiago barged into the Homicide Department, sputtering like a bomb about to explode. He tugged at a red and blue striped tie and shrugged out of a dark-blue polyester sport jacket. His shirt was drenched despite an air temperature in the low seventies.

"I hate these things." He glowered at the three detectives, as if waiting for a challenge.

"What d'ya hate, Cap," Harris was a master at friendly banter, "the tie or the jacket?"

"Both. Neither. Oh, shit. I was talking about the goddammed news conference, Jack. You know, I'm in no mood for your antics, you welterweight piss-ant. Go catch that bastard and leave me in peace. The fucking 'Angel of Death.' Boy, Eddy Roush really knows how to stir the pot."

"He's not as bad as most, Bob." Harry Klein stood and stretched.

"He went along with Al. Held back the real story for nearly two weeks. You gotta give him a little leeway now."

"Yeah, I suppose. Where's Warner today? Chasing a hot new lead, I hope." Santiago folded the tie and shoved it into his jacket's pocket.

"No such luck, Boss." Harris leaned back, crossing his ankles. "He had a doctor's appointment this morning. Still having mucho nightmares from Leordano. Or maybe from the slug off the noggin. Whatever, he doesn't sleep well, that's for sure."

"He's seeing Carlsen?"

"Yeah, finally. If anybody can shrink his head, it'll be Sven. Al's held up pretty damned well, for so little rest," Harris said.

"He and Sharon are a twosome again, and she's better for him than any shrink'll ever be."

Harry Klein looked up, waving a copy of *Penthouse*.

"Dalwin's gang are digging into any connection they can find with the photo spreads. We've been going over the little articles about the four vics in the magazines. My wife refuses to believe that reading all these lovely, colorful things is really an assignment. Can you write me a note, Teach?"

"Sure, Harry," Santiago laughed. The old cop always knew how to defuse the Captain's temper. Bob was going to miss him when he finally retired.

"Anyhow," Klein continued, "we're checking the stories to see if anything there might point us in the right directions." He spread the *Penthouse* on his desk. "He must have got info from the articles. Like we found chocolate truffles at the Atkins girl's apartment, and she says here they're her one weakness. And Sutton's article said she wanted to get into movies."

"Okay. Makes sense." The captain hung his jacket on a coat

hook in his office. "The Feds finish with the crime scenes?" he asked through the doorway.

"Yep," Klein answered. "and there're pretty much done with the evidence files. They're working up their profile, but I'm not sure how much that'll help, Boss.

"Meanwhile, we're contacting other South Florida girls in that *Playboy* feature. Al's cluing them in about the danger and who to look out for. And he's assigned tails to the local women in the mags, for their safety. Poor guy, having to talk to all those hot babes all by himself."

"Better him than me," Harris chuckled. "I'd be so busy dreaming about humping them, I'd forget why I was there. At least Warner's got Sharon. With a dame like that, who needs to look somewhere else."

"All right, enough of this bullshit," Santiago said. "Back to work. I gotta prepare a report for the chief."

"Sure, Cap." Harris settled himself behind his desk and picked the July *Playboy*. He opened the magazine and folded out the centerfold. He definitely needed more assignments like this.

He licked his lips. *Damn, what a pair of bazookas.*

Mama mia. Sometimes, he loved this fucking job.

SEVENTY

Warner fidgeted, nearly engulfed in the folds of the deep armchair. Why was he here? Because Sharon coerced him into it, arguing her case in true legal style. This was to placate her, but he didn't really expect much.

Sven Carlsen settled across from him. The man, huge in every dimension, wasn't a stereotypical psychiatrist. At six-foot-seven and a good three hundred pounds, he was an imposing, even intimidating, sight. Probably not a plus for someone in his line of work. His thick shock of curly, dark hair and his neatly trimmed Van Dyke were shot with veins of gray. But, when Al looked at his gentle, sympathetic face, the force of his overpowering size evaporated.

Al watched him as he readjusted his bulk in the other, extra-large chair. *Do I really want to be doing this?*

The psychiatrist smiled.

"So, Al, it's still the dreams, eh? Ivan told me he's examined you and found nothing physically wrong. You're fully recovered from your head wound. Physically, at least." He paused, watching the detective closely.

"You've been through a trying time. It's never easy to take another's life, even one as despicable as Luis Leordano. That alone can be quite traumatic. The fact you were so seriously wounded certainly compounds the psychological strain. There's no shame in that." His smile widened.

"You are, after all, human. Tell me about the dreams."

Warner paused, took a deep breath, and began his tale haltingly, slowly responding to the psychiatrist prodding. Before long, however, the words started gushing forth, a dam broken by the flood-swollen river of his pent-up frustrations and self-imposed restraints. Twenty minutes later, he sat motionless, sweating lightly, finally empty of all he had held back.

The mental earthwork he had erected against his fear had crumbled. He spoke of the frustrations of Leordano, exacerbated now by the Angel of Death, and the anger, then and now, associated with an investigation going nowhere. There was the momentary terror of his deadly encounter with the Baby Butcher, his own near death and lengthy struggle to regain his strength, both physical and mental.

"The dreams got started after I came back to work." He squirmed in the chair. "They're intermittent. They come several nights in a row, maybe for as long as a week. Then they'd quit for days at a time. If I was at Sharon's, I was usually okay, but not always, even then. And whatever sleep I do get ain't providin' any real rest."

Dr. Carlsen sat quietly throughout this outpouring of long stored anxiety. Finally, Warner's eyes blinked several times, refocusing from some dark abyss he had been staring into. He was back in the here and now.

"Very interesting, Al. Quite a catharsis, once you got past your own reluctance to examine your feelings. You know, dreams are a metaphoric window to what's on our mind at any specific time. More from our subconscious than the conscious. They're much like an ancient Greek play, where all the characters wore masks. The actions in dreams are rarely literal thoughts." The big man leaned forward.

"You've had several repetitive dreams, and in each of them, you are in perilous danger. There's the faceless man with the gun, Leordano you think, about to shoot you. There's the vicious dog from Hell, chasing you up a never-ending staircase. And the car hurtling toward a massive stone wall, about to crash. All life threatening."

"Yeah. Plenty scary. I wake up shakin' and soakin' wet. Sometimes I don't even know where I am, and when I figure it out, it's like I don't belong there. What do they mean, Doc?"

"What do *you* think they mean? That's what's important."

"Geez, how should I know? I just wake up scared and very worn out."

"Well, that's definitely the first part of it. They tell us you're dreading something. Paralyzingly afraid. But these terrors aren't of a person or thing. More likely, you're expressing fears about you—something you feel is dangerous to you. Something you are unwilling to face. Any idea what that might be, Al?"

"Not a clue, Sven. I'm no hero, in spite of what the press calls me, but I'm not easily scared, either. That's what makes this so unsettlin'."

"What, or how, did you feel, after you killed Leordano?"

"I had a terrible headache, Sven," his acidic humor showing itself for the first time. "A bullet off the skull'll do that, y'know."

"But afterward," Carlsen pressed, in spite of his own chuckle. "After you began recovery, and you had time to think about what happened. After you realized you had killed another human being, regardless how despicable. How did you feel then?"

"Did I have any regrets?" He ran fingers through his thick, curly locks. "No, not for a minute. He deserved to die, after what he did to those seventeen kids. Hell, he deserved to die after the first girl. The other sixteen were just frostin' on his funeral cake. I'd kill him again, without blinkin' an eye."

"Not the slightest remorse? No moral quandary."

"Not a bit. And I'd jump at the chance to do the same to this new lunatic, this Angel of God. Death's Angel." Warner was upright in the chair, dark eyes burning with intensity as he snarled this out, echoing his frustration.

"So, how does *that* make you feel? Knowing that you've killed without remorse and are ready and willing to do it again.

"And what about others who commit heinous crimes? Are you really ready to be judge, jury and executioner for them all?"

"Geez, Sven, I never thought . . .." Stunned, Warner slumped back, his mind spinning. The doc was right. He was angry and bitter enough at these atrocities to want to end it all by himself, without the due process he was sworn to uphold. That realization made him afraid, but only of himself. What had he become, in his quest for justice?

"Now, don't go off half-cocked. This is just our first session. We're only discovering possible venues for these dreams. None of this is cast in stone.

"I've known you for a long time. You're an honest, compassionate guy. Some of what's going on with you is obviously PTSD from Leordano. You killed and were nearly killed in return. Now you're faced with a similar psychopath, and much of what you've suppressed during and after Leordano is bubbling up to the surface." The psychiatrist edged forward in his chair, watching Warner intently.

"Understandably, you don't like what these guys bring out in you. You've become obsessed with catching them, and that's your job. Your uncommon humanity makes this much more important for you than most. You want Justice, with a capital 'J.' And you may be terrified as to what levels you might be willing to go to achieve that end."

Carlsen paused, steepling his fingers under his chin.

"You just have to face up to that fear, because in the end, you must realize that your real human nature will force its way through. The real Al Warner will step forward."

"Shit, I think you're right. Never realized it, but I guess I thought of me as an avenger for those kids of Leordano's, and now these girls. I'd set the scales right for all the victims, and the only way to do that is with this guy's death. He thinks he's the Angel of God, redeemin' sinners, and I wanna be *his* Angel of Death."

"Yes, that's a big part of it, but there's more—things you're still unwilling to face. Things from your youth and how they affect you now. There's more work to do."

"Dammit, Doc, you've already lifted an elephant off my back. Ain't that enough?"

"It's a start, but if we don't uncover the rest, you'll still be handcuffed by some level of uncontrolled anxiety. There's still much more to do on what we've covered. We may have made some progress on the nightmares, but you can't do it all in one session, despite how terrific an analyst I am."

They smiled as they rose from their chairs. Warner reached out for the bigger man's hand.

"Thanks, Sven. I don't know why I was so reluctant to come see you. I feel a whole lot better, and I bet I even get a good night's sleep, for a change."

And he did, that night and several thereafter. Feeling so much better, he neglected to make a follow-up appointment with Dr. Carlsen, despite Sharon's pleading. He felt he was "cured."

But it was only temporary.

SEVENTY-ONE

Warner studied the overflowing squad room, mentally ticking off "heads:" three Sheriffs and their deputies from the Tri—County area, about a dozen police chiefs from various cities and towns from the same vicinity, with their top homicide and Major Crime detectives, plus, the heads of most of the Patrol Divisions. No one who might help was left out.

He turned to the Special Agent in Charge, nodding.

"Looks like the whole gang's here, Ed. Hope you guys got something useful."

Agent Dalwin shrugged. "We'll see. At least everyone should be on the same page, after this."

Warner sighed, turned to his captain, and tilted his head toward the lectern.

"You're up for the intro, Bob."

Captain Santiago threw back his shoulders and walked to the podium where the patrol sergeant usually gave the morning briefing to his troops.

"Okay, ladies and gents. If you'll settle down, Special Agent in Charge Dalwin and his crew are going to clue you into whatever we've got to go on. Let's hope the BAU's dug up something new." He turned to the group of six FBI agents, gathered behind him. "Agent Dalwin?"

"Thanks, Captain," Dalwin said, stepping forward, trailed by members of his team. "It's been about a year since I've seen most of you. I wish it were under better circumstances. It's a shame that it's usually serial killers that bring us together.

"Unfortunately, I'm afraid that, again, we haven't found much new to add to what you already know. You've got another Unsub with a sketchy profile, but here's what we do know.

"He's a white or Latino male, mid-thirties to early forties, about six feet, fit and *very* strong. Not a pumped-up guy—just lean and powerful."

"He's probably physically attractive," Agent Whitehead pitched in, "and smooth and charming with the ladies. He's the ultimate gentleman, not pushy or aggressive with his potential vics, which makes him more appealing."

"And he's a researcher," Agent Anita Salto added. "He studies the articles about these women, zeroing in on their favorite things and aspirations. He knows what buttons to push to turn them on."

"The man's clearly psychotic," Agent Pauletti said, "and delusional, thinking he's an agent of God. That probably gives him a feeling of invincibility, which may eventually lead to his downfall—but also makes him inordinately dangerous."

"While these things are all pretty clear," Agent Dalwin said, "what we don't know are the stressors that set him in motion. This is a man who lived a normal, probably uncomplicated life until something set him off.

"It could be an event or a person. Possibly a deteriorating

relationship with a family member. His fixation with beautiful women who've posed nude or nearly nude may come from a puritanical upbringing. If so, he has either embraced it, or is rebelling against it. It's unusual that one with that bent would have sex with these girls before killing them."

"It may be," Agent Ashkin stepped forward, "he has to prove to himself—or to God—that these women *are* wanton, and in need of his brutal form of purification."

"Unfortunately," agent Dalwin said, "that's about all we've got now. I know that's not much new to work with. It leaves us awaiting the Unsub to select his next victim, and hoping he make a mistake. We're admonishing every local girl who has appeared in those magazines to be extra cautious.

"We're going to be right here with you guys, working with whatever comes up, until we catch this sick puppy." He paused, eyes sweeping the room.

"We're not interested in stepping on your investigations, but bring us whatever you've got, and we'll help any way we can. Our unified goal is to put this guy away before he does any more damage. Questions?"

"So, he looks like any normal Joe Blow?" a homicide detective from Fort Lauderdale asked. "Doesn't give us much to go on."

"You're right," Agent Ina Yeager responded. "We're probably handcuffed until he takes his next victim, and maybe makes a mistake. Unfortunately, the only living eye witness is catatonic in a mental ward. If he comes out of it, we'll probably have a description, but his docs aren't too optimistic that's gonna happen anytime soon."

"Right," Dalwin said. "All we can do is get out on the streets and cover all the bases we do have. Clue in your patrol units, too. Good collars come from observant street cops."

"Okay, that's a wrap," Captain Santiago says, stepping to

the front. "Special Agent Dalwin and his team have set up their command post here, since we've had the first, and most murders. But they're available to any of you in the Tri-Counties. Take a moment to introduce yourselves to his team and leave contact info. You're all on the distribution list for anything new we discover. File it with them and they'll see everyone is kept up to date.

"Let's go out and catch this crazy bastard. I'm tired of serial psychos making South Florida their playground."

A feral rumble bounced around the crowded room, as over fifty law enforcement professional disbursed, heading for their turf. Hope that the Angel of Death doesn't visit their little backyards was tempered by the excitement of the possible notoriety if they happened to be the ones that eventually nabbed him. Killing the Baby Butcher, just a year before, had brought Al Warner fame as the Hero of Miami—and put him in the hospital and out of action for nearly six months.

Of course, one of the truisms about serial murderers is, many are *never* caught.

Al Warner mulled that scary thought as he returned to his office. As usual, he was worn thin by a night filled with terrifying dreams.

He hoped he'd have better luck tonight, but somehow knew that was unlikely.

SEVENTY-TWO

"No. God, no." He jerked bolt upright, perspiration beading on his body in rivulets, his heart a pneumatic drill, pummeling his chest. The damned dream again.

Warner gasped for breath, struggling to restrain his rampaging heart. Slumped over, perched on the edge of his bed, he stared numbly out the window. The last of daylight was ebbing like a strong spring tide.

Shit. He'd slept the whole day. He'd awakened that morning shivering, racked with chills and sporting a 102-degree fever after a night of doing battle with *The Dream*. He'd reluctantly called in sick, made some tea and toast, and went back to bed, vowing never to eat sushi again.

The whole day. Unbelievable. But at least those body-racking chills seemed gone, replaced now by a cold terror still holding a diminishing grip on his soul.

The Dream. Almost always the same one now—the slavering three-headed beast hounding him up those dank, narrow, spiraling stone stairs. Getting closer.

Closer. Close enough to feel the heat and smell its fetid breath. His stomach heaved.

The Dream. All night, then again, all day. He'd thought his visit with Carlsen had finished them, but he was wrong.

Lurching shakily to his feet, he stripped off his drenched pajamas, intent on a hot shower. Gotta get a grip, and right now. It was time to go back to work.

The Angel of Death wasn't napping.

He was out there, looking for his next victim.

SEVENTY-THREE

Sharon hung up the phone, jumped up, and did a little soft shoe around her office. The team from *Playboy* had just called with the schedule for shooting her photos for the upcoming feature.

Next Tuesday.

They rented a yacht to sail out to Elliot Key in Biscayne Bay. They'd shoot a bunch of shots aboard the boat, on the beach and in the water. It was just what she needed—a day of sun and sand to wash away the accumulated tension of this often-thankless job.

She paused in the middle of a twirl, catching her lower lip between her teeth. Would Al understand this urge to express her independence? It worried her every time she thought of this ribald little adventure. She sighed.

Why challenge him like this?

But he did love her. One of the things he always said he admired most was her adventurous and unconventional spirit. Would he see this in that light? Well, whatever his reaction, she'd win him over eventually.

Better tell him about it before the issue hit the stands, but that's months away.

Plenty of time to prep him.

But uncertainty fed procrastination, and *that* fed trouble.

With a capital "T."

SEVENTY-FOUR

"Boca Raton Homicide. This is Detective Fanucci."

"Hey, Vinny. This is Julan Watts, Lantana PD."

"Hey, Julan. How's it going up there? Lot quieter, I bet, then when you were cruising Liberty City."

"Yeah, I suppose. But we still got brothers killing brothers here. It's real depressing."

"Yeah. So, what can I do for you, my friend? The Boca PD's at your service, unless you really need something. Then I think the brass won't be so helpful."

The chuckle on the other end of the line was mirthless.

"We got a corpse you might be interested in. Sounds like the same MO as that FAU girl you had last month, and a lot like those down in Miami."

"Beautiful young dame, who modeled in a men's magazine? Crushed windpipe while in the act of getting it on? *Vengeance is Mine* in red lipstick on a mirror? That describe it pretty well?"

"Yeah, more or less. Not a model, though. One of those topless hot dog cart vendors. She danced nude from time to time at the Crystal Palace in Boynton."

"A hot dog vendor? One of the dames on Lantana Road? Which one, Julan?"

"One Rosa Bianco, AKA Tiffany White, when she was dancing at the Palace."

"I think I knew her. A little slip of a gal with a big pair of boobs. Real natural looking ones. If she's the one I'm thinking of, she was kinda sweet. A very friendly gal. Real cute face?"

"Yep, that's her. I hear she *was* friendly—to cops. Maybe figured it was a way to stay out of trouble. Didn't do her any good this time. Say, exactly how friendly were *you*, Vince?"

"Whoa, there, sport. Why would she cozy up to a Boca cop? I just bought a dog or two from her and admired the view. Anyway, from what you're telling me, she was offed by our Angel of Death. Not a gal from *Playboy* or *Penthouse*, but I guess nude dancing and selling dogs with her boobs hanging out might be close enough for this nut. Where'd you find her?"

"At the Clarion, on Congress. The maid found her this AM, and the message was on the mirror in hot red lipstick.

"Her boyfriend's been looking for her. He found her cart

chained to a light post. Been driving the detectives crazy. Now he's screaming a cop killed her. Insists she'd only lie down for a badge. Sez they were going to get married and raise a family, soon as they saved up a big enough stash."

"He don't want to think she'd cheat on him," Fanucci laughed. "Hell, that cunt'd pop between the sheets just because she loved it. Didn't have to be a cop."

"You get more than dogs from her, Vin? What else you get?"

"Just what I heard. You oughta call Al Warner at Metro-Dade. Your boss was at the Feds profiling down there. Warner's coordinating everything. He's had the first and most body bags. Talk him into sending up Moe Gold with the BAU team. To help your forensics guys. Their little wizard can turn lead into gold."

"Good idea. So, I'll e-mail you what we got, in case it rings a bell on your case. Can you send me a copy of the file on yours?"

"Sure. I'll send a car. Too much to e-mail. This bastard's sure snuffing some really hot chicks. What a waste." The two detectives passed a few more pleasantries before hanging up.

Fanucci sat silently for a moment, thinking hard.

Shit. Just what he needed now. Anna playing patty cake with someone, and now this. If it got out he'd boffed Tiffany, he'd be in a real hot spot. The Captain would toss his ass in a big pot, and Anna, that two-timing bitch, would probably light the fire.

What fucking bad luck.

SEVENTY–FIVE

"Look man, it had to be a cop. Rosa and me, we was gonna get

222

married. No way she'd hop in the sack, 'less she was muscled. I'm all the stud she needed. Some cop's been pushing her. Fuck him or he'd close her down. She tole me, man. She tole me."

"Sure, Santos. What else she gonna tell you? 'Hey, baby, we're getting married, but I'm getting a little on the side in the meantime, 'cause some other guy knows how to do it better than you.' Gimme a break, will ya." Detective Watts studied the man across the desk from him. "We'll check it out, but this got all the earmarks of that Angel of Death killer, not a cop."

"Yeah? Sez you, man. And who says this Angel can't be no cop? Some of you guys has done worse, ain't ya?"

Santos Carrera was boiling. Some bastard had just cashed in his meal ticket. And Rosa, AKA Tiffany, had definitely been a blue-plate special. Between dancing at the Crystal Palace, and the money she took in from her little mobile lunch vending cart, Santos was living very high on a very healthy hog.

That Rosa was also sweet, loving and hot in the sack, well, those were all bonus points. She had a firm, willowy body and a terrific pair of boobs, and men paid, and paid well, for the chance to see them, to be close to them, to fantasize about them. And Santos, for one, was going to miss them very much. But not nearly as much as the cash those lovely twin mounds provided him. The loss of Rosa Bianco wasn't nearly as disturbing as was that of her income.

"What 'bout her jewelry, Man? I'm her fiancée, so I should get her jewelry." Maybe he could salvage something.

"What jewelry?" Detective Watts asked, looking up from the papers on his desk, eyebrows arched.

"No mention of any jewelry on the inventory list. I was at the crime scene, and don't remember anything on her body."

"Bullshit, man. See, some fucking cops picked her clean." *Probably you, or one of your nigger buddies.* "Rosa wore gold earrings, and a big gold neck chain. An opal ring and a good watch, too. Where the fuck are they, huh?"

"A good question," Watts said, making a note on his pad.

"Give me a description of the stuff, and I'll get some men on it. If the killer took her baubles, it may lead us to him."

The young Latin pulled up some photos of the lovely young woman who had died so tragically just two days before. Santos pointed out the necklaces and earrings, plainly displayed in one shot of her in a bikini. Another picture showed the watch and ring, as she held up a wineglass in an apparent toast.

"These are good," Watts said as he studied the shots. "I'll print copies for the Robbery boys. Maybe this prick'll try to fence 'em. Anyway, it's a shot."

"Sure, sure. Here's my phone. My poor Rosa."

"Yeah, thanks. I can see you're all broken up over your loss." Sarcasm dripped coldly from Watts' remark. "I'll get this back to you in the morning."

As the still fuming man left, Detective Watts looked after him, shaking his head in disbelief. He turned to his partner, Mike Corwyn, with a rueful smile.

"That fucking Spic's only interested in making a profit. The poor dame was in trouble if she'd lived to marry that bum."

"Yeah. Too bad she hooked up with scum like that. But, maybe this Angel of Death finally made a mistake. Better send Warner and Fanucci copies of the pics, in case the stuff shows up on their turf. Stranger things have happened."

"Yeah, but I doubt our "Angel" lifted 'em. Not his style. Somebody else found her first."

SEVENTY–SIX

Warner slid onto his chair and stretched his arms high over his head, yawning. The first six of the last nine days were only interrupted once with nightmares. Good timing, because they'd just run the first boot camp for a trial group out of Juvie.

That didn't go off as smoothly as they'd hoped. One tough, smart kid, Carlo Delgado, had orchestrated a revolt, and they lost half a day rounding up the other sixteen kids and regaining order. Jose wanted to kick him back into detention, but Warner had a gut feeling this kid could make it, and become a positive influence on the rest. Delgado had become his personal project.

But that would have to wait, because he had a lunatic to nab, and the dreams had come back in the last three days, bad as ever. He was going to have to see Sven again after all. Damn.

He glanced at his ex-partner, busily reading one of Jarrett's old *Playboy* mags.

"Anything new on the hot dog girl in Lantana, Jack?"

"Rosa Bianco. A hot little Cuban gal with poor judgment. Damn, how could anybody hurt something as sweet as that?"

"That's who he thinks he's doin' it for, Jack. God. Any news from forensics?"

"Yeah. Moe and Agent Haskins finished up there this morning. Boy, you should have heard the Hawk grumbling about the mess Lantana CSU made of the scene. But there's no doubt it's our Angel of Death. How he strangled her, the message on the mirror, all identical to the first four. The Hawk's running DNA on the sperm, and he'll put it through all the databases again, but it's a waste of time. We already know this bastard ain't in the system anywhere."

"So, nothin' new?" Warner scowled and shook his head.

"Just the missing jewelry," Harris said, glancing at his notes. "And there's a three-county sweep looking for that. Broward Sheriff and Fort Lauderdale PD have pulled out all the stops, too. Guess they figure he might hit them next. The Hawk's crime team picked up a few strands of dark-brown hair, but we already know his hair color. Everything was wiped clean, as usual."

"Damn this careful, crazy bastard. How 'bout the Sutton girl's boyfriend? You check on him recently?"

"Talked with Doc Carlsen yesterday. What little change there's been is for the worse. The guy's almost catatonic. Keeps mumbling he can't believe she fucked the guy. Not she's dead, but that she would actually open those long lovelies for someone else. I wouldn't count on nothing from him anytime soon."

"Terrific. This nut's got everything goin' for him. Even our one eyewitness is useless. We gotta come up with something. The press is grillin' our asses." Warner threw down his pencil.

"Five vics, and no progress. We're looking like dummies. The Feds are sendin' agent Pauletti, their behavioral guy, to help with Tazwell," he continued, "but Sven's as good as anybody. The Chief wants to keep the investigation in house."

"For sure. I just can't figure why he took Bianco's babbles. He left lots better stuff, and even some thick bundles of dough with his other victims. It just doesn't figure."

"I've been thinkin' about that, Jack. I bet someone found the body first, lifted the stuff, and didn't report the stiff. Are the Lantana detectives checkin' out the hotel staff?"

"Don't know, but Watts is pretty sharp for a black boy raised in the inner city. Just goes to show you what a little schooling and real dedication can do for a so-called disadvantaged guy. I'm on liaison with him. Should I mention it?"

"Can't hurt. I'd hate to spend any time on a red herring."

"Okay, Boss. Will do." The little man picked up the phone.

But Detective Watts was already way ahead of them.

SEVENTY-SEVEN

226

She answered on the third ring.

"Sharon Clark." Her normally musical voice was strained.

"Boy, you really sound tired, Sher. How's the trial comin'?"

"Oh, Al, how nice to hear a friendly voice."

"That bad, huh?"

"No, not really. The DA's just about finished his case. I did the cross on the rape victim today, and when she saw that I wasn't going to rough her up, she relaxed a little. But, she's sure about her ID of my client. Without her somehow showing some doubt . . .."

"How much longer, Babe?"

"Two or three days. I don't have many witnesses. I hoped to impeach theirs."

"Can you make any time for us?" Warner hesitated, then rushed on. "I've had five miserable days, with the nightmares gettin' worse than ever. You know he hit again in Lantana?"

"I heard. You got anything new to work with?"

"Not a damned thing. Some jewelry missin', but I doubt he took it. This is like runnin' in quicksand."

"You sound exhausted. Have you made another appointment to see Dr. Carlsen? You'll never dispel those dreams without his help."

"Seein' him tomorrow mornin'. I'm not so uptight about it anymore. I do believe he can help, and I gotta find a way to get more rest." He sighed. "I got a little caught up there for a while, but I've lost it all in these last few days.

"So, any chance you can pencil me into your busy schedule?"

"Probably not until after this trial, lover." She groaned. "My evenings are at the law library. Then I pass out in bed when I finally get home. But it won't be long now." She sighed. "And— and there something else I need to talk to you about."

"Anything you can say over the phone. It's not bugged. I check it every day." A small joke, falling on deaf ears.

"No, it's something we have to do in person. Don't worry, I still love you madly. Just a little thing I'd be more comfortable discussing face to face."

"Okay, mystery woman." Warner paused. "Say, I just had a thought. Doesn't the girl wear glasses?"

"Girl? What girl?"

"The girl who was raped. I saw her file at your place. Doesn't she wear thick glasses? How'd they stay on after the rapist pulled her down behind the hedge?"

"Al, you're a genius. Her glasses make Coke bottles look thin. I'll recall her tomorrow and see if she can still ID anybody without them. If this works, we'll see each other sooner than I thought. I love you, you clever cop, you."

"I'm waitin' with bated breath. I love you, too, Sher. Lots and lots."

"You'd better. Talk to you soon, hon. 'Bye." The phone was dead in his hands, the receiver momentarily dangling idly from his fingers.

What was so special she couldn't talk about it on the phone? She could be so devious when she was playing games.

Well, he'd find out soon enough.

But some things never go as planned.

SEVENTY-EIGHT

"So, you're back," Carlsen said. "As are the dreams, I suspect."

"Yeah. Just as scary and exhaustin' as ever. Had about a week of relatively peaceful sleep, but that's done. What the fuck's wrong with me, Doc?"

"I told you we've just scratched the surface, Al. You're a good guy, with a strong, basic moral fiber, but you've also got some deep-seated problems. Some of those undoubtedly predate your run-in with Leordano, and are possibly from your childhood. They're only surfacing now because of these other pressures. The wound to your head may have exacerbated things." The big man shifted in his chair.

"There's no quick fix. It's going to take continued therapy, but you'll come out of this a happier person. I'm sure of it."

"It can only be an improvement, Doc."

"So, what's happened in the last ten days? Have the dreams changed at all?"

"It's mostly that scary three-headed dog, chasin' me up those spiral stone stairs. He seems closer now. I'm still runnin' in slow motion, but I'm nearin' the top, and his stinkin' breath is hot on my neck. I'm shittin' bricks over what's gonna happen when I run out of stairs. That thing's gonna get me then."

"Try to relax, Detective. Remember, it's only a dream, however frightening, and dreams are purely metaphorical. Whatever you've buried so deeply, something you're afraid of, is getting closer to the surface. It's my job to put a spade in your hand, so to speak, so you can finish digging it up." He leaned forward. "Once we get it out in the light and take a good look at it, I'm sure you won't find it so scary."

"That's it, huh? Just get it out in the open and it'll go away?"

"No, it won't go away. We're not magicians, Al. These things have probably been a part of you for a long time. But, if you can get them into the open, you can deal with them. Stop them from crippling you emotionally. That, my friend, is our task. So, you talk, I'll listen, and we'll see where that takes us."

Warner slumped back into the comfortable, big leather chair, squeezing out a soft groan. The flow of his thoughts trickled out slowly at first, then as before, gained steam, rushing forth in a verbal geyser, venting his sulfuric frustrations.

The hour sped by, with Carlsen injecting few comments during Warner's diatribe. Carlsen looked at his watch and called a halt as Warner's thoughts rumbled slowly to a stop.

"We're out of time, Al. I think this was a very good start. You've vented feelings that should provide clues about what's going on inside of there." Carlsen pointed to his patient's head.

"Boy, I'm bushed. This was more tirin' than runnin' from that fuckin' dog-creature. Did all my ramblin' do any good?" The detective pulled himself upright, trying to shake off a thick lethargy enfolding him. "It seems so disconnected to me."

"That's because you're still sitting too close to it. When we finally sort things out, it will be much clearer. You've unconsciously done a clever little dance around whatever's disturbing you. It's somehow connected with how you see yourself. We'll dig it out, and may use hypnotic regression later."

"Hypnotism?" He grimaced. "I don't know about that."

"Don't worry. It's not at all threatening. In fact, most patients feel very relaxed and peaceful when we're finished."

"Okay. You're the doc. When do you want to see me again?"

"How about Friday? I'd like to see you twice a week for the next few sessions, so we can make quicker progress."

Warner agreed, and left, more at peace than he had been for a long time. Maybe this thing was really going to help.

But even simple things rarely go as planned.

SEVENTY-NINE

The door of the Public Defender's office imploded, slamming back and forth on screechy hinges. Sharon Clark, hair tousled and blouse a bit askew, waltzed through the opening, singing merrily.

Shuffling to a stop, she dropped into an elaborate curtsy, generating giggles and stifled laughter from her captive audience. Humor was rare in a place where so much human misery was exposed and examined in such minute detail.

"I take it things went well in court today." Mark Barber, her boss, grinned, black eyebrows arched.

"Is an acquittal considered 'going well,' chief?"

"An acquittal? Wow, how'd you manage that, Counselor? I know you were convinced he was innocent, but the victim made a positive ID. She was unshakable."

"Yeah, well I put her back on the stand and got her to admit her glasses were knocked off when the assailant jumped her. Hers are like Coke bottle bottoms. So, I asked her to take them off and see if she could still pick out her attacker." Sharon smiled.

"She's always very deliberate, putting them in her glass case, then in her purse. Finally, she looks up and points to the defendant chair. 'That's him.' she says. 'That's the man what done me.'" Sharon's squeaky rendition of the victim evoked more giggles.

"I asked her to take her time and be sure there was no mistake. She squinted hard, then pointed again, saying that's him, she's absolutely sure."

"So, how'd that get you an acquittal, Sharon? She made the ID, even without her glasses."

"The hell she did. She pointed to his chair all right, but while she was fumbling with her glass case, he slid down under the table, and Billy Hartmann took his seat. I cleared it with the judge first. The prosecutor almost dropped a load right there in

231

his pants. Billy and the defendant look about as much alike as King Kong and a chimp. The acquittal took less than an hour."

"Great work, kid," Barber said. The whole office jumped up, offering a resounding round of applause. "How'd you think of that gimmick, so late in the game?"

"Actually, it was Al Warner. We were talking yesterday, and, almost like an afterthought, he tossed out the idea that she might not see too well without her specs. It was so simple, but only he thought of it. How can I help loving that guy."

Sharon retrieved the briefcase she'd dropped while making her dramatic entrance. Heading for her desk, she was urged along by several congratulatory pats on the back. She flopped in her chair, kicked off her shoes, and leaned back, interlacing her fingers and stretched her arms above her head. It was good to finally relax. She'd have to think of some special gift for Al as a reward for his help.

She just hoped he wouldn't be too upset when he learned of her forthcoming photo session with *Playboy*. But he always claimed to love her independent spirit.

She prayed that would be enough.

EIGHTY

Warner lazed in his chair, his hands clasped across his flat abs, thoughts far from the Angel of Death, so dubbed by Eddy Roush. Instead, he was retracing his two sessions with Doctor Carlsen.

He had been such a jerk to resist going. He was almost

giddy after spilling his guts to the doc. He'd malingered, almost terrified of finding out what's really lurking inside his thick skull—something secreted there he was evidently hiding from.

Wow! You're ready to be judge, jury and executioner. But guys like Leordano and this new nut, they should die. Save the State bucks, and the victims' families lingerin' grief. Gotta respect the law, but what if some slick shyster even gets him off? Diminished capacity, or whatever.

They had to get this guy and kill him. He'd kill him, if he got the chance, despite what Sven said. Just this once: judge, jury and executioner. Ending this might stop his nightmares, as well, and he'd finally be at peace again. He didn't know why, but he sensed his dreams would die with the Angel of Death.

"Boss." Warner's head jerked up as he climbed lethargically out of his reverie. Rafael Olvida was holding up his phone, waving in his direction.

"It's Watts, the detective from Lantana. Line three."

"Thanks, Ralph." Warner shook off the mantle of brooding and punched the winking button on his phone.

"What's up, Watts? Good news for a change?"

"Nothing significant. We found Bianco's jewelry, but it's no help. A room service guy found her growing cold when he collected their dirty dishes and helped himself to her baubles. Left her for the maid to find in the morning. He copped to the theft when we busted him trying to pawn the stuff."

"Didn't he see our perp when he delivered the food?"

"No such luck. Said the shower was running. Rosa signed, putting it on the tab."

"How about the desk clerk. Didn't he register?"

"He was too clever. Rosa signed the register and paid cash. The clerk never noticed any guy. Bitched that they got stiffed on the food charges."

"Yeah. I bet the only reason he let Sutton's boyfriend see

him was he planned on doin' them both. Figured Tazwell'd show after his phony meetin' didn't pan out, and he'd take him then. Something musta scared him off, but he got lucky when the guy flipped out. So far, our wayward angel's had all the breaks, but it's gotta be our turn soon."

"I hope so. I'll let you know if anything else comes up, but I'm not confident."

"Thanks, Julan. Talk to you later." Another fizzled lead. Like Leordano, they kept coming up empty.

He hadn't expected much from this one. Stealing jewelry didn't fit the MO. After all, he was a minion of God. Material things were of little value to him.

"Ha. Tell it to the fuckin' tele-evangelists," he muttered. "Those bastards took every penny my righteous, bible-thumpin' parents ever made."

Meantime, they had a clever killer to catch. And it wasn't getting any easier.

EIGHTY-ONE

"You're very relaxed. Nothing can harm you." Dr. Carlsen had required little more than five minutes to put Warner into a deep trance.

"You're descending steps, and have arrived in a very beautiful, peaceful garden. Do you see the colorful flowers: the blues, the reds, the violets?"

"Yes." His voice soft, unstrained.

234

"You're safe here. There's a bench in the shade of a gazebo."

"I see it."

"Good. Lie down. It's very comfortable."

"I'm there." His voice was mechanical, like some futuristic robot.

"Fine. Now we are going to take a little trip back in time. Just your Higher Self and me, as your guide. Your body will remain on this bench, resting peacefully, until we return. Your Higher Self is free now to lift *up* in a bubble of safety. Rising *up*; rising *up*; rising *up*. You can see your body, lying peacefully below."

"Yes."

"Now there is a tunnel of light, pulling you *back*; pulling you *back*, *back* to another time in this life. *Back* to your childhood; *back* to a time of trauma. Can you see yourself there?"

"Yes."

"Where are you? Do you recognize the location?"

"My backyard, in Antioch." It was the voice of a child.

"Antioch?"

"Antioch, Illinois. My father sells minnows and fishin' tackle to fishermen on the Chain-O-Lakes." Warner was drawing back into the depths of the chair as he spoke.

"How old are you now?"

"Eight."

"What are you doing in your yard?"

"Hidin' from my father. He wants to strop me." His head twitched back and forth, a small boy, scouting for danger.

"Strop you?" Carlsen was very alert now. Warner seemed quite agitated, cringing, almost disappearing into the cavernous folds of the big chair.

"He beats me with a razor strop 'cause I cut bible school again. I'm afraid."

"You have nothing to fear now. You won't experience that pain again. You can just watch it, like a movie." Warner began to relax again.

"Does your father beat you often?" He scribbled on his pad.

"Yes. I'm not religious like them. Calls me a sinner, and says God wants me punished."

"Are you a sinner? Look at your behavior and attitudes then, like a movie on fast forward on your VCR. Judging by your current adult values, are you a sinner, at that time, as a child?"

"No. I believe in God." He was still the eight-year-old boy as he spoke. "But not like them. I get good grades, and hardly ever get in trouble at school. Why does God want him to beat me?"

"It's okay. You're safe here. Let's move forward to some of your teenage years." Warner's knotted muscles eased, the planes of his face again placid.

"Are you there?"

"Yes. I'm sixteen. I won't go to church. I don't think religion should have so much fear in it. He's gettin' out his strop."

"What do you do now?"

"I'm bigger and stronger now. I take it away and knock him down. No more God's vengeance on me, or drunken beatin' of my Mom. Never again." His face morphed into hard, flat planes, his mouth a razor slit, eyes pinched closed, white-knuckled hands clutching the arms of the chair.

"Try to relax, Al. Nothing here will hurt you. What happened to your father after this?" The doctor looked at his watch, then his tape recorder. He hated to end a session producing so much therapeutic material, but their hour was nearly up. He wanted some time to talk to Warner at the conscious level.

"He seems terrified, a shell of himself, clinging to his 'Old-Time' religion."

"Okay, we have to come back to the present soon. Do you

see anything else important, before you leave that time?"

"Dad's crazier than ever. He buys a bullwhip, but I take it away from him, too, when he tries to beat Mom, and he runs off. It was finally his turn to be scared." He fidgets in the folds of the chair.

"I start hangin' with a gang of rowdy football players, gettin' into trouble, but then two men straighten me out. They . . .."

"Okay. We'll look at that next time. Now, it's time to return. We're going to travel *back* to the garden, *back* to the present *back* . . .."

EIGHTY-TWO

As Carlsen's count hit *five*, Warner opened his eyes, glancing around warily. Seeing he was still sitting safely in the big chair, he knuckled his eyes and stretched.

"That was weird. I'd forgotten most of that stuff. It happened so long ago. Was that important, what we did here today?"

"You tell me. Do you think those memories have a bearing on what's troubling you now?"

"Shit, I don't know. My crazy father chasin' me with that big razor strop? Boy, that thing really burned when he connected."

"He was sort of like an angry dog, huh?"

"Yeah, exactly, Doc. Like a pit bull."

"Like a demon? Maybe even three demons: him, his strop, and the God he said he was punishing you for. Almost like he had three heads?"

"Oh, shit, Sven. Sure. Like that fuckin' Cerberus. Boy, is that

237

suddenly obvious."

"And the heat of its breath is like the burning from that strop, when he hit you?"

"You bet. Boy, how come I never saw that before?"

"What do you think of your father now, Al?"

"He was twisted up, angry at those he saw as sinners. He had a warped image of God, like our Angel of Death, only not so deadly."

"And you started having those dreams about the time this new killer showed up, didn't you, Detective?"

"I suppose. But we just learned he was redeemin' gals he perceived as sinners in his own weird way."

"Consciously you didn't know. But you told me several times there was something you felt you were missing. Maybe subconsciously, you knew his mission all along. After all, you'd lived a milder version of holy retribution as a victim yourself, didn't you?"

"I guess so. It sure felt like Hell to me then."

"And could that be why you have the strange sense of affinity for this guy. He reminds you of your father."

"Holy shit, Doc. What a fucked-up world we live in."

"You're right there, Al." Carlsen had turned off his tape recorder and picked up a note pad and a pen.

"But I want to use these last few minutes to talk about this Angel de Dios. I'm working up my psychological profile for your captain to hopefully help you guys find this very sick puppy. I've got some interesting ideas that the BAU crew may not have considered, and I want to get your input."

"Sure. Any help you could give would be appreciated. So far, we got mostly 'zip'. What d'ya want to know?"

"What's your gut feeling about this guy? Your subconscious sense of who he is. Not a name, but *who* he is."

"Shit, Sven. That's your department, not mine."

"I know, but this is your third serial felon in five years. Who'd have a better feel of him than you, Al?" he edged forward in his chair.

"Yeah, well, there's nothin' I can really put a finger on. He seems to fit the most common profile: white, late thirties, give or take, quite charmin', and very intelligent. He's methodical and careful, and he's got an agenda. But that fits 85% of all serial killers." Warner interlocked and stretched his fingers.

"His victims suggest maybe he was abused by women as a kid, but I don't see it that way. There's something about how he goes after these gals, and even fucks 'em, waitin' until he comes before he sends them off to meet their maker." He shrugged.

"I get the feelin' he enjoys the work too much to be gettin' even for things a woman, or women, did to him as a child. No, something else got him goin'. I can sense it."

"That's very insightful, Detective. It's obvious why you have such a good record. I suspect your killer may have met his match for intelligence. It's only a matter of time. This bolsters what I'm working up. You've given me new food for thought, though." The therapist lumbered out of his chair.

"Glad to oblige, Doc." Warner also rose. "I only hope you think of something to help us snag this bastard before I gotta look into many more body bags."

They shook hands as the psychiatrist ushered the younger man from his office. The next patient, an overweight, balding, middle-aged man in a crumpled blue suit, sat, biting his nails.

Warner hardly glanced at him as he strode out into the hallway. He was pondering the results of the day's session with mixed feelings of both relief and anxiety.

He didn't know why.

EIGHTY-THREE

He quickly braked, slipping the blue Dodge in front of a raggedy yellow Mustang, ignoring an angrily blared horn at the insolent intrusion.

Fuck 'em. He needed at least two cars between him and the little red Miata convertible. Damned hard enough to see it in front of two larger cars.

White-knuckled hands squeezed the steering wheel, his eyes narrow slits against the glare of the western Sun.

"Going to a little party, are we, my pretty?" he muttered.

"Well, I'm watching you, whore. Only God can redeem you and your immoral lover, whoever he is. I'll happily do his bidding." He grunted, visualizing her throat in his hands instead of the faux-leather steering wheel. His grip tightened.

The little sports car darted into the parking lot of a small strip mall and adjoining office complex, one of many lining South Florida thoroughfares. He continued on and turned into the second entrance.

Damn. She was coming directly at him. He spun into a vacant space, the red car passing behind him, continuing toward the three-story office building. His nondescript stakeout car wasn't noticed. Not being seen was something he was very good at.

Glittering dark eyes, hooded by the peak of his cap, traced her hurried arrival to the building, waiting until she entered before he followed. It was a small complex, with only four offices per floor. He'd observe where the elevator stopped. If the directory didn't give her away, he'd make his way up, finding a safe place to await her return. Time to bring this shameless harlot and her lover to justice.

At the door he noticed his reflection in the tinted glass—

broad-shouldered and muscular. He smiled mirthlessly. An intimidating sight, except for the peaked cap. Somehow, a ballcap made you innocuous. Peering through the glass, he saw the elevator close. He pushed through the doors, watching the floor indicator skip past two, stopping at three. He scanned the directory and didn't have far to read before he saw the name.

It had to be him.

"You pompous, godless son-of-a-bitch. Fucking another man's wife and feeling pretty good about it, aren't you? Soon you'll both pay."

He quickly left the foyer, fire burning in his coal-dark eyes. They were sinning and needed to be taught a lesson.

He'd be their tutor.

He grinned, his lips a narrow slit across his face.

It was work he'd enjoyed doing.

EIGHTY-FOUR

"Public Defenders. This is Ms. Clark."

"Hi Sherry. How's it goin'?"

"Great timing, lover. I was just thinking about you. What time are you picking me up?"

"Sorry, babe," Warner said. "I gotta call it off tonight."

"Trouble?"

"Yeah. We got victims six and seven today. Hot lookin' twins in West Palm. Our Angel of Death was a busy guy. Did 'em both at the same time. I volunteered Moe Gold to assist the BAU and the local CSU to go over the scene. They're good guys, but our little Hawk's in a class by himself. Maybe three heads'll be better than one." He paused, his voice tense.

"Anyhow, I'm goin' up there this afternoon with our files. Cap'n Lawson from West Palm's runnin' the case himself. God knows when I'll be back. We'll get together later in the week, okay?"

"Whenever you say, darling. My evenings are all free, and I still have something to discuss with you. Call whenever you get back, I don't care how late. I know this nut's getting to you, and I want to be sure you're all right. Promise?"

"Yeah, sure. But don't worry. My work with Doc Carlson is startin' to pay off. Had nightmares last night, but they were the first in nearly a week. I'm doin' better now. Talk to you later, Babe."

"Fine. I love you, sweetheart. You know that, right?"

"Yeah. Love you back, more'n anything. Bye."

Warner leaned back, hands clasped behind his head.

Amazin' to be loved by a gal like . . . He shrugged and shook his head. There were more urgent things to consider.

Their deadly angel was really getting bold. Two at one time. He wondered . . .?"

"Hey, Harry. Break out those mags we took off Jarrett and see if you can find anything with the Entman twins. Start about two years ago and work back from there. They're probably there, and maybe we can learn something useful."

"Sure, Boss. It's dirty work, but someone's gotta do it." He chuckled. "I might need a note to the wife, though, if she wonders why I'm so horny tonight." The older man sauntered over to the large storage carton filled with back issues of *Playboy, Penthouse, Hustler*, and other men's magazines.

"Warner." Captain Santiago shouted from his office. Al rose.

"Yeah, Bob? What's up?"

"You got the report from West Palm on that double murder yet?"

"Yeah, it was our guy. I'll buzz up there this afternoon with

242

Moe. They'll run the DNA, but it's the same MO. Just a few little differences. What a pair of identical beauties. He's pickin' only the crème de la crème." He sat on the edge of the desk, flipping open his notebook.

"The girls modeled scanties for guys lookin' for a cheap thrill. Probably some touchy-feely for an extra tip. But they were surely hookin' on the side. The doorman at the joint where they worked saw 'em talkin' to a guy in a car about two AM. Green or blue Plymouth or Dodge."

"A year? A plate number?"

"Of course not. Anyway, he says one of the girls gave him a piece of paper, and they split. Lawson's team found a note with their address and phone number on it, stuffed up Heather's— well, you know. It was covered with sperm."

"Bastard. This guy's laughing at us."

"Yeah. We must look pretty funny to him, runnin' in circles. He even managed to fuck both girls. Looks like he handcuffed Hillary to a bed in the other room while he was doin' Heather." He ran fingers through his curly, dark hair. "Musta just thought it was kinky sex, and Heather probably died very quietly. Then he covered her like she was sleepin' and did Hillary in the same bed. She mighta got spooked and started to struggle, but these were little girls, and our guy is defiantly an ox."

"He leave the message?"

"Yeah, but not on the mirror. He laid them next to each other and wrote across their tits and stomachs. Real gristly."

"Sounds like he's getting bold enough to start making mistakes."

"I sure hope so, Cap. He's gettin' farther and farther into left field. Almost like he's lookin' to get caught. If we don't find him quick, this whole town'll be turned upside down again."

"You got all the assets on it we can spare. You coordinating with the BAU, Boca, and West Palm? Sending them everything we got on our three?"

"E-mailed what little new we had this morning. The rest's goin' by car this very minute. What really scares me is, I'm bettin' Forensics won't uncover more'n we already got, and that's zip. This guy may be loony, but he's smart. And very careful."

*　*　*　*

Warner was engrossed with his notes from the latest crime scene, when Harry Klein tapped him on the shoulder.

"Here it is, Boss. *Playboy*, December, 2016. Hot Heather and Hillary on a cold winter eve. It's every guy's fantasy to make it with this kind of double trouble."

"I guess it was available for a price, Harry. They did private room lingerie modelin' at some joint in West Palm. You'd think this kind of exposure in *Playboy* would get them something better, wouldn't ya?" He rose and circled his desk.

"I'm leavin' now to go up there. Make copies of the article and I'll take 'em with me, just on the chance something there might help their investigation."

"This is six and seven, Al. We aren't getting any closer, are we?" The older man frowned.

"I don't know, Harry. If we are, I sure can't see it. Maybe by doin' two, he got a little careless. I sure hope so, 'cause this is gettin' pretty damned depressin'."

Warner gathered his files as the other detective headed for the copy machine, *Playboy* in hand. Seven beautiful dead women, and very little to work with, spelled frustration.

His jaw muscles bunched with clenched teeth, and he shook his head. Something better happen quick, because there was no end in sight, and he hated the idea of more dead beauties. The scariest idea was, this guy might just stop killing, and his victims' families would get no satisfaction.

Not if he could help it.

EIGHTY-FIVE

Sven Carlsen heaved himself up from his chair and glared at the papers littered across his desk. He lumbered restlessly back and forth across his office. The psychiatrist did his best thinking when he paced, undistributed.

There were two separate dilemmas nagging him: Al Warner's deep-seated emotional blocks were still destroying the peaceful regeneration we require during sleep; and secondly, developing a really definitive profile—a persona—of this killer, this self-styled Angel of Death who had terrified three counties. Two more victims had succumbed the previous day, beautiful twin girls, bringing the death toll to seven in less than three months. That's unusual activity, for even the most aggressive serial killer.

But Warner was a perplexing case and the first thing on Carlsen's agenda. Sven regressed him for the third time that very morning, uncovering still further layers of the physical and emotional abuse suffered at the hands of his demonic father. And while this provided understanding and some sporadic relief from his traumatic dreams, it was not enough.

An impenetrable barrier still sealed off a corner of his mind. It obscured something so dire, so terrifying, that Carlsen was unable to wedge it open. Not even a small chink he might eventually widen, until they finally discovered whatever was secreted away in the dark confines of that mental vault.

Even his most creative efforts were blunted. He had come to know Warner well during his years working with Miami-Dade Homicide. Now, through these sessions, he knew him even better—an intelligent, complex and highly moral person who really cared about the people he served. Carlsen knew of no other cop within the department who shouldered as much integrity.

The manifestation of his neuroses reared up sometime during the Leordano case. The death of that madman, and the bullet wound Warner received to his head, seemed the dual events releasing these long-standing traumas. But there was something else, something very important—to Warner, at least—still locked tightly away in that walled-off nook of his mind. They must dig it out and expose it to the light of reason or he'd never achieve real peace of mind.

Then there was Angel de Dios, the Angel of God, who stalked the streets of South Florida, first seducing, then brutally killing some of the area's most beautiful young women. Clearly highly intelligent and charming, his lovely victims willingly accepted his sexual advances, even in these times of caution. Plenty of DNA evidence to identify him, if and when he was found, but nothing to help in the actual search to locate him. The police, even after seven murders, were clueless.

Carlsen had pulled several files from patients, past and current, with inclinations to abuse women. Two of them were area police officers whose wives he discreetly counseled. But this embodiment of Death's Angel was a bit different. He sought women who exposed their bodies for the pleasure of men, clearly a sin against God—at least in his warped mind. Like Al Warner, this killer had a moral code. He just chose a socially unacceptable and deadly manner of enforcing this credo. Something had driven him over the edge, into a deadly psychosis.

Now Carlsen was comparing his files with psychological profiles of similar serial killers. He felt instinctively he might know this man, even have treated him in the past for some unrelated problems. That seemed an unlikely coincidence, but the premonition lingered.

The psychiatrist was unhappy Captain Santiago told the press he, this locally famous expert, was working separately from the BAU to help find the killer. All Sven might provide was a better understanding of Dedios. It would be pure, unadulterated luck if he somehow identified the man.

Regardless, the article in the *Herald* made it sound like he was hot on the heels of the madman. The police needed to show progress in the investigation, but Carlsen would issue a statement tomorrow clarifying what he was doing. Still, the persona he was developing did seem somehow familiar.

Stopping his restless prowl, Carlsen returned to his desk where he began to collect and straighten his files. It was late, and he had already missed his usual dinner alone at one of his favorite restaurants—the lonely life of a bachelor. As he picked up the last of the folders, a nagging thought suddenly burst from where it had been hiding in shadows. His huge hand slammed nosily down on the desktop.

"My god! I've been so dense. Why hadn't I'd seen that?" Shaking his head, he scribbled notes to follow-up on in the morning.

He paused, looking up. A noise in the hallway? Someone trying his locked door? Yes. The knob wiggled, but before he could react, the door imploded with a sharp crack, the splintered jam casting shards of wood across the room. The shadowy figure of a powerfully built man stood framed in the opening.

"Who's there? What do you want?" Icy fingers trilled up his spine, bathing him in a cold sweat.

The apparition glided across the room, visible now in the light from the desk lamp. Carlsen's hand moved slightly, depressing a button on his Phone AnswerMate.

"You. What are you doing here? You have no appointment."

"I've come to punish you for your sins." The voice hoarse and cracked.

"Me? That's a laugh." Carlsen's voice quavered. "You—you're the sinner."

"You know your guilt. Pray God forgives you."

The dark man sprang across the desk, grabbing Carlsen by the shirt, yanking him to his feet. Despite his size, the psychiatrist was no match for the other's physical strength.

"No. Please, I don't know . . .." Powerful hands encircled the doctor's neck, thumbs burrowing into his trachea, cutting off his voice. The psychiatrist's hands clawed at the other's arms, but his strength quickly ebbed. A moment later, the attacker's powerful grasp cut off his life. The man cast the bulky corpse aside, sprawling face down across his desk.

"Maybe God can forgive you, I can't," he mumbled. Pivoting, he left, wiping off the doorknob on the way out.

All was quiet—deadly quiet—except for the soft whir of the telephone answering machine, continuing to record the silence.

EIGHTY-SIX

Sharon lifted the large manila envelope, an icy shiver slithering down her spine. Was this eagerness, or trepidation?

The *Playboy Publications* return address predicted its contents: a prepublication issue of the magazine with her as one of eight young female lawyers posing for the feature.

Heart fluttering and hands clammy, suddenly numbed

fingers fumbled with the little copper clasp. Flipping the flap open, she upended the packet, dumping its contents on her desk. Out came the expected magazine and a letter.

Why was she so nervous? There were seven other attorneys for around the state. The *Playboy* staff were all very professional—perfect gentlemen. She'd readied an arsenal of barbed comments to fend off any sexual by-play, but they were unnecessary. It was a fun, invigorating day in the surf and sun.

It was Al's potential reaction that worried her. Would he understand? Accept her right to rebel against constraints to a woman's freedom to do as she wished? She *had* to tell him before he saw this issue on his own. She'd already delayed too long.

She flipped over the magazine, which had landed face down on her desk. As her eyes swept the cover, she flushed, gasping for breath. Her knees buckled, her vision blurring as tingling little feet skipped across her scalp.

Her face, in a collage with two other women, each in almost-revealing poses, smiled at her from the cover, hazel eyes twinkling merrily.

Holy cow! The cover. The whole world will see her.

Calm down. She'd made a choice, and it was too late for cold feet. Cover or not, the whole world was *still* going to see it. She'd better tell Al tonight for sure. Damn. Why hadn't she talk to him first, even before agreeing to pose? Would he ever understand?

So, what would she have done, asked his *permission*?

Never. She was an independent woman and had no need to ask any *man* what she should do. Still, she loved him, and he had a right to know. And what if she *had* told him in advance? He would have tried to stop her, that's what. Just more motivation to do it, regardless of how he felt.

Terrific. A knee-jerk rebellion, not very considerate for the guy you love. Occasionally, her zeal for independence clouded her better judgment. Actually, *more* than occasionally.

Gotta realize I don't live in a vacuum. Shit.

She collapsed onto her worn leather chair. Picking up the thick magazine, she thumbed through, searching for her photo.

There. Geez. The final page all to myself.

Damn, she looked hot, didn't she? Only one other gal got a whole page. Shit, who knew they were going to show *everything*? Well, what did she expect? She got what she bargained for, and there's no turning back now.

Al was certainly going to be upset—even angry. Was she subconsciously trying to give him a reason to dump her?

Stupid, stupid, stupid.

He was the best thing ever coming into her life. A guy who really cared for *her*, not some illusion of looks and position. Her ego, and a nagging urgency to prove independence, may have screwed up this relationship. She needed his love.

She sighed, scanning the letter that arrived with the magazine. Jerking upright, eyes wide and breath coming quickly again, she reread the second paragraph.

Wow! They want me for a centerfold.

Playboy must think she was pretty hot stuff. How many thirty-three-year-olds had they ever featured? Probably none.

She slumped back in her chair as a wind-tossed sea of mixed emotions crashed through her. Eyes closed, limp from her turmoil, she vowed to talk to Al. Tonight, for sure.

EIGHTY–SEVEN

"Right. We're on the way. Just keep the place clear of onlookers and the press 'til we get there, will ya?" Jack Harris hung up the phone and looked at his ex-partner. Warner was at his desk, reading the file on the Entman Twins.

"Boss." Harris averted his eyes. This was trouble.

"Yeah, Jack? What's up?"

"We got another murder. It might or might not be related to our Angel of Death."

"Another model."

"No." Harris paused, and sighed. "You ain't gonna like it."

"Spit it out, Jack. Can't be any worse than what we got so far."

"Oh, yeah it can. It's Sven Carlsen."

"Carlsen? He's at the scene?"

"In a manner of speaking. *He's* the vic. Strangled last night in his office."

"What?" He lurched to his feet. "Carlsen dead? The same MO as our guy, Jack?"

"That's for us to find out, I guess. There are only a couple of uniforms there. We'd better get going."

"Let's move." Warner dropped the file on his already crowded desk. "I'm not gettin' anywhere with this thing, anyway.

"Fuck. Sven Carlsen. What's next?" The two detectives left the squad room in a rush.

*   *   *   *

Warner and Harris burst from the elevator on the third floor. A cop stood at the doctor's door to fend off a gaggle of civilians, including three reporters, Eddy Roush among them. He tried to waylay Warner, but Al waved him off, shaking his head. "Later," he mouthed. The detectives pushed through the crowd and into the office. Another uniformed cop hovered near the reception desk. He looked up and gestured toward the other door.

"He's in there. Nobody's touched anything."

"Then how did you know he was strangled?" Warner asked, eyebrows raised.

"Oh, you could see the marks on the back of his neck plain enough. I guess there coulda been something else, but he was sure strangled plenty hard enough to kill him, I'd guess."

"Okay. Keep the gawkers out," Harris pitched in, "and don't touch nothing out here. You never know where the killer might have been."

The young cop threw an offhanded salute as Harris followed his partner, who had already entered the inner office. Jack found him sitting in a huge leather chair, head in his hands, shaking slightly. Was Warner actually crying?

"This one hit you kinda hard, huh, pard?"

"Yeah, I guess. This whole fuckin' case is gettin' to me, Jack. Sven was such a gentle soul. He was a big help to me, and I'm gonna miss him."

Harris moved to the desk and looked at the dead psychiatrist.

"Not much of a struggle, was there?"

"Doesn't look like it." Warner heaved up, a brief shudder racking his head and shoulders. It was time to go to work.

"Judgin' from the trauma on the back of doc's neck, the perp was very strong. Sven was big, but probably not very powerful." He scanned the desk. "Nothin' else seems out of place. Looks like the perp killed him and just left. Lots of papers scattered around, like he was reviewin' some files. Have to wait for Moe and CSU. When they move the body, we can see what's there." He massaged the back of his neck. "Why would Dedios want to kill Carlsen?"

"Beats me." Harris was studying the desk intently.

"Think it had anything to do with the announcement Carlsen was helpin' on the Angel of Death case?" Warner asked. "The captain made it sound like he might even identify him, instead of just workin' on a profile."

"You think he was killed to shut him up, Al?"

"It's possible." He looked at Harris who was crouching next to the body, head cocked to one side. "What're you looking at there, Jack?"

"There's some notes on that pad under his arm. Can you read it?"

"Yeah, most of it. Let's see. 'I've been so blind.' Something, something '. . . seen this before. I've got to recheck his file. It's all there, right under my nose'." Warner looked up.

"Maybe he found more than he bargained for. I wish to Hell Moe and the Feds would get here. Sven may have left us the clues we need to finally catch this lunatic."

"Yeah. Hey, look." Harris nudged Warner's arm. "His answering machine is blinking for a *Personal Memo*."

Warner produced a small pocketknife and slid the blade under the cover of the tape cassette compartment, flipping it open without touching anything that might contain fingerprints.

"Look, the cassette's fully expended. I bet that sly old fox taped his conversation with his killer. Where the fuck is Moe?"

A small commotion erupted in the outer office. Warner's wish had been answered. The Hawk and the Crime Scene Unit had arrived, along with Agents Dalwin and Ashkin.

An hour passed before the Medical Examiner had finished with the body and Moe Gold had gone over the desk for forensic evidence. Finally, Warner and Harris were given unobstructed access to the victim's inner office.

Jack photographed Carlsen's last message from the pad on his desk, while Warner rewound the tape in the answering machine, eagerly awaiting what they hoped would be the voice of the killer. After a few seconds, the playback began.

"You. What are you doing here?" It was Carlsen, sounding annoyed, but not yet afraid. "You don't have an appointment."

It was someone he knew. Now a new, hoarse voice, cracked with tension.

"I've come to punish you for your sins." Warner's skin prickled. The motive of Angel de Dios. Though strained, the voice sounded familiar.

"Me? That's a laugh. You—you're the sinner." Fear now laced Sven's voice.

"You know your guilt. Pray God forgives you." There was a clatter, followed by gasping and grunting and Carlsen's final pleading before he died, rather quietly.

"Maybe God can forgive you, but not me," The killer muttered, and then silence.

"It's him, Al. It's the Angel of Death. Could be he thought the doc was getting close to identifying him, so he offed him, too."

"Makes sense, Jack. Except, how does that make Carlsen a sinner? It was definitely someone Sven knew. That voice really sounds familiar to me, too. Let's see what else he's got on his desk. There're files all over the place."

"There's a stack of five right here. Hey, yours is here, too."

"Yeah, I saw him that morning. Still fightin' bad dreams. See, this guy had the appointment right after me. I think Sven reviewed patient's files each evening before he put 'em away."

Warner turned back to the desk, picking up an open file. It had been pinned under the body. A glancing at the label sent a chill coursing down his spine, raising goose bumps and the hairs on the back of his neck. He *knew* that voice was familiar.

This was doctor/patient-privileged information, so they'd need a subpoena to gain access to it. Still, Warner scanned the first page, and one statement glared back at him: "HISTORY OF ABUSING WOMEN." He quickly replaced the file on the desk.

"Jack. Call the captain and ask to get a subpoena to examine these files. But I already know the perp on this one."

Agent Dalwin picked up the file, noting the name. Eyebrows arched he glanced at Warner.

"Wow, so fast? Is he the one killing these girls?" Jack asked.

"Don't know. Maybe, maybe not. Meanwhile, ask the Captain to call Boca PD."

"You asking for Fanucci's help on this?"

"He's already helped too much," The agent said. "Warner believes Fanucci killed Carlsen, Jack."

"What?"

"Yeah," Warner said. "I recognized his voice on that tape, but didn't place it 'til I saw his wife's file open on Sven's desk. He could be the Angel of Death, too. He's got a history for it, it seems. But it's almost certain he did Carlsen. Go make the call while I poke around some more here."

"Jesus H. Christ. Vinny Fanucci. What's this world coming to? I'll get right on it, Boss." The little detective returned to the outer office, already dialing his cell phone.

Things might finally be coming together.

EIGHTY–EIGHT

Captain Santiago hung up his phone and walked to the door of his office, looking for Warner.

"Al, they're bringing Fanucci up for interrogation. Who's working him with you?"

"Agent Whitehead and Jack Harris'll start, but in the end, I think it'll be me he'll talk to. Good of Boca to give us first crack at him."

"Yeah. Well, he killed Carlsen in Miami. Go on. He should

be there by now." He plucked Warner's sleeve as he rose, catching his eyes.

"What d'ya think, Al? He the Angel of Death? Kinda sad if it is, but it sure would make my day."

"I don't know, Bob." He shrugged. "He sure don't strike me as the type, but these psychos can be very deceivin'. He's got a thing for abusin' women. His wife was seein' Carlsen because of that. We'll see what we can find out."

"Look, Vinny, we know you did it. The doc turned on his recorder when you came in the office." Fanucci sat in a straight-backed chair, manacled to a plain, 4 x 6 metal table bolted to the floor. The windowless room sported the usual large one-way mirror, with an observation room behind.

Harris leaned across the table. "They're running a voice match. You know how reliable that is. Why don't you just make it easy on everybody, and fess up."

Fanucci sat silently, glaring at the detective. His eyes softened when he turned to Warner. Al was a kindred spirit. He'd understand. Warner knew that look. Special Agent Whitehead had departed and was probably in the viewing room.

Al gesture to the cop, lurking by the door. "Uncuff him."

"Regs say . . .."

Warner cut him off.

"I don't give a shit. Uncuff him. He's a cop."

The officer hesitated, then complied.

Warner turned to his prisoner, whose hands were now free.

"Tell us what happened, Vin. They're hopin' to pin the deaths of these seven girls on you, too. What you said to Carlsen is pretty damnin'. Same as the motive of our so-called Angel of Death. Why'd ya do it?"

"Shit, Al," Fanucci glowered. His eyes were red-rimmed, his face shadowed with a day's black stubble, his lips quivering with—what? Fear? Guilt? Anger? Warner couldn't tell. The Boca Raton cop sagged, shuddered, then glanced at Warner.

"You don't really think I did all those girls, d'ya? Why the fuck would I do a thing like that? I love women. I wanna fuck 'em, not hurt 'em."

"Their killer fucked them, Vince," Harris said. "They were probably feelin' very much loved—'til he snuffed them."

"It wasn't me. I'd never seen any of them before they died."

Harris sneered, barking a harsh laugh.

"What about Rosa Bianco," he asked. "You didn't know her, either, huh?"

"Yeah, well that was different. She was a hot little cunt with a terrific set of jugs. And one Hell of a fuck. She was just doing me so I wouldn't harass her or run her out of business."

"You telling me that street smart little cunt didn't know a Boca cop couldn't touch her in Lantana? C'mon, Vince."

"We're gettin' off the subject," Warner interjected. "We wanna hear about Carlsen. We know you did it, Vinny. The question is, why?"

Fanucci glared at him, then sighed. There was no way to duck this. Too much damning evidence. Slumping back in his chair, he moaned softly, massaging his temples.

"He was boffing Anna. A big oaf like him. I couldn't let him get away with that."

"Carlsen and Anna? Are you nuts?"

"She was having an affair. She met the guy twice a week. I followed her to his office last week. She was there for a good hour. Probably boffing her right on his couch."

"Oh, Vinny, you idiot. She was his *patient*, not his lover. He counsels wives of cops who're mistreated by their husbands. You really fucked up, Fanucci."

"She was having an affair, Al. I know she was. I could tell."

"Why? Because she wasn't lovey-dovey anymore? You

257

knock 'em around enough, and they tend to lose those tender feelin's. She was seein' Carlsen to try to learn how to deal with you. She wanted to save your marriage. You killed the man tryin' to help you and Anna stay together." Warner eased back, crossing his arms.

"She wasn't having an affair?" His voice quavered. His whole body seemed to collapse inward. This large, strong cop seemed suddenly very small and frail.

"No, Vince," Warner sighed, tired and let down. No Angel of Death here today. "She was just his patient. Now, are you gonna tell us what happened last night?"

Fanucci groaned and shrugged, his face creased with resignation. Warner handed him a cup of hot, acrid coffee.

"Yeah. But I didn't do those seven girls. I swear it."

"Okay, we'll talk about that later. Now tell me about Carlsen. I want it all, Vince. All the details. You been read Miranda?"

Fanucci nodded.

Jack Harris pushed a tape recorder out on the desk as Fanucci started his confession. It took just over ninety minutes. Al Warner sat back, listening with half an ear.

There was no way this poor, dumb bastard was the Angel of Death. He said the wrong things that night, but it was just a coincidence. They'd investigate it, and maybe they'd even charge him. But the DNA wouldn't match or there'd be another girl killed, and they'd be right back in the thick of it, with that lunatic laughing in their face.

Warner sat quietly while Harris handled the details of the interrogation. Glancing at the mirror, he shrugged and shook his head, figuring Whitehead was on his way to tell Agent Dalwin they still had work to do.

Warner sighed, anticipating tonight's quiet dinner with Sherry. He could use some TLC when this day was done.

He hated finding a cop who had gone wrong.
He hated that more than anything.

EIGHTY-NINE

Sharon saw it was Al Warner through her recently installed doorbell camera, just as she expected. It was his voice over the intercom, but she was super-cautious, with that lunatic still out there.

Sucking in a breath, her heart galloping to her own rendition of William Tell, she said a silent prayer, then opened the door.

Warner stepped in, sweeping her in his arms, nuzzling the hollow of her neck, working his way seductively up to her ear. She sighed, stroking the back of his head, as electric little explosions set her body trembling. God, she loved this surprisingly tender and complex man. Hopefully his love would transcend his expected disapproval of her posing for *Playboy*.

She struggled with her ambivalence. Again, she silently chastised herself. What a *stupid* thing to do, knowing how he would feel. Was she challenging his commitment—or just trying to destroy it? Love was relying on your partner, joining him, not independent of him. Why was that always so difficult for her?

She'd learned, through therapy while in college, she was nothing like her mother, who let her husband dictate her every move. It seemed she still needed to keep proving this to herself.

They kissed hungrily, her heart hammering fiercely, her legs wobbly and disjointed.

"I've missed you," he whispered, as he molding her to him, his hand luxuriating in her hair.

"After a shitty day like this, comin' to you is so—so . . .."

"Oh, Al." Her voice husky, she pressed against him, her legs still rubbery. He drew his head back, eyes searching hers.

"God, Sherry, are we ever goin' to make this permanent? I love you so much."

"Do you mean living together," she was breathless, "or was that a sly offer of marriage?"

She struggled for air, trembling, uncertain if she were thrilled—or terrified—at either option.

"I never really expected you'd consider marryin' me, Sherry." His voice a husky whisper. "I'd ask in a minute, if I thought you'd say yes." His lips nipped softly at her earlobe.

"I wasn't sure you'd even consider livin' together."

"Why? I'm hopelessly in love with you. How can you doubt that?" She grinned, realizing the preponderance of her emotional evidence leaned toward thrilled, rather than terrified.

"People in love do marry, you know." She struggled free from his tender grasp, her balance still shaky, and steadied her breathing, his hands in hers.

"This is stuff we shouldn't discuss in the heat of passion. I'll grill a pair of juicy steaks, and there's a lovely Chilean wine. We can talk about our future later, once we're more relaxed." Her sweet smile belied the tango beat of her heart.

He nodded, grinning. "Great. I'm starvin', and I sure need to unwind. Let's eat."

Warner mopped up the last of the gravy with his second buttermilk roll. He leaned back, hands clasped happily over a full stomach, and sighed.

"Boy, that was a terrific steak. I haven't had a good Porterhouse in ages. And that corn was so sweet."

"Fresh from the Farmer's Market. With all our careful eating, I thought this'd be a nice treat. It's fun to cheat once in a while."

"Geez, I'd almost think you were tryin' to soften me up for something."

Caught, red-handed.

"Wait for dessert. Then you'll really be under my spell."

"Already there, babe. Let's relax, and let all this good food settle a bit. I gotta use the john, then maybe we can have a little something sweet, *before* dessert."

He winked, lips twisted into a lopsided grin, as he headed for her bedroom, with its adjoining bathroom. Sharon began pacing, starting and stopping in fitful bursts.

Why didn't she tell him? Can't keep putting it off. Gotta do it tonight. Damn, how terrible if he finds out on his own. She'd do it after making love, when he's mellow. Yes. After making love.

The moisture of expectation dampened her panties.

NINETY

Warner sighed as he zipped up his pants. How had he gotten so lucky to be loved by such a terrific gal? Would she really marry him? Might even consider early retirement then. Hard to make a real relationship being a cop

Leaving the bathroom, his gazed swept her bedroom. They'd be back here soon. He loved how she decorated it, warm and feminine. He noticed a small pile of books and magazines on her nightstand.

She was an eclectic reader, with widely varied tastes.

261

Curious as to what interested her now, he picked up the thick magazine on top, flipping it over. His brow knit, recognition wedging itself into his momentarily bewildered brain.

His eyes widened, his face flushing, blast furnace hot. Sucking in a slow, shuddering breath, everything suddenly plunging out of focus. Acrid bile swamped his throat as he stumbled from the room, colliding noisily with the doorframe.

Sharon spun around. Something was wrong. His face was twisted in obvious torture. "What is it, darling? Are you okay?"

"What the hell's this, Sherry?" his voice a venomous hiss. The magazine landed at her feet. She blanched, shivering, suddenly chilled, as if an Arctic wind roared through her.

"Al. Oh, Al. Please. I can explain."

"Explain what? That I fell for a tawdry slut?" Snatching up the magazine, he fanned the pages, finding her photo in the eight-page feature. Warner groaned, a sharp knife of agony ripping through his heart. His stomach churned, gorge again rising in his throat.

"You—you did this and didn't even ask my opinion. They paid you, right? You're a—a whore."

Sharon stumbled back, collapsing on the sofa, cringing. *Oh, god, what to do*? What to say? How *stupid*. She ruined it. Ruined everything through arrogant, willful pride. Her wild hazel eyes beseeched him, rivulets cascading down her cheeks.

"Please, Al." A little girl's voice, pleading for forgiveness. "Please, darling. It was a mistake—a big mistake. I wanted to tell you. I was going to tell you tonight."

"Yeah, when? After softenin' me up with a steak and some hot sex? You'll be the laughin' stock of Miami. *I'll* get it big-time at the department. Stupid Al Warner, in love with an elegant cunt who likes to show it off. My mistake. I thought you were different."

"Oh Al, don't say that. Please don't be spiteful. I love you."

"Spite you? I don't wanna hurt you, Sherry. I *can't* hurt you. You've done that yourself. You didn't need anybody's help with *that*." He snatched up his sport coat.

"I gotta get out of here before I'm sick to my stomach. Don't call me. And don't expect to hear from me. Damn, was I stupid, thinkin' we were something *special*."

"Oh, Al. Al. We're still the same two people. I love you. I need you, darling. I'm sorrier than you can imagine. Please don't go."

"If we *are* the same people, then I guess I didn't really know you. I can't take this. This, . . ." he flourished the magazine in her face, ". . . is not what I'm lookin' for in *my* woman —*my* wife." He gritted his teeth, shaking his head, like a dog, just out of the lake.

"The woman I love would *never* demean herself like this. Now, you may have marked yourself for death. This is exactly the kind of woman our Angel is seekin' out. He may be a homicidal maniac, but I sure do understand some of his moral ethics."

"Oh, Al. Don't. I was foolish and pride-full, but not immoral."

"Yeah? Well, he doesn't know that. Be careful, Sherry, now that I'm gone. And make no mistake, I *am* gone. There's no one to keep you safe except your own good judgment. This may disgust me, but I certainly don't wanna see you dead." He turned toward the exit.

"Maybe, with some time, I'll get over this, but don't count on it. The one thing I absolutely need from my woman is the one thing you didn't give me, Sherry. Trust."

He stormed off, slamming the door behind him. Sharon collapsed on the sofa, her body torn by racking sobs. Bands of pain crushed her chest, wringing out a torrent of tears. She gasped for breath.

"Oh, Al," her wretched cry ripped away by the wind of despair.

"Al. I love you. I love you."

Silence.

"I love you," she whimpered softly.

But there was no one left to listen to her hollow lament.

NINETY-ONE

"Warner. My office."

"Yeah, Captain. What's up." He stood in the doorway.

"Close the door and sit down."

The detective slumped wearily in the armchair across from his boss, legs stretched out in front of him.

"You look like shit, Al."

"Thanks, Bob. It's always special to start off the day with a compliment."

"Well, it's the truth. Is it Sharon?"

"Why Sharon?" Warner groaned softly. "Oh, I suppose you've seen the magazine. It's been on the stands for all of one day."

"Yeah, I saw it. I can't imagine what possessed her to do that." He sat back and studied Warner's face, creased by lines and craters from exhaustion.

"Me either. She *is* an independent soul." He sighed. "Just went way overboard to prove that. Mostly to herself, I think. Gotta admit," he mused, a tiny grin ticking at his lips, "she looked pretty terrific. Most beautiful gal in the whole spread."

He shrugged and worked his fingertips over his temples, exploring the hidden furrow, throbbing with an agonizing heat.

"Yeah," Santiago responded. "Really terrific. But why are you so down in the mouth? You ending something as good as the two of you over one indiscretion, Al?"

"One indiscretion? That's putting it a little mildly, Bob. And it's more about trust than bad judgment. Yeah, it's over. For now, anyhow. Maybe time'll heal the wounds—for both of us." He looked up, his eyes hooded. "I said some pretty nasty things.

"I suppose everybody's seen the magazine, huh?"

"Yeah, pretty much. But you won't hear about it here. They got too much respect for you, and no one wants to end up in the hospital because of a careless remark. It's a cross you gotta bear yourself, but give it some serious thought before you bury this for good. Sharon Clark's a terrific girl, and everyone's entitled to make a mistake. Real love is about forgiveness, Al."

"I know. I've been thinkin' about that. It's something I gotta work out. How come all the concern? You the new psychologist, now Carlsen's dead?"

"I got an ulterior motive, besides a real concern for my chief of detective's mental health." Santiago stood and began pacing.

"The DA's charging Fanucci with the Angel of Death murders."

"He didn't do 'em, Bob. Even the BAU team doesn't think so." Warner voice was listless, without energy.

"I know you feel that way, but there's some pretty damning evidence. They're pushing for a quick DNA match."

"It's all very circumstantial," Warner said. "They'll know they got the wrong guy when that bastard kills another beauty."

"I agree, but the DA's feeling the heat to produce a suspect, and they think they've got enough to nail Fanucci. Meanwhile, they'll try him for the Carlsen murder. Vinny's up to his neck in hock, so it's going to the Public Defenders. They're already making noises for Diminished Capacity."

Warner stared at his captain, and his stomach balled into a

painful knot. He sucked in a deep breath, lips pressed into an almost invisible slit, fighting to relax.

"You guessed it, Al," Santiago said, nodding. "It's gonna be Sharon Clark. It's your case, Warner, but I'll turn it over to Jack Harris, if you want."

"No, I'll handle it. There ain't much she's gonna want from me, anyhow. The evidence is pretty straightforward. Don't worry about me, Boss."

"But I do worry about you, Detective. If you're not in top form, my investigations suffer. Are you getting any rest, Al? You look all rung out."

"It's the same fuckin' dreams, Captain. I was doing pretty good while I was seeing Doc Carlsen, but with his murder, and now this thing with Sharon, well, they're back in force. I guess I should find another shrink and get him Sven's files on me."

"Dr. Eva Guttenberg's taking over his cases for the Department. She's top drawer."

"Thing is, I knew Sven, and was comfortable with him. Spillin' my guts to anybody else—a stranger—would be tough. It ain't easy."

"Yeah. Well, give her a try. At least you'll enjoy the view."

"Huh?"

"She's a beauty, in a dark, sultry way. Meantime, Ms. Clark wants what you got on Fanucci. Might be a little less stressful if you take it to her office."

"Okay, but d'ya mind makin' the appointment. I'll go, but I ain't ready to talk to her on the phone just yet. And give me Doc Guttenberg's phone number."

"Sure. For now, I haven't officially closed the Angel of Death investigation, since my chief of detectives has some doubts. Stay on that for a while, and see what you come up with. I'd sure like it to be somebody other than a cop."

Warner wearily nodded. "DNA'll settle that in a hurry."

As he left the office, all eyes were averted, an eerie silence replacing the usual ruckus in the squad room.

NINETY-TWO

Warner stuck his head through the door of the conference room.

"Got a minute, Ed?"

"Sure, Detective," Agent Dalwin said. "What's up?"

"Thanks. It's the Fanucci thing."

"Yeah. That's got to be pretty upsetting. A local cop, and someone you know pretty well. What about him."

"He surely did Doc Carlsen, but I don't make him for our Angel of Death.

"Me either. None of the team does. Your lab's rushing the DNA, and when there's no match, that should take care of that."

"Right. The DA's pushin' for an indictment. It's gonna make all of us look stupid when the DNA falls through, or if the loony takes another gal. We still gotta catch our wayward angel."

"I agree. So, we're still here to help, but I don't know what we can add to the investigation, unless something new pops up. Agent Pauletti is making daily stops at the psych ward to see if our one witness shows any signs of coming around."

"Well, that's a relief. Just wanted to be sure you guys weren't buggin' out. We need as many heads on this as we can muster."

"Don't worry. We're not going anywhere until the real Unsub is nabbed. The Fanucci thing's a temporary distraction."

"Thanks. Just checkin' we're still in sync. I'm gonna be tied up, off and on, on the Fanucci case and Doc Carlsen's murder."

"No worries, Al. We'll stick until we get this psycho."

"Swell. I'll check with you later. I got an appointment now with the PD who's defendin' Vinny."

"Right." They shook hands. "We'll keep you in the loop."

Filled with trepidation over what was coming next, Warner headed for his office to retrieve Fanucci's file.

NINETY-THREE

"Detective Warner, to see Ms. Clark."

"Yeah, she's waiting for you in Conference Room B. Don't worry, she's got all her clothes on."

The young and very foolish attorney's smirk quickly turned to panic as a powerful hand snatched a handful of shirt and hauled him physically out of his seat. He hung limply, legs unable to support him, as he stared into the two dark laser beams of Warner's eyes. With a look of disgust, Warner threw him back into his chair where he cringed in utter terror, until Warner turned and headed for the conference rooms.

Sharon saw the interchange through the large plate glass window. That poor green kid just learned a lesson in discretion. At least Al cared enough to protect her dubious honor. Could there still a chance for them? Better play it very cool. No pressure.

Warner knocked and entered at her summons. He handed her Fanucci's file, then moved to the end of the conference desk and flopped onto a chair, studiously examining his fingernails.

Sharon spread the contents of the file in front of her and started making notes. She would photocopy whatever she needed when she finished. Warner covertly watching her work as his heart pounded, the roar of his blood in his ears.

He still loved her. In spite of what she'd done, he still loved her. She was a wonderful, caring person who made a stupid mistake. Was he man enough to forgive her, though? His parents never would have, but he didn't want to be anything like them. Maybe, in time. Just maybe . . ..

She looked up and her smile flooded the room with light. His heart thundered, crashing against the rocky shore of his ribcage.

"Thanks for this, Al. He was very distraught, wasn't he?"

"Vinny? Yeah, distraught. You lookin' for me to support his Diminished Capacity plea, Sharon?"

"It would help, if you really believed it."

"I think he was crazy with paranoid jealousy, but that's no excuse for murder. He was sane enough to wipe the place down before he left. Call me to testify, and that's what I'll say."

"Good. That'll help. As far as the other murders, I don't think he did them."

"Neither do I."

"What? But you've indicted him."

"Not me. The DA. I told 'em they've got the wrong guy. So have the Feds, but he needs a patsy to take off the heat. Captain Santiago hasn't closed the investigations, and I'm assumin' Angel de Dios is still out there. The DNA won't watch, and another dead beauty'll turn up. Then the fat will be back in the fire." He watched her with obvious concern.

"You just be sure you're not his next victim, Counselor. I may be angry and feelin' betrayed, but I sure don't wanna see you dead. I'm tryin' to get over this—this thing, but it ain't easy." He looked away, his jaw muscled bunched in hard ridges. "It's as if you lied to me, not trustin' me enough to tell me the truth."

"I know, Al. I feel so rotten. I let you down. I let us *both* down. I wish I could take it all back, but I can't. I just hope you learn to forgive me. I'm waiting for that day, however long." Tiny rivulet spilled silently across the swell of her cheeks. She looked very frail and beautiful, and he wanted to take her into his arms, but he couldn't bring himself to make a move.

"Aw, cut it out, Sherry. You know cryin' melts me down. It's dirty warfare."

A small smile edged across her lips as the deluge from her eyes ended.

"All's fair in love and war, Al. You know that."

He laughed. Somehow, the exchange released a mountain of tension. Maybe things would work out, after all.

"If you're done with those files, I gotta get back to work. I still got a serial-killer to catch."

Sharon smile widened through the remnants of her tears. She felt lighter, the crushing weight of guilt that smothered her since that dreadful evening began to evaporate. Her heart swelled and pumped freely, without painful restraints of remorse, for the first time in days. She, too, felt they were on the road to making amends. She longed to hold him again.

"Give me a few minutes to photocopy these things." Her hazel eyes glistened with the last of her tears. "I'm glad we've had this chance to talk, Al. I feel much better. Like, well, maybe we'll be able to work things out now. I do love you, you know."

"Yeah. This went easier than I expected. I think I still love you, too, but I ain't sure we can ever get back together again. Not that way. I need more time. We both do. Meantime, I'll be happy to be your friend, if that's okay."

"Better than okay. It's a good first step. I promise to be patient, and we'll be spending some time together on this case. You'll keep me apprised if you get any new development?"

"You'll know anything as soon as I do. I promise."

"Thanks, Al," she laughed. "I'm glad you're still on the case. Vinny's got a better chance with you there."

She stood, and they shook hands, self-consciously.

Ten minutes later, Warner exited the building, whistling softly, happy for the first time in days. Maybe they *could* patch things up.

He had his first appointment with Dr. Guttenberg that afternoon, then was going to hit the sack early, hopeful he'd get some real rest for a change.

NINETY-FOUR

Sharon found a parking spot on the well-lit street, close to the secure front door of her building. She didn't relish walking from that poorly lit lot, late at night. Hobbling under the burden of two large briefcases, she pensively scanned the shadows.

Warner's scary warning that her exposure in *Playboy* made her a target for the Angel of Death was not far from her mind on this inky, moonless nights. Dropping one case, she fumbled with the lobby door lock before releasing it and scooting inside. The door closed automatically behind her, bringing a sigh of relief. She wearily lugged the cases toward the elevators.

He watched from the dirty green Dodge, parked in a tree-shadowed spot, a hundred feet from her door. Intense, dark eyes followed her until she disappeared.

Angel de Dios looked at his watch, the luminous hand indicating 12:50 AM. It *was* her: the beautiful, hazel-eyed lawyer, naked in this month's *Playboy*.

A sinful, wicked woman.

A Jezebel. A temptress.

She must be punished for her sins. The Lord called for her. It was he, the one they called Death's Angel, who would redeem her. Not tonight, but soon. Only time, and the detective, Al Warner, stood in his way. He feared neither, because he knew he was master of them both.

He would deliver Sharon Clark, shameless sinner, to his Lord.

Soon. Very soon.

NINETY-FIVE

Warner stared into space, tired, and what was worse, listless. Normal boundless energy levels were dissipated by exhaustion, fired by the dreams, worse than ever. His first visit with the lovely Dr. Guttenberg had done nothing to dissipate them.

Last night he struggled, like sloshing through waist-deep water, up those stone stairs, and ran out of room. The lichen-covered walls of the tower were so wet they seemed to bleed.

A dank, sour odor overpowered his senses. The great, stinking beast lurked close behind—closer than ever before, its hot breath singing the hairs on the back of his neck.

He stumbled into a small round room at the top, one high window illuminated by a full moon and star-spangled night sky.

Trapped. He turned as the three-headed beast lunged, fangs flashing in the moonlight. Ducking and weaving, he slipped in, hands snatching two of the throats, but the weight of the monster drove him down. Desperate, he heaved the creature back on its haunches, seeing its faces for the first time. Wild, red eyes glowed eerily in the slivery light.

Shit. His father's craze-distorted face hovered on his left, and Leordano, razor-sharp fangs dripping blood, snarled at him on the right. The center face was shadowed and indistinct. Only iridescent, coal-black eyes shown as that featureless head bore closer—closer, its slavering maw opening, immense jagged canines glinting, reaching for this throat. He couldn't hold it back. It took him in its mouth . . ..

He lurched awake in sweaty panic, shouting, arms flailing. He scoured the shadows, but there was no creature. Only he, lying on the floor, the tangled sheets wrapped tightly around his neck. He struggled up, face in his hands, crying softly.

NINETY-SIX

Warner prowled restlessly around his office, the dream still clearly etched in his mind. The third head must be the Angel of Death. He was getting closer to him. Somehow, his intuition, acted out in the dream, told him it was finally going to come down to a deadly contest between them, just as it had with Leordano.

If Doc Carlsen were still alive, he could explain why Al joined his father with the Baby Butcher and Angel de Dios in this dream. Because they were all lunatics? He had made progress in excising his father's demons with Sven's help, before that paranoid fool, Fanucci, killed the psychiatrist.

The trauma of this new dream left him more exhausted than if he had not slept at all. It was like starting all over again with Doctor Guttenberg. He was actually looking forward to his next visit.

Warner's thoughts slowly surfaced in the present, summoned by the insistent buzzing of his phone. He stared blankly at it for a moment before realizing his private line was demanding his attention. He sighed, lifting the receiver.

"Warner," his voice dull and flat, without enthusiasm.

"Al, I'm so glad you're there," Sharon said. "I almost hung up."

A trickle of electric energy charged him, dragging him from his miasma of lethargy. How he'd longed for her, in spite of his anger.

"Ah, Sherry. Glad you called. I've been thinkin' about you—us."

"Oh, I'm so glad. I've missed you. I cry myself to sleep every night. It was so stupid to pose for those shots. A selfish thing to do without talking to you first."

"Yeah. An important part of love is considerin' your partner, wantin' them to be happy. I always felt best when I did that for you."

"You succeeded plenty, darling." Her voice was soft.

"It's good to hear that. How'r things goin', with no nosy cop around, gettin' in your way?" Talking with her was a catharsis.

"Well, that's one reason I called."

"What's the problem?" He swiveled back and forth in his chair.

"I'm a little scared. I think I was followed last night. I came home late, and I sensed somebody was stalking me." He jerked upright, coming off the edge of the chair, very alert.

"Could you make out the car, Sherry. Color, model, anything?"

"It was green. A Plymouth or a Dodge. I remember seeing it parked in front of my building two nights ago, when I was working late. Do you think it could be—him?"

"Don't know, but it's certainly possible. You put yourself into his category of potential victims. Bein' on the cover may make it worse. I still don't know what you were thinkin', especially knowin' how this lunatic was pickin' his victims."

There was a soft, stifled sob from her.

"Shit, I'm sorry. That was a low blow. I guess I'm still a little bitter over how I found out. I'm tryin' to get over it. I certainly don't want anything bad happenin' to the most wonderful woman I've ever known."

A soft sigh drifted across the fiber optic line.

"Thanks, Al. I can't tell you how good it is, hearing that. You think you could come over this evening? I'd feel safer."

"Yeah, I'll come but it'll be late. Get home early, and don't let anyone in unless you know 'em very well. I mean anyone. Okay?"

"Yes sir, I promise. Maybe—maybe you can stay the night? I keep hoping we can be like we were before. I love you so much."

"I guess I still love you, too, despite everything. Maybe I *will* stay. I haven't had any rest since—well, you know. I always sleep best when I'm with you. You were certainly good for my peace of mind. And the dreams have been really bad lately. I came face to face with the three-headed dog last night. I'll tell you about it later."

"Oh, Al, I'm so happy you're coming. I'll make a light supper."

"Swell. I—I just realized how excited I am about seein' you. Remember, no one gets in unless you're sure you know them well. This guy could be anyone."

"I'll be careful. Nobody but you tonight."

"Good. See you later."

Warner hung up, dropping into his chair and closed his eyes. It was time to make up. How did a woman like that come to love someone like him? He loved her more than life itself. He just had to get some of the starch out of his stiff neck, and make amends.

She had apologized and apologized. It was more than

enough.

He'd go home early and take a little nap. The investigation was going nowhere, and he wanted to be awake and sharp tonight, if there were going to be any trouble at her place.

NINETY-SEVEN

He left the shelter of the building's vestibule, striding up the street, oblivious to the light rain. Gray, water-laden clouds lumbered across the sky, obscuring the moon and stars, shrouding him in a black velvet darkness. He paused beside a battered, green Dodge coupe, scanning the street, intense obsidian eyes boring into the night.

No one else was out and about, and that pleased Angel de Dios.

He smiled. Tonight, he will take another sinner for the Lord—that slut attorney, brazenly displaying her exquisite body for all to see. His breath quickened and a shameless stirring between his legs foretold his intense lust for her. She would be his that very evening, willing or not, for the Lord called.

Entering the car, he drove off, eagerly anticipating the coming encounter.

Sharon peered down from her window. The wet blacktop pavement shimmered and glistened under street lights, a million rainbow-hued starlets, sparkling brightly. Cars hurried below, casting aside plumes of spray. She didn't see Warner's, but he usually parked on the next street.

Was that a green car? A Dodge? She'd caught a bare glimpse

from the corner of her eye. Whatever it was, it hadn't slowed. She pivoted away from the glass and resumed pacing her living room. Where the heck was Al?

He was late. Smiling ruefully, she remembered he was frequently late, but that made her no less nervous. Afraid was more accurate. But Al was coming, and he would protect her. Life had to go on.

She returned to her kitchen and checked the chicken and pasta casserole in the oven. The pungent odor of garlic and oregano assailing her. Almost ready.

She jumped, startled at the doorbell's ring, and the oven door slipped from her grasp, banging closed with a loud thump.

"Finally." She scurried to the intercom, sucking on a slightly singed finger, and depressed the "Talk" switch.

"Who's there?" Her voice a tense squawk.

"It's me." It *was* Al. The poor guy sounded exhausted. A flood of compassion overshadowed her tension. He needed *her* as much as she needed him. She toggled the buzzer, and a few moments later, he knocked at the door.

She checked the doorbell cam, still cautious, and verified it was indeed Warner, dressed strangely in a black crew neck and sweatpants. She opened the door and quickly closing it behind him, throwing the deadbolt. No one lurked in the hall, but she wasn't taking any chances. Sharon turned, finding her lover smiling bleakly, his face haggard and drawn. Wordlessly, he opened his arms to her.

"Oh, Al." She rushed into his grasp, clinging fiercely to him, heedless of his rain-dampened clothes. "I've missed you so."

Tension sluiced away, leaving her dangling weakly in his grasp. Raising her face, they kissed, tenderly first, but then with rising passion. Sweeping her up, cradled securely in strong arms, he started for the bedroom.

"The dinner," she whispered. "It'll burn."

"Let it. *I'll* burn, if I don't make love to you right now."

Sighing softly, she snuggled closer, arms draped around his neck. He stumbled through the doorway and slithered onto the bed, but in spite their raging need, he loitered over her careful arousal.

Kisses, in concert with a moist tongue, ventured over her eyes, her ears, her mouth, the hollow of her neck. Somewhere along the way, their clothing disappeared.

His lips and fingers lingered over her thighs, her belly, her breasts, her buttocks, teasing and inciting her with promises made, playfully broken, then skillfully remade. Sharon soared on a cloud of euphoric passion, intensified by their recent separation.

In the full throes of her passion, she rolled him on his back, straddled him and took him inside her with one slow thrust. She began to undulate, rising and falling, rising and falling, rotating her hips from side to side, driving both toward ecstasy.

She was an erotic goddess, bringing rapture to her one love—and to herself.

NINETY-EIGHT

Their orgasms detonated almost as one, sweeping her away to some ethereal nether world, floating weightlessly on a cloud of sensual bliss. Slowly she descended from that exotic plan e, drawn back by the hoarse rasp of his voice.

How strange. He rarely talked so soon after making love. Her mind still fogged by the intensity of her passion, she barely made out the words, but the voice sounded like—someone else.

Suddenly their startling impact began to register.

"You've sinned, Sharon, whorishly displaying your body for the pleasure of others. You must seek redemption at the side of God."

His hands moved up from their erotic attention to her breasts, softly stealing across her shoulders, to a final gentle caress of her neck.

"The Lord Calls," he whispered, his voice brittle, as his hands circled her long, elegant neck, his thumbs pressing against her throat.

"Al, stop! You're hurting me!" she screamed, snatching futilely at his wrists.

What was he doing? She was strangely aware of wetness running down her thigh. Was it his sperm, or had she peed from fright? Nothing to worry about if you were about to die. Her strength was ebbing as she pried weakly at his fingers.

"Warner is gone." His dark eyes impaled her with a manic intensity. "I am Angel de Dios, bringing Gods judgment to sinners."

"No." Her pain-fogged mind barely grasped the enormity of his words.

Al, the Angel of Death?

"No. You can't be. You *are* Al Warner." She squawked as he cut off her air. Her hands clutching at his.

"A good man," her voice a hoarse whisper. "Not a killer."

She neared unconsciousness when the pressure on her neck eased. His face, so close to hers, was a distorted mask, filled with both anger, and now, uncertainty. Sharon coughed, her throat on fire as she sucked up air in short, ragged gasps.

This is wrong. It must be a nightmare.

"No." His voice a harsh caricature of the Warner she knew.

"I am God's instrument, sent by Warner's father to bring redemption to sinners. Leordano's bullet set me free. You are a harlot, and must be redeemed."

His grasp began to tighten again, but it lacked the swift

279

resolve, so quickly extinguishing seven other young beauties. This *was* Sharon Clark, someone Al Warner, imprisoned behind those two black lasers, loved desperately.

"No. Please." She struggled ineffectively. "You *are* Al Warner, the man who loves me. The man who pledged to destroy the Angel of Death." She stared into the bottomless depths of his eyes, two obsidian orbs, sensing a flicker of uncertainty.

Fighting for consciousness, for her very life, she cast one final, frantic stone as the steely bands cinched ever more tightly around her tortured throat, her words a breathless gasp.

"He's here now, Al—the Angel of Death. Destroy him. Chase him from your mind. Don't let him hurt me. Make him go away. Please, make him go away."

She hovered at the edge of consciousness, when the deadly bands paused, then eased. Suddenly she was free, falling, crumpled like a rag doll, sprawling across the bed. The man— was it Warner or the killer—stared at her, then his hands, his mouth working soundlessly.

"Please. Please don't hurt me," she whimpered and curled into a fetal ball.

"Sharon?" The voice, filled with surprise, softened, once again her lover's.

"Sharon, what's happening? How did I get here?" His head pivoted erratically, scouring the room, his eyes flared.

"Al, don't you know?" Her voice was strained, barely a choked whisper. Every word was a searing burn, but she had to make him understand.

"Know? Know what? I took a nap to be fresh, and . . .."

"You're—you're him, Al. You become The Angel of Death. Some kind of split personality. You almost killed me." Her hands fluttered at her throat, purpled now with darkening bruises.

"Me? That deadly lunatic? Are ya crazy? It can't be *me*." His eyes darted furtively, searching the dark corners of the bedroom. There were no answers there.

"I'm—I'm trying to catch the bastard. You got it wrong, Sharon. It can't be me."

"He told me. *You* told me. After we made love, you started strangling me, and you said something about carrying out your father's will to redeem sinners." She wiggled into a seated position at the edge of the bed. "I was so scared."

"No. Not me. I was always at home asleep when he killed these girls." He stared blankly at his hands, turning them back and forth, as if uncertain they were his.

"Maybe that's it, Al." Strength seeped back, as her mind began clearing.

"Angel de Dios must come out when you're asleep. That's why you were always so tired. You weren't *really* sleeping. *He* was in charge, doing his dirty work on those seven poor girls."

"Can't be. I'd know, wouldn't I? How could I hide that from myself?" "

"Maybe." She struggled to stay erect, trying to swallow. She coughed, her throat in flames, but she had to make him see the truth. Get him the help he so desperately needs.

"You said Carlsen told you that you've walled off a nook in your subconscious he couldn't penetrate. Something so terrible that you refused to face it. That must be where you kept Angel de Dios locked away."

"Impossible. How could I hurt you, Sherry? I love you more than anything—more than life. I was coming tonight to patch things up, not *kill* you."

She leaned against him, her hand massaging her brutalized neck, her voice a raspy whisper.

"Look how you were dressed," gesturing at the dark heap beside the bed. "Not the Al Warner I know. But it's not your fault. *He* was in control, not you."

She touched his cheek. "You need help, now that we know the truth. Professional help."

NINETY-NINE

Warner lurched to his feet, gingerly gathering the items so recently discarded in their race to get at each other. He stared blankly at the black crew neck sweater and sweatpants. Shaking his head, he probed the pants pockets, withdrawing a set of car keys. He held them before confused eyes, blinking rapidly?

Sharon sat numbly, arms wrapped around her shins, head resting on her knees, gulping up air in short, painful gasps. They were Chrysler keys. The Entman twins' killer was seen driving a green Dodge. A similar car had stalked her. She sensed the cogs of his mind spinning, building a good case of circumstantial evidence against himself.

He looked at her, his eyes filled with agony, seeing the raw, red welts on her long, graceful neck. He pressed his palms to his temples and groaned. She knew then it was going to be okay. Al Warner was back to stay.

The room filled with his soft moan, growing to an anguished wail, his fists pounding against his head.

"This ain't possible. There's gotta be another explanation."

She wriggled her way to the edge of the bed, still weak and unsteady. Her throat was closing up, making it more and more difficult to talk, but she couldn't quit now. Her hand gingerly caressed her traumatized neck, as she tried to bring reason to a place where none could exist. Here, reason was utterly unreasonable.

"Partly my fault." Her voice was barely audible. "Shouldn't have posed for *Playboy* without telling you. A shameful, headstrong thing to do."

She watched him battling inner demons, his body twitching convulsively. Her eyes flooded with compassion for this tortured man.

He suddenly became very still, then raised his head, regarding her with a strange coolness. Moving quickly, he settled beside her, drawing her into his arms. She sighed, snuggling against his shoulder as he stroked her back and neck.

"It'll be okay now." She held him tightly, protectively. "We'll get you help. We can beat this."

Cupping her face in his hands, he leaned back slightly, smiling coldly, his voice soft but harshly strained. It was no longer Al Warner's.

"Warner's gone, whore, sleeping again while I do God's bidding. I've delayed too long. I must send you to the Lord for redemption before he returns." Hands that had been tenderly resting on her shoulders pressed her back on the bed, again beginning their deadly mission.

Sharon strength was nearly gone. She flailed around, beating weakly at his hands, face, and chest, with what little energy she could muster. The Angel of Death was back, and he would kill her, unless she could get Al Warner to stop him. Thrashing, she screeched a painful plea.

"Stop! You *are* Al Warner. You love me. Don't let him kill me. Stop him, Al. S*top him.*" Her flailing hands knocked something from the night stand onto the bed–a digital alarm clock.

Her vision dimming, unable to blurt out even one more plea for help, her finger circled the clock. On the verge of oblivion, panic fueling a burst of adrenalin, she slammed plastic case against the side of his head, just where the bullet wound had unleashed this monster.

Warner—or Angel de Dios—grunted, lurching back, slipping off the edge of the bed. Sharon coughed, sucking a searing breath through the blast furnace that was her throat, and forced her swollen eyes open. Squinting, she saw the top of his head (was it *him*, or was it Warner?) awkwardly canted back against the side of her mattress. She scrambled for the other side of the bed, but her arms and legs wouldn't support her. She flopped face down onto the soft quilt, managing to slip over the edge, sprawling onto the floor.

Wheezing with labored breaths, unable to make it to her hands and knees, she snake-crawled across the floor, her naked breasts friction burned from the carpet. She had to make it to the living room and the other phone. The one on the nightstand sat too close to her attacker to chance it. Once there, whom would she call? 911?

Did she want this tortured soul arrested for things he didn't even remember doing? Well, maybe better than dying in the clutch of those powerful hands.

No. He needs help, not prison. She arrived at the doorway, regaining enough energy to lurch to her hands and knees.

"Jack Harris," she muttered. *I'll call him. He'll' know what to . . ..*

"What about him?" The voice was cold, emotionless, as strong arms and warm hand encircled her waist.

"That pipsqueak can't help you now, whore," Angel de Dios said. "You're in the hands of God's servant and you *will* be redeemed—made pure again at his side."

"No, Al, no." She thrashed, trying to squirm from his grasp, arms and legs flailing with renewed energy.

"Struggling will avail you nothing, whore," he grunted, hoisting her under one arm like a bundle of rags.

"You're a shameless devil, displaying your naked beauty for all to see—to plant seeds of evil lust. Warner was trapped by it. Even I almost succumbed. You *must* be redeemed." Hauling into the bedroom, he dumped her again on the bed.

Straddling her body, he loomed above her, pinioning her flapping arms. His bottomless dark eyes, devoid of emotion, consumed her.

"Al, I know you're in there," she squawked. "Don't let him do this to me. Fight him, Al. Fight him."

"Warner's asleep, my beauty." Strong hands slipped over her arms, across her smooth shoulder, resting again on her already bruised neck.

"And now, the Lord calls for your wicked soul." He tightened his fingers, then hesitated, and she saw something flicker in his eyes.

"No." Her voice a strained screech. "No. Come back, Al. It's Sharon. Don't kill me, Al. Don't—kill—me."

ONE HUNDRED

She wiggled and squirmed, trying to pull free. Warner *was* there. She just had to drag him out from behind those cold, dark eyes. Kicking violently, her right knee caught him squarely in the groin.

Angel de Dios woofed, eyes glazing, as he rocked back on his haunches, his hands now resting on her shoulders. His lips twisted, spitting out an angry snarl. His eyes flared, surprise morphed across his face, and he shook his head in short, sharp snaps.

"No! Stay down, you spineless wimp." He growled like an angry dog, body quivering. Glaring at her, he snarled, "I've got God's . . .." He paused and blinked, his jaw sagging open.

Slowly, tension seeped from his body, his hands relaxing, falling to his side.

It was Al Warner sitting across her groin, wild-eyed, his mouth gapping.

"Sharon?" he stammered. "What's happenin'? I—I don't remember . . .."

"You—you were him again." She struggled up on her elbows, barely able to whisper. "You fought your way back, somehow. He's gonna—kill me. Gotta stop him. Keep him away." She swallowed painfully, but she had no saliva left.

"Said you—sleeping while he—killing me. Don't—let him—hurt me." It was the plaintive whimper of a little girl.

The man looked in awe at his hands, then again at the growing bruises on her throat.

His face crumpled, a look of contempt and loathing blossoming, and she was terrified. She knew the expression well. It was there the day he found her photo in *Playboy*.

"Asleep? He said I was sleepin'?" He shook his head furiously, jumping to his feet. She sagged to one side, unable to sit up on her own.

"The dreams." He paced fitfully, hunched over, angrily opening and closing his hands—the hands so recently stifling her life.

"Was it *me* I'm runnin' from in my dreams? *I'm* the vicious creature I've been huntin'? The fuckin' Angel of Death?"

He hung his head, staring blankly at his powerful fingers, curled now, like claws. Shaking violently, he pressed his palms tightly against his temple, as if trying to squeeze out the agony. Tears filled his eyes.

"And I said I did this for that crazy bastard father of mine?

The maniacal religious nut I despised."

"How can *I* be the fuckin' three-headed monster, killin' off all those girls? I'm a cop. A good cop. An *honest* cop. He's the bastard I vowed to stop—to kill—just like Leordano." He paused his meandering and looked at her, eyes flooded

"What've I been doin'? Chasin' *me?*"

"You didn't know." She battled through her pain. "You were dreadfully abused as a child. What many killers are made from, but you fought it off. Somehow, Leordano's bullet released that hidden anger. But you can fight it, now that we know."

"Oh, Sherry." Eyes glittering with moisture, his whole body sagged. "What good will it do? I'm a fuckin' murderer. Seven beautiful young girls. It's not my parents. It's me that's responsible. *Me.*"

"But you're *not. He* did everything, not you. No one will blame *you.*"

He paused his restless pacing, his face a frightening, contorted mask.

"Yeah? What about the families of those kids? Will a heartfelt apology for my 'other self' make 'em feel any better?

"Dammit, Sherry! Whether it was *him* or me, these are still the hands that strangled 'em. And all for a man I hated?"

He squeezed his eyes shut and shuddered. Then he looked at her, his eyes dark pools, filled with pain, a plea for forgiveness—and something else.

It scared her. Not for herself, but for him.

"No. They'll never forgive me. Doesn't matter what some shrink'll say. And I'd never forgive myself. In the end, we're responsible for ourselves, no matter what the excuse."

"But, darling . . .." She had made it back to the edge of the bed, sitting wobbly, feet dangling to the floor.

"No *but's*, Sharon. What'll they do, lock me away in an institution? Are there any guarantees *He* won't reappear to kill again? I gotta stop him now, or he'll kill you the first chance he gets. I can sense him inside my head, fightin' to get out. Tryin' to get at you one more time."

She flinched, drawing back, a chill racing down her spine, her arms crossed in front of her breasts. She had to stay calm. Reason with him.

Seeing her recoil, Warner barked a harsh laugh. He snatched something off her dresser, and stalked from the room.

"Al." Sharon staggered off the bed, legs barely holding her.

"Al, it's not your fault." She had to explain to him. Make him understand. But what if that deadly minion of God returned? Sharon clenched her jaw. She *had* to try.

"You can get help, now that we know," she called. Too weak to stand by herself, she summoned some hidden reserve, snatching the bedpost for support before tottering across the six feet to her door to catch the jamb. He was in the other room, talking to himself.

"You're a fuckin' murder, Warner." His voice a gravely snarl. "The ultimate sinner. Ready to kill the woman you love more than anything in life. All for God." He shook his head.

"*Stupid*. Gotta rid the world of the murderin' bastard, once and for all."

"Al, what're you doing? Not your fault." Her ravaged throat burned with the effort.

"Too late for me," his voice calm. "I'm beyond forgiveness. Got no right to live. I said I'd kill this Angel of Death, and now's my chance. I got him in my sights, and he doesn't know it."

What was he saying? *He's* Angel de Dios. If Warner kills him, he'll . . . .."

"Stop! What are you . . .?" Realization ignited a surge of adrenaline, kick-starting her wavering muscles. She lurched through the doorway, catching her balance on the sofa.

He stood naked in the middle of the room, his 9mm pistol

in his hand, dangling at his side. Tears filled his eyes as he watched her battling for balance, resolutely working her way toward him, one piece of furniture at a time.

"Always remember, I loved you—more'n life itself." He raised the gun to his temple and closed his eyes.

Sharon scrambled shakily across the room, urging trembling legs, shouting despite her traumatized throat.

"No. Don't."

"The Lord calls," his voice toneless and devoid of emotion. She launched herself at him, her wail of despair drown out by the muffled roar of a single gunshot.

They collapsed together, her arms around him, spinning to the floor. She had spent every reserve she could muster. There was nothing left. She lay atop him, limbs tangled, her face misty with tears. Wiping her cheek, she was surprised at its stickiness.

Fingers, streaked with red, appeared in front of her eyes. *Blood.*

The smell of gun powder—and the casserole burning in the oven—permeated the air, as Sharon Clark fainted.

ONE HUNDRED ONE

Jack Harris skidded to a stop in front of the apartment's door, suddenly unsure of what was expected of him.

Sharon's call was filled with panic and nearly incoherent. Something was up with Warner, but Jack loathed inserting himself into a lover's quarrel—and those two had plenty to fight about after her *Playboy* fiasco. Between her strangely raspy voice and continued blubbering, he couldn't decipher if Warner was troubled, causing trouble, or *in* trouble.

He rang the bell, identified himself, and was buzzed in. Sighing, he ran fingers through his rumpled mop, gritted his teeth, and knocked. Ten seconds later there was a dull thump, and the door slowly swung open. Sharon appeared, her face crumpled with bleary bloodshot eyes, her hair a snarled nest. She hung onto the door for apparent support. A black, man's sweatshirt draped her like a sack.

Jack's eyes popped, his lips twisting when he saw the raw bruises on her slender neck, and what looked to be a large bloodstain on the shirt. Wordlessly, she snatched his forearm and dragged him inside, slumping against the door as it closed.

"Sharon. What the Hell . . .?"

She blurted out a prolonged groan, tears cascading across her cheeks.

"Jack. Oh, Jack. I—it's—Al. It's Al . . . .."

"Al? What about . . .? Where *is* Al? That blood. Is it . . .?"

She snatched his wrist, tugging him after her as she stumbled toward the living room.

"Al's. It's Al's. Shot. Hurry."

"Al? Al's shot again? What the fuck . . .?"

He jerked to a stop at the sight of Warner, sprawled naked across the carpet, blood pooling around his head.

Pulling free from her feeble grasp, he raced to his best friend's side, dropping to his knees, feeling for a pulse.

"He's alive." Rolling Warner over, Jack snatched a cloth from the coffee table, pressing it against the still seeping head wound.

"What the fuck happened, Sharon?" He glared at the woman, who had flopped to the floor, sagging against an armchair for support.

"Angel of Death," her voice slurred, a hoarse whisper.

"Angel de Dios?" Harris shot a glance at Warner's Beretta, lying by his side.

"He was here? Shot Al in a gunfight?" Harris scanned the room, but they were alone. No sign of another body.

Sharon nodded, then shook her head and shrugged.

"It's—complicated." Seeing he'd pulled out his cell phone, dialing 911, she stretched out, gripping his hand.

"Don't. Not yet. We gotta—talk first." Strength ebbed back into her voice. Her jaw was clenched, her lips a narrow slit.

"We'll talk while we wait for the medics. He's lost some blood."

"No. Gotta *talk* first. Get things straight." Her eyes pleaded with his.

"Straight? Straight about what?" Harris eased back on his haunches, eyes darting between this battered woman and his friend, motionless on the floor.

"The Angel of Death," she whispered.

"What about him? And where is that bastard? Al's gun's been fired. Didn't he hit that lunatic?"

"Yeah—in a sense." She took his hands, squeezing with what little strength she had left. Tears again crept from her eyes as she nodded toward Warner.

"There he is."

"Yeah, I see Al. Where's Dedios?'

"Oh, Jack. Jack." The water gates were in full flood, spilling down her cheeks.

"It's Al. *He's* Dedios. *He* killed all those women."

"What? Are you nuts? He's been obsessed over catching the bastard. It's been givin' him nightmares."

"No, Jack. He did it like sleepwalking. The dreams—that's when he was out as Dedios."

"Sharon, you're delusional." He snatched her forearms. "How did you concoct such bullshit?"

"He told me. *Bragged* about it, when he was in that murderer's head."

"Warner? Warner told you?"

"Uh-huh. But not when he was Al. When he turned into that monster—and tried to kill me." Her fingers trailed lightly over the darkening bruises on her elegant neck.

"What? How the hell . . .?"

"Dedios said it was the head wound. Leordano's bullet. Somehow, that trauma set free some bad stuff put there by Al's crazy father, years ago. Al didn't know."

"Al became Dedios?" Harris' eyes were wild, his jaw hanging open.

Sharon struggled onto her haunches, adjusting the sweatshirt, and nodded, glancing at her fallen lover. She shrugged, and groaned softly.

"When I got him back—separated him from that deadly beast, I made him realize he was—the assassin he was chasing. That's when he—he decided to finish what he'd set out to do."

"Finish? Finish what?" Harris' eyes swept back and forth between the woman and his friend.

"Kill the Angel of Death," she whimpered. "Somehow, I got to him in time to spoil his aim a little. Did I save him?"

"What! He tried to kill himself?"

Sharon nodded weakly.

Harris peeked under the cloth, examining the furrow cut by the 9mm slug. The bloody wound was beginning to clot.

"Yeah, I think he'll live. Looks like he bounced another bullet off his thick skull, just about the same place Leordano did. Just hope it didn't scramble his brains this time."

Sharon sighed and sat back, her eyes riveting the little man.

"That's what I'm hoping for, Jack. Maybe just a little scrambling."

"What d'ya mean? Are ya nuts?"

"Well, a bullet wound brought out the Angel of Death. Could another, in the same spot, have sent him packing again? Maybe Al killed Dedios after all."

Harris rubbed his chin, glancing back and forth between his fallen friend and the woman huddled next to him, her arms wrapped around her shins.

"Okay. I see where you're going with this. I don't know what we can do for him, though. Ya got something in mind?"

She straightened her shoulders, knuckling her bloodshot eyes. "It's going to sound crazy, but here's what I thought . . .."

ONE HUNDRED TWO

COP KILLS ANGEL OF DEATH
THE HERO OF MIAMI IS BADLY WOUNDED WHILE RIDDING SOUTH FLORIDA OF SECOND SERIAL KILLER THIS YEAR

Eddy Roush suspected he didn't have all the facts. The body of Angel de Dios was mysteriously destroyed. Al Warner took a bullet off the head, his second in a year, in almost the same spot as the first. Once again, this hardheaded cop's skull was badly cracked, but there was no terminal injury to the brain. He remained in a coma in "guarded" condition.

There was something very suspicious about the whole thing, but Eddy had a fantastic story. The best cop he ever knew had ended the reign of terror of this lunatic while nearly losing his own life for a second time, protecting the woman he loved. Might even be a Pulitzer in it.

According to Captain Santiago, Angel de Dios was destroyed as Warner fought with him in Sharon Clark's apartment, where the killer was wounded. In the brief gun battle that followed after Warner chased him down to his car, the killer's Dodge erupted in flames with him in it, then exploded. It was during this melee Warner was wounded.

Eddy had seen several car fires on his beat, but only one other so disintegrated as that pile of twisted scrap. Virtually nothing was left of the vehicle, and its occupant was immolated. What remained was a pile of ash and a few bone-shaped pieces of charcoal that would never give up even a trace of DNA.

Roush once saw a car blaze, reputedly started by an electrical short and fed by highly flammable upholstery and plastics. It was so entirely consumed, nothing was left inside but heat-twisted seat springs.

This one was worse, as if there were extra accelerants, but cars have tanks full of gas, and that's often enough. If something phony were going on, he didn't want to know about it.

Especially if it had to do with Al Warner.

If in his zeal to be sure Angel de Dios was gone for good, he got a little carried away, so be it. Warner was a good guy and a brave cop who gambled his life to free the Gold Coast of another lunatic. That's all anyone needed to know.

Captain Bob Santiago said the Angel of Death died in that fire, so Roush decided to take what he had. It was plenty good enough to make him famous, and maybe even rich, if the book he intended to write was the success the publisher promised. Still, he wondered what *really* happened that evening.

Sharon Clark's wobbly lurch across the room was barely in time to snatch Warner's arm, deflecting his aim enough to save his life.

She convinced Jack Harris, who served as an explosive

expert with the Army Rangers, to take a wild chance on his best friend.

They found the green Dodge parked up the street. Using two gallons of gasoline siphoned from the old car's tank, Harris rigged it to burn and blow.

Some quick and fancy footwork at the morgue—only two miles away—and a friendly medical examiner conveniently on "coffee break," provided the body. A homeless guy known on the streets as the Carp, had just bought it with a heroin overdose. Then Jack orchestrated Angel de Dios' fiery demise, while Sharon rushed Warner to the hospital.

Only the two knew the whole truth, and they intended it to stay that way, until—and if—Warner woke up. They'd worry about the reality, once they learned what Warner remembered.

They agreed that if the Angel of Death was "dead," they'd eventually have to clue in Captain Santiago. They need him in on the plot to have enough eyes to be sure the real Al Warner was the only one surviving. If the captain wouldn't go along— well, they'd face that at the time.

Of special interest, the neurosurgeon who examined Warner discovered a small sliver of bone pressing against his brain. Micro surgery was required to remove it, with minimal intrusion to the actual brain mass. The surgeon, when pressed by Sharon, admitted it may have been residual from the earlier Leordano bullet trauma that they somehow had missed. It was lodged in an area that may easily have been the culprit behind all his nightmares.

Sharon and Jack wondered if it were also the "key" that liberated Angel de Dios from his cage inside Warner's head. If so, maybe that demon *was* banished forever.

Sharon rarely left Warner's side for the twenty-six days he was unconscious, sleeping in the other bed, left vacant by the hospital. A .38 snub-nose lay under her pillow, forced on her by

Jack Harris, in case "the wrong guy" woke up.

"Better safe than sorry," he'd said. "Al would want it that way." Harris gave her regular breaks so she could grab a hasty bite in the cafeteria and check in at work.

She shunned the television and news of the aftermath of the "death" of Angel de Dios, instead reading Sherlock Holmes novels aloud at Warner's side. She wanted him to know he wasn't alone. That despite everything, she was still there for him. He was, after all, the man she loved. It was the Angel of Death who terrified her, not Al Warner.

Who *was* lying in that bed, anyhow? Was it the crusty yet tender detective, or that cold, deadly charmer, Angel de Dios? The head wound was exactly like the one spawning that malevolent creature. Might this one, along with the removal of that tiny bone fragment, have banished him back into permanent confinement?

Was the Angel of Death truly dead, as Captain Santiago assured the press, or was he still lurking there, just under the surface, awaiting his chance to again begin his deadly quest? Not knowing was a terrible dark mist permeating her.

She wished *she* could find a way to sleep now, without anguish-filled dreams traumatizing her each night. She would awake in a cold sweat, with the specter of *him* perched lightly at the side of her bed, dispassionately crushing the life from her, his last words from the nightmare still ringing in her ears.

"The Lord calls."

EPILOGUE

". . . so, while we've got many psychological profiles of these psychotic killers, we can only categorize them to a limited extent."

The taxi driver had tuned in a station interviewing University of Miami Professor, Robert Greenbaum, a noted authority on Criminal Behavior and sometime consultant to the FBI's BAU. An interesting and sought-after speaker, the subject that day was a postmortem of the Angel of Death.

The interviewer asked, "So, did this man, who called himself the Angel of God, fit the usual serial-killer's mold?"

"In many ways, yes. He was white, obviously intelligent, charming, in his late thirties, more or less, and a killer of women. But we know nothing specific about him or his background. No family or acquaintances have stepped forward.

"Of all the modern-day serial killers I've studied, he's the only one with no apparent history. We have no idea who he was or where he came from, or what stressors suddenly sent him on this deadly quest, and frankly, that bothers me.

"The man finally tracking him down, nearly giving his life while delivering us from this clever sociopath seems to know little more."

"Are you saying this Angel de Dios may have once been sane and normal? That some terrible event, or string of events, transformed him into this monstrosity?"

"Quite possibly. There's usually a final "stressor" that sets these deadly lunatics in motion. Sadly, he may be one of those killers remaining an enigma. We'll probably never know what event or chain of events set him off ... a modern-day Jack the Ripper. We only know the terrible results. Seven lovely young women perished, six families rent apart by their loss.

"His death may bring them relief, but I suspect very little solace. Only his chance encounter with Detective Warner brought an end to his reign of terror.

"So, of Angel de Dios we know little but the results of his acts. But in the end, he's gone, and for the nonce, we are once again safe, thanks to some luck and the bravery of a single, dedicated police officer, Detective Alan Warner.

"I wish him a speedy recovery and hope he will once again be able to join us in pursuit of evil. This community needs more men like this tough, honest cop."

Sharon Clark, scrunched in a back corner of the cab, tears trickling across her cheeks, applauded softly. She slumped back and adjusted the light silken scarf draped around her graceful but still discolored neck. She and Jack Harris were the only ones who knew exactly what happened that horrendous evening, but, except for Captain Santiago, they intended to keep it to themselves.

Yes, dear god, please see to his full recovery again. The swelling of his brain was nearly gone. A tiny bone, missed during his healing from his previous head wound, had been removed. Significantly, its location was consistent with possible development of split-personalities.

Now conscious and cognizant, he had no apparent memory of those last moments, nor the truth about The Angel of Death. The bullet's furrow along his skull intersected the older scar at nearly right angles. "X" marked the spot that hatched a vicious killer. She hoped that monster was now forever buried there.

Though she still loved him, she'd be always haunted by what he unknowingly became. That, and the sacrifice he sought to make for her in the end, filled her dreams and plagued her thoughts.

Who would he *really* be, once he recovered? Could she ever be with him again without fear? Her fingers fluttered at her throat, and a shiver chilled her at the memory of strong thumbs burrowing slowly into her windpipe—a vivid image etched in her mind.

She had to get out, unable to bear this city any longer. Too many painful memories here. Maybe, after a while, when things settled back to normal ....

She sighed, tears glistening like tiny diamonds in her hazel eyes, as the taxi approached Miami International Airport. The airline ticket in her purse was to Buffalo, and home.

One-way.

The End

If you enjoyed this novel, please take the time to recommend it to friends. I hope you will leave review at Amazon, Facebook, Twitter, and Goodreads, if possible.

You may want to continue the Al Warner adventure. Read the 2nd in the series, **Born to Die,** to discover how Warner survived and moved on.

In this exciting, 5-Star reviewed novel, Detective Al Warner is on medical leave, stemming from the conclusion of *Death's Angel.* He meets nurse Casey Jansson, and with forced inactivity weighing heavily on him, he agrees to help investigate a mysterious rash of Sudden Infant Death Syndrome (SIDS) deaths of six-month-old Palm Beach baby boys. Only Nurse Casey is suspicious, but Warner can think of no logical motive or opportunity for the infants' deaths. Casey's compulsion leads to a stunning conclusion, putting her life in mortal danger. Only Warner can save her if he gets there in time . . . but he doesn't know where to look.

You can find *Born to Die* on my web site:

https://georgeabernstein.com

or at Amazon:

http://amazon.com/dp/B016V6P7EK

Available as an eBook, paperback, and at audiobook.

Happy reading.